PAWN TO QUEEN FOUR

PAWN TO QUEEN FOUR

A NOVEL BY
LARS EIGHNER

ST. MARTIN'S PRESS
NEW YORK

Design by Sara Stemen

Library of Congress Cataloging-in-Publication Data

Eighner, Lars.
    Pawn to Queen four / Lars Eighner.
        p.   cm.
    ISBN 0-312-13581-5
      1. Gay men—Oklahoma—Fiction   I. Title.
    PS3555.I54P39   1995
    813'.54—dc20   95-23541

First edition November 1995

10 9 8 7 6 5 4 3 2 1

To the memory of
B. K. "Bunch" Brittain

Been combin out this hair, Lawd, too many years.
Been combin out this hair, Lawd, too many years.
Been combin out this hair, Lawd, too many years.
Seems like I'd be a stylist by now.

"A Work Song"
Crumbelly Croissant

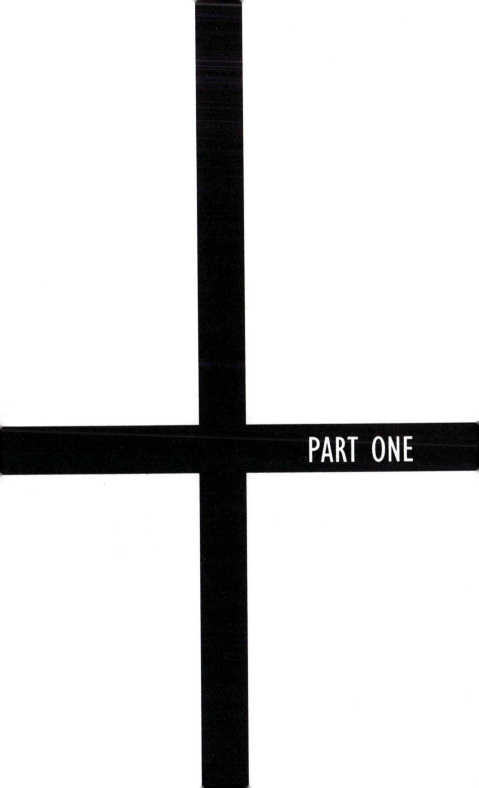

PART ONE

ONE

J IM opened one eye. A snowy egret glowed at him. *No, he thought, that cannot be correct.*

The squish and thud of his pulse in his ears reassured Jim that it was another Sunday morning. Jim decided to lie very still for a while. *Maybe it will go away.*

He opened the other eye. *Oh, it is a stained-glass window depicting a snowy egret. That's much better. A stained-glass window makes much more sense, except that it is set in a stone wall which leads to a vaulted ceiling and somewhere, deep inside this place, someone is playing a real pipe organ. My arm is missing.*

No, not missing. His arm was asleep. *My arm is asleep,* Jim thought, *because this angel's head is on my shoulder. That explains the organ and the vaulted ceiling and the stained glass. I was run over on my way home from Sleazy Sue's. I have been carried off to Heaven and this angel is sleeping on my arm.*

No, that's not right either. One cannot go to Heaven by way of Sleazy Sue's unless some great error has been made in theology. Yet it looks a great deal like an angel with its snow-blond hair and its look of peace and contentment.

The fugue swelled as a nine-foot door groaned and opened into the room. Jim did not feel up to meeting the distraught parents or the cuckolded lover, but his gut told him that any escape by means of sudden movement was out of the question.

A red-haired beachboy carried a silver service into the room. *A beachboy,* Jim thought because of the rounded deltoids, the striated pectoral plateaus, the brown-flecked, peeling sunburn, and the tiny bone-white chamois loincloth. Since this could not be the distraught parent, Jim assumed it was the cuckolded lover. *Placating this one may not be so bad as soon as I am feeling more myself.*

"Good morning, sir," said the beachboy. "If you will awaken Master Phil, I will serve your breakfast."

Jim pulled his arm from beneath the angel. The angel's eyes opened. They were gray.

"Hello, Jim," the angel said.

"Hello . . . uh . . . Phil."

"Are you okay?" The angel sat up gracefully and looked inquiringly into Jim's eyes.

"A little hungover."

"Madam Agnes thought that would be the case," the beachboy said as he set the silver service across the angel's lap. "She sent you these." From the waistband of the bone-white chamois loincloth, the beachboy extracted a tiny gold box and presented it to Phil.

Phil opened the box. It contained two zebra-striped capsules. Phil offered the open box to Jim. Jim looked wary.

"Oh, these are okay." The angel seemed amused. "Agnes has something appropriate for every occasion." Phil placed the box on the silver tray, removed one of the capsules, and swallowed it with a gulp of Bloody Mary. "Now you."

Jim removed the leafy garnish from the other Bloody Mary and took the remaining capsule. He had relaxed a bit when he discovered that the beachboy was a servant. But the mention of this Agnes person was disconcerting.

Phil closed the box and tucked it into the waistband of the beachboy's loincloth. Jim flushed when he saw Phil pat the bone-white chamois bulge. Phil caught the look in Jim's eye.

"That will be all, Thomas," Phil said to the beachboy.

"Very well, sir. Madam's audience will be in an hour." The beachboy left through the nine-foot door. The organ music muted and the hinges groaned as the door swung shut.

"Did I have a good time?" Jim asked, trying to sound as if he were making a joke but wishing he could remember even an instant of the night with the angel.

"I hope so," Phil replied, "because I certainly did."

"Where are we?"

"Agnes calls it the Imperial Court of the Jade Chimera." Phil spread marmalade on a muffin.

"Are we still in Austin? Are we even in Texas?" While poking about on the near end of the silver tray, Jim discovered what he took to be a gourmet treatment of an egg. Whatever it was, was not sunny-side up.

"Yes, of course. Actually this is a townhouse on Eighth Street. You've probably passed it a hundred times. The outside looks like a weird boutique."

"Oh." The egg had the consistency of reheated mozzarella. Jim toyed with it for a moment but decided it would be safer to butter a muffin. The zebra-striped capsule, however, began to assert itself. By the time he had finished the muffin, Jim found his appetites much revived. He devoured the egg, gulped the whole Bloody Mary at once, and even ate the garnish, although it was green, crunchy, and served before noon. Then Jim leaned back to peek under the silver tray. An angelic lump in the sheets seemed promising.

"Who exactly is this Agnes?" Jim asked.

"You'll love her. Everybody does."

"I take it Agnes is an old queen."

"Well, Agnes is rather mature and regal. But yes, Agnes is a man in a technical sense, if that is what you are asking."

"Uh-huh." Jim detected, or thought he did, an increasing lumpiness in the angelic lump. Evidently the confrontation with the cuckolded lover was still to come. Jim meant to compound the felony if he possibly could.

Phil wiped a smudge of marmalade from the golden hairs at the far corner of his mouth. Jim pounced to lick the near corner with his tongue and reach under the tray with his free hand.

"You'll spill the tray!"

Jim did not care about the tray. But he was surprised at himself. He had never been much of a morning person.

"We both need a shower anyway." Phil slipped from Jim's grasp and placed the tray on the face of a crimson dragon in the carpet. With a cricket-flick the angel stood beside the bed.

Jim could not understand. Jim had not felt any resistance, certainly no muscle force opposing his own. Yet at one moment he had a hold of the angel, and at the next the angel was free. The tight curls of the snow-blond angel hair formed a halo. The almost six feet of angel reached for Jim's hand.

"No, get back here right now." Jim patted the empty spot on the bed. *This isn't even lust,* Jim thought. *It's the urge to defile. No one should look that sweet on a Sunday morning.*

"That is a side effect of the pill. You'll get over it. Besides, whatever you have in mind will be much more interesting on the roof garden." Phil tugged on Jim's hand. "Come on."

Jim pulled back. Phil dropped the hand and disappeared into the drapes behind the bed. After a moment Jim saw that Phil was really gone. Jim got up and looked for his pants. All of his clothes were missing. Nude and embarrassed, Jim fumbled with the drapes until he found the opening.

The roof garden seemed to be a twelve-by-twelve-foot-square redwood deck set down in a tropical rain forest. Jim was not impressed. He had been in bars that achieved much the same effect. The shower that sparkled over Phil's body appeared to fall from a banana tree.

"Come on in," Phil called, "the water's fine."

Jim noticed with some concern the number of nearby taller buildings. He imagined what a tenant in one of those buildings might think, looking down and seeing Jim naked, with Jim's urge to defile bobbing its head. Perhaps without the foreign drug in his system, Jim would have exercised some prudence and resisted the invitation of the beckoning golden boy, slick with soap, gleaming in the water and sunlight. Perhaps not.

The slickness of the soap, the Sunday-morning sun, and the fresh Austin air conspired with the drug. Jim found the urge to defile sated more quickly than he wished. Almost immediately, in fact.

"See?" said the angel without a trace of disappointment. "I told you it would be more exciting out here."

"Yeah, but how exciting was it for the neighbors?" Jim thought his nervousness over the neighbors might do as an excuse.

"Probably not very. They must be used to it by now. Agnes often entertains out here. Which reminds me, we must make ourselves presentable for her audience."

"Audience? You mean she wants to watch?"

"I expect that if she did, then she has." The angel nuzzled Jim's chest. "No, her audience is a kind of formal meeting. She has a peculiar way of putting things sometimes. You'll get used to it."

Jim doubted he wanted the chance of getting used to anything Agnes did. Still, he wanted to redeem himself with Phil. Perhaps by the time they returned to the bedroom, it would be defiling time again.

Phil took one of the two Turkish towels from the green chaise longue and dried himself. Jim followed his example.

"You know, I won't be able to get very presentable without my clothes. Do you happen to remember where I left them?"

"Oh, I'll ring for Thomas." Phil tweaked the spine of what appeared to be a century plant. "We had them laundered for you."

Jim felt a bachelor uneasiness at the thought of his laundry being done. "Look, I'm not sure I can stay for this audience thing or whatever. I've been putting off doing some things around my apartment."

"I understand," said Phil, looking as if he understood too well. "Humor Agnes a bit. Then Thomas will drive you right home."

"I suppose I could."

"Please. It's really quite early."

A slender, dark young man in drawstring pants and a gauze shirt suddenly appeared from the foliage. Jim grabbed a damp towel and wrapped it around his waist.

Phil smiled. "Thomas, please have our clothes laid out if they are ready."

"Right away, sir."

Jim watched the boy leave and spotted the other entrance to the roof garden. "I thought the redhead was Thomas."

"All the staff is called Thomas. When they are together, Agnes calls that one Tomás. The real Swede she calls Tom. The redhead she calls Tommy—he isn't really Irish, but she likes to think he is. That's the way Agnes is. I knew all of their names at one time, but I've forgotten."

"Does she call you Thomas too?"

"Oh no. It's not like I was one of the staff."

"I see." Jim wrinkled his nose as if he smelled something disappointing.

"No. I don't think you do see. But you will." Phil grabbed the towel from around Jim's waist, flipped it over his shoulder, and led the way back to the bedroom.

Jim was sorry to see that the bed had been made. His clothes had been laid out. His jeans had been pressed for the first time since they left Hong Kong.

The bathroom was splendid. Jim thought it was strange that the brass fixtures had been allowed to become faded and scratched. Then he realized: They were not brass at all but a softer, paler metal. The sealed toothbrush was obviously meant for Jim. "Do you always shave with a straight razor?" he asked Phil.

Phil blushed. "I hardly have to shave at all. That is for you. I can send for whatever else you'd prefer. Electric? Safety? What?"

"This is fine." Jim stropped the razor out of habit, although he could see that the factory edge was unmolested. "Did we discuss shaving last night?"

"No. I don't think so. Is anything wrong?"

"Everything is fine." *But why would a brand new straight razor be left out for me unless he knew what I shaved with? And how would he know?*

One of the ornate devices was meant to be peed in. Jim waited until Phil had used it, just to be sure it was for use as well as for show. Jim had almost finished buttoning his fly when he remembered his new policy. He readjusted the elastic of his underwear so that it passed under what it was designed to pass over. He rebuttoned his fly and found a passable bulge in the mirror.

"Now where are my shoes?"

"These are for you."

The joggers that peeked out from the foot of the bed were Jim's brand. They were his color. But they were not his shoes.

"No. These are new. Where are mine?

"These are exactly your size. The others . . . well, you know, the stitching and the grease and all. They've been discarded. I hope it's all right. I'm sure I could send for any you would rather have."

Jim managed to say, "Oh, these will do fine," before the high-speed-elevator sensation of threat and loss overcame him. His laundry had been done. A straight razor had been laid out for him. Now his own personal shoes were gone.

As he put it on, Jim noticed that his flannel shirt had been starched. "Look, I'm not sure I am up to this audience thing." Jim tried to assume a wan effect. "Why don't I just slip out. You know, give me a raincheck."

"Please. It won't take long. I promise. Thomas will have

you home before you could walk." The angel seemed guile-
less enough.

"Well . . ." Jim knew that he was weakening.

"I haven't asked you for anything else. Please, for me."

"I suppose."

"Good. It's time, anyway. Follow me. And be sure to
compliment her on her nails." Phil opened the creaky door.
The stone steps to the lower floor projected from the wall.
At the landing Phil and Jim confronted two more great
doors, these slick with black and red enamel and glinting
with gold leaf. The doors opened inward to a long room.
Agnes stood.

"Welcome to the Imperial Court of the Jade Chimera."
The imperial gown glowed with silken figures: harts, uni-
corns, lions, and two great part-goat, part-serpent creatures
confronting each other. There was ample room: Agnes was
six-seven and weighed three hundred pounds.

The imperial dais groaned as Agnes sat back on the imperial throne. "Please be seated." One of her two-inch nails
curved toward a pillow at her feet.

"Go ahead," Phil whispered. "I must excuse myself."

"But . . ."

"Sh! You'll see me again in a minute."

Agnes toyed with a jade and onyx chess set while Jim
squatted on the pillow. Jim watched desperately as Phil
withdrew and two new Thomases closed the doors.

"We trust you slept well."

"Yes, thank you."

"And that you have recovered yourself."

"Oh yes! Those pills were great. I wish I had your connection."

"We do not have a connection. We have a sensory stylist."

"Oh, I see."

Five Thomases in all arrayed themselves to the right of the throne. First, a Japanese Thomas in a cadet uniform. Second, the one that Jim took for the Swede. Then the beachboy and the one called Tomás and finally a tall one in a flannel shirt and jeans.

"Well, Jim, we have seen you about town, but we must say that you are much better-looking at close quarters."

"Uh . . . thank you. And . . . gee, I love your nails."

"How sweet you are to say so." Agnes fanned her emerald claws. "Of course, they're real. Except for the color. A petty vanity of our old age. Would you care for a cocktail before we begin?"

"I don't want a drink. Begin what?"

"No doubt you are wondering about all of this."

"This hasn't been my usual Sunday morning."

"Indeed. None of them ever are. We understand that you have been somewhat political."

"I try to do my bit."

"Excellent." Agnes touched the ornamental comb in her raven wig. "But you do not care much for old-fashioned girls like ourself."

"They served their purpose." Jim felt this had not come out right.

"Never mind. We know what you meant. Indeed, we served our purpose. We know you suppose you invented gay power by parading around half naked and kissing men in front of law enforcement officers." Agnes adjusted a chesspiece.

"Yes. Well, liberation and all that." Jim's foot had gone to sleep. He crossed his legs the other way.

"That is all very well. But more subtle methods are often necessary. You are about to see a little of that." Agnes snapped her fingers. "Tommy, the first photograph."

The redheaded beachboy opened the manila folder he had been clutching under his arm. He presented Jim with a color photograph of a man who was holding a Bible in front of his chest like a shield.

"Do you know who that man is?"

"I've seen the picture before. I don't remember."

"Tommy, the second photograph."

The same man with the same white crew cut stood in front of a towering mosaic of the Creation of Adam.

"Oh, it's that college in Osage, Oklahoma."

"Correct. Holy Word of God University and Technical Institute."

"Then the man must be Brother Earl."

"Correct again. What do you know about him?"

"He's a nazi pig."

Agnes cleared her throat. "Yes, we suppose one could put it that way. Suffice it to say, you know he is the enemy."

"Yeah."

"What was that?"

"I said yes, ma'am."

"What you may not know is that we have had him in check for a number of years, owing to the existence of certain other, shall we say, less seemly photographs." Agnes rolled her eyes.

Jim smirked. "I sure would like to see them."

"Indeed, child, so would we. Unfortunately, the sister who was holding the photographs has passed away. Some difficulty has come up concerning the estate. We cannot be sure we will retain control of the photographs. That is why we have summoned you." Agnes spun the largest of the black pearls at her throat.

"But what do mean, you have him in check? He's always ranting about threats to the family, unnatural perversions, and sodomites."

"Child, we have no interest in preventing the man from making a living. We realize that a certain amount of that rhetoric is required by his profession. We merely mean to see that he does not get ideas of carrying things too far. Live and let live, you know."

"What's all this got to do with me?"

"You are going to recapture the photographs for us. Failing that, you are going to be instrumental in obtaining a new set of photographs."

"That means going to bed with Brother Earl?" Jim drew back.

"Only as a last resort."

"Never."

"The situation would be carefully controlled."

"I don't want any part of this."

"We urge you to reconsider."

"Why me? You seem to have plenty of flunkies who can do it." Jim swept his arm at the line of Thomases.

"Our staff is not to be referred to as flunkies. The reason it has to be you is that you are Brother Earl's type."

Jim clamped his eyes shut and shook his head. "Ick. No way."

Agnes clicked her nails impatiently on the chessboard. "We want you to do this because it is a just cause. We feel you are the sort of person who will put the welfare of our people ahead of your selfish whims. We must call to your attention, however, that you will find it much to your advantage to cooperate.

"Some wonderful things have happened to you in the last week." Agnes leaned back and smiled broadly. "The telephone company has inadvertently credited your account with the huge sum you owe on long distance. You had an excellent job offer. The coupon you sent to the magazine sweepstakes bears the winning number. You will become mildly wealthy—unless, of course, the coupon is lost in processing."

"How do you know all that?"

"We know it because we arranged it. Needless to say, we are capable of unarranging the whole thing as well. Oh, and there is one more thing: Tom, show Jim what is behind the curtain."

The blond, awkward Thomas in the khaki shorts walked to the opposite end of the room, slapping the marble floor with his big bare feet. He parted the green curtains. Phil stood in a loincloth, chained at four points to the limestone wall.

"Hi there!" Phil shouted.

"Should you be successful, you will have the use of Phil for a whole year."

"The *use* of Phil. What are you, some kind of pimp?"

"The chains are merely to make the presentation more dramatic. Actually, Phil has agreed to stay with you for the year. After that, you may have him only so long as you can keep him. We happen to know that Phil is just your type. That's not pimping; that's matchmaking."

The bubbling nausea of his laundry done, the straight razor laid out, and the discarded shoes began to coalesce into a lump in Jim's stomach.

Agnes continued, "Of course, if you refuse, Phil will remain with us so long as his looks last. You won't see him again."

"So long as his looks last? How horrible! Why should he agree to stay with you? He can make it anywhere."

"Tom." Agnes called to the far end of the room. "Close the curtains." As the curtains closed, Phil tried to blow Jim a kiss from a manacled hand.

"We will pay him well. If he saves his money, he will get by once the bloom fades. We know he can do better. So do you. But we said he is just your type. He is none too bright. Just as you like them."

Jim looked as if he had been slapped hard. "Now that's a ridiculous lie."

"No more ridiculous than Fred, or Martin the bartender, or Peter, or Scott, or John Fletcher—you don't remember John's name. He's the Einstein you took home a fortnight ago. A whole string of dim bulbs. You may not know it, but you like them dumb. We could go on."

"I think you've gone far enough."

"Then, we take it, you accept." Agnes interwove her fingers and fluttered her nails like butterfly wings.

"What?"

"Look here, child. Justice, the riches of the world, and a fair young thing whose fate hangs in the balance. Mercy! Is chivalry dead at last? Of course, you need not take Phil if you don't want him. If you wish, we will discharge him with a generous settlement upon the completion of your mission."

The lump in Jim's stomach began to dissolve. "You promise?"

"You have our word."

"I suppose I could look into it." There was, after all, the magazine sweepstakes to consider.

"Excellent. Now put this on. It will help you in more ways than you can know. It's quite butch enough for your style." Agnes extracted her finger from the gold ring. A creature, part lion, part goat, in gold inlaid with jade, clasped a tigereye orb. Jim put the ring on his right hand

and turned the gem palm side, showing only the gold band on his finger.

"See," Agnes said with satisfaction, "it fits. Now Thomas will drive you home." Agnes indicated the Thomas of least rank and waved toward the door.

When the doors were closed again, Agnes picked up the jade queen's pawn. Her nails clicked against the stone. She snapped the chessman down sharply on the marble board.

Pawn to queen four.

TWO

Jim blinked as the garage door disappeared, absorbed
quickly and quietly somewhere above. He blinked at
the strong August afternoon sunlight. He blinked again
at the steepness of the ramp as the car plunged down
into the alley. He had not seen Thomas glance at the convex
mirrors that were mounted in the alley. He had not even
seen the mirrors. He supposed this was only another reckless act in a day filled with reckless disregard for his own
sensibilities.

The steep descent impinged upon his being: It tickled his
prostate. That sensation reminded Jim that he was, after all,

still single. This he took as a reassuring thought, but one that ought to be put to the test as soon as possible. Thus it occurred to Jim that the Thomas who was driving was easy to look at. Jim looked at him.

"What is your name?"

"Thomas."

"No, I mean your real name."

"Thomas. I'm the only one who was born Thomas."

"Thomas, doesn't it seem to you that we look a lot alike?"

"If you say so, sir."

"Come on. I'm serious."

Thomas glanced at Jim. "Yes, it's true."

This Thomas was slightly shorter than Jim and two or three years younger. Thomas's black hair showed the wave that Jim's developed when it was allowed to become a bit longer. Encouraging the comparison was the lumberjack drag the Thomas also wore, despite the heat. Jim was not sure whose eyes were the bluer. He wished he could compare them in a mirror. But then other interesting possible comparisons came to Jim's mind.

Jim did his best to pump up his arms and chest without being obvious. Then he removed his flannel shirt. Jim thought it was too hot for flannel, and the starch was scratchy. But mostly he hoped the clear wisdom of his example would encourage Thomas to remove his shirt too. Thomas appeared not to notice.

A residual itch from the starch could have accounted for Jim's ruffling the black hair of his chest. Thomas appeared not to notice.

Jim could have been sleepy or stiff from a morning of staying quietly around court. That could have accounted for his broad stretching and flexing motions. Thomas appeared not to notice.

"Yes," Jim tried again, "I'd say we are pretty much the same type. I don't see why Agnes wouldn't have thought you were as much Brother Earl's type as I am."

"Speaking as a flunky, all I can say is that there is no second-guessing Madam Agnes once she has a plot afoot."

No wonder he isn't responding to me, Jim thought. *I have offended him.* "Well you know I didn't mean—"

"Damn it!" Thomas pounded on the steering wheel with his fist.

"Hey, I'm trying to say I'm sorry."

"No, it's not you. Don't turn around. Look in your side mirror."

Jim saw the shaky image of a blue MG with its top down. The driver was a ruddy man in a loud sport shirt. His short hair was the muddy color that auburn becomes on its way to gray. The MG was close on their tail, but Jim could not see anything special about it. "So?"

"So, it's my little shadow. He follows me everywhere."

"He probably wants your phone number, like anyone with good eyesight." *There. That ought to make up for my "flunky" remark.*

"No. He's after Agnes."

"Whatever for?"

"It's a long story. He thinks she runs a sex slave ring for chicken hawks. Now we'll drive very slowly and carefully for a while to throw him off guard. He used to be a lot more subtle about following me. But he's given up that game."

"Chicken hawks, huh? Small wonder. All of you Thomases must be less than half Agnes's age."

"No. He's not talking about gay guys who know the score but may be a few months shy of legal. He thinks Agnes kidnaps *little* boys, like seven or eight years old, and ships them around the country." Thomas slowed, hoping to catch the MG behind the timed traffic signals.

"Well, does she?"

As their T-bird approached Fifteenth Street it was hardly beating a walking pace. In the last moment of the traffic signal's yellow phase, Thomas goosed the accelerator. The T-bird sped through the intersection. "Does she what?"

"Sell little featherless chickens."

"Are you crazy? Have you ever heard of such a thing?"

The MG ran the light. The tactic was not going to work on a quiet Sunday afternoon with no cop in sight. Thomas turned left twice, heading the T-bird back to town. "Fasten your seat belt. I've got something up my sleeve I've been waiting to try out on him."

Jim tried to figure out how to fasten the belt. "You sometimes read about cases . . ."

"The guy's name is Professor McThacry. He's not talking about your occasional weirdo. He thinks there is a real trade in boys—you know, hundreds per week. He also thinks that all of us are in on it."

"All of the Thomases?"

"No, all queers. Hold on. Here goes."

Thomas sped up and turned sharply from the center lane of the one-way street. Out of sight of the MG, Thomas turned the T-bird into the ramp of a parking garage and raced up two levels.

"Hey, that was the *out* ramp. You could've killed us both."

"I didn't think it very likely." Thomas brought the T-bird to a halt, pulled a shoebox from behind his seat, opened the door, and set the box on the pavement. He flicked a toggle switch on the side of the box. The garage was filled with sounds of squealing tires. "Now we'll slip quietly down the in ramp. He'll spend a few minutes chas-

ing the sound up and down the garage before he catches
on." The T-bird rolled away from the squealing box and
nosed down the entrance ramp.

"But you could have killed both of us."

"I said I didn't think it very likely. Who's going to be
whipping out of a bank garage on a Sunday afternoon? Besides, I've been waiting a week to test the device. I made it
myself out of spare parts."

Back in the sunlight, the T-bird headed north again. "So
anyway, he thinks we are all conspiring to trade little boys
like baseball cards. He's planning to teach a course on the
subject this fall. His texts are mostly Rechy's novels. He's
popular with the Izod and boatshoe crowd because he
grades easy and sometimes cries at the lectern. So the people
who are going to be running this state won't know anything else about us."

Jim was trying to figure out how to unfasten the seat belt.
"McThacry? Seems I've heard the name."

"You probably have. He's the token liberal at Hogg
University. His job is to say outrageous things that make
headlines and give the impression that academic freedom is
getting out of hand. When the AAUP comes to investigate,
the administration points to McThacry to prove the university shouldn't be blacklisted."

"Queer-baiting doesn't seem very liberal to me."

"Well, he made his reputation teaching a sociology
course on how Americans have not always been especially
nice to black people. At Hogg U, that's as liberal as it gets. I
took it once. You know, a multimedia thing. The queer
course looks like it will be a real dog-and-pony show."
Thomas turned the T-bird into the shade of Avenue H.

Jim had been trying to discern any change in the drape of
Thomas's jeans in the general area between brass button

and knee. "Look, I'm sorry about that flunky stuff. This has all been kind of unsettling for me."

"Think nothing of it."

"I mean you are obviously well educated, and that gizmo was a stroke of genius." With a man who considers himself clever, Jim believed, it is impossible to lay it on too thick.

"Nothing to it. Really, it was all old junk."

"And this car. I bet you maintain it too."

"Yes."

"I'm wondering: It looks like a T-bird. But not exactly."

Thomas chuckled. "In fact, it looks exactly like a T-bird. It's the famous hardtop convertible. Agnes had always wanted one. It's kind of funny working on a car that is older than you are. I had hell restoring it. Agnes kept wanting to stick doodads on. I kept telling her there was no point in having a classic if she was going to screw it up. If she'd had her way there would be fake fur all over everything. The color was her idea. I was against it. But the people I talked to said there really was a titty-pink original. So I gave in." Thomas stopped the car in front of Jim's apartment complex.

"Hey, how did you know where I live?"

"Oh, Agnes owns these apartments. At least she owns a corporation that owns a corporation that owns them."

That, Jim noticed, did not answer the question. "Why don't you come in for a drink." Jim got out and hung his shirt from his belt.

"I think I had better. I have your instructions. And you still have a surprise coming." Thomas carefully locked the car.

Jim knew it was Sunday, but his coming-home routine included looking into the mailbox. While he opened the empty box, he noticed that Thomas went directly to the door of his apartment. Jim felt he'd already had all the surprises he really cared for—unless the next one was that Thomas would stop being coy.

The apartments were well maintained by Austin standards, yet they were beginning to show their age. They had been thrown up in the 1960s to capitalize on the baby boom's coming of age. Jim's apartment was on the first floor and opened onto the pool area.

The pool had been something of a disappointment to Jim. He had chosen the apartment for what he assumed would be a picturesque view. But the pool was only for show. It was too small for men to swim in, and few made the attempt.

The surrounding apartments kept most of the area in the shade. Those prepared to move at intervals to follow the heavenly progression might sunbathe. But none of the other male tenants found the effort worthwhile. After the first few weeks, Jim closed his drapes.

Out of habit, Jim went directly to the thermostat as soon as he opened the door. Although he nearly tripped over the new luggage in the living area, he did not actually notice it until he had started the air conditioner.

"This, I take it, is the surprise."

"Agnes likes to send her boys off to college in style."

Jim did not like being considered one of Agnes's boys. "She must have been pretty sure of herself. What if I had said nothing doing and run home to find all of this?"

"Agnes is used to getting her way."

"I don't like it." Jim stepped into the kitchen, which was only the space behind the bar, and looked for something that might be presented as a drink.

Half a dozen bottles in the cabinet contained a swallow each. Three bottles of unnaturally colored liqueurs had been tasted once and thereafter left to gather dust. Together, what was left of the good scotch and what was left of the rotten scotch might make one drink. Then what was left of the passable scotch might make another. But Jim decided to serve beer and schnapps, thinking it might take more than a couple to break the ice. Fortunately, Jim was always well supplied with beer and schnapps.

Jim fished in the bottom of the sink and found two shot glasses. They did not feel quite right. *Oh,* Jim recalled, *it is only the aspic which has melted on them.* He washed the glasses. The only dish towel he could find was the one that resided at the foot of the refrigerator. When Thomas was not looking, Jim dried the glasses with his flannel shirt.

Jim's apartment had neither desk nor bookshelves. The carpet was chocolate; the walls, dark paneled. Together, the feeble lamp in the living area and the amber swag over the dinette table could, even on a sunny afternoon, scarcely produce enough light for reading. The apartment developers had had the keen inspiration that no student would rent a place suggestive of studying.

Nonetheless, Thomas set the carry-on piece of luggage on the dinette table and withdrew a letter-sized expanding file. He laid the contents, pocket by pocket, in little piles on the table.

"Here is your plane ticket. This is your letter of acceptance, which is genuine; Tommy, the redhead, compromised their computer. This is your transcript, which is falsified. Over here are appropriate ID cards and some other stuff you will need to read over. You have been admitted as a seminarian at Holy Word of God University and Technical Institute. Classes start a week from tomorrow. Your courses are not so bad, except for a really horrid required seminar on Christian family life. The subject matter is bad enough, but—well, you can cross that bridge when you get to it."

"Wonderful." Jim placed the shot glass and the beer at Thomas's right hand.

"With a little luck you won't have to attend the university at all. The first thing is to search Leslie's house—Leslie is the dear departed—to see if you can find the photographs there. Here is the address and a key. Also, you have a membership card for the only known gay bar. It's called the Reservation. You will find Oklahoma liquor laws amusing. Naturally, do not get the membership card mixed up with the school stuff."

"Naturally not. But all of this my being Brother Earl's type aside, why doesn't Agnes get one of the locals to do this?"

"Your health." Thomas downed the schnapps. "I've said there's no figuring Agnes when she's plotting. But the truth is, while in theory Osage is in Agnes's realm, some kind of split occurred years ago. Agnes and Leslie had a falling out.

"That's why Agnes doesn't have the influence or contacts that the Jade Court used to have. It is also why she doesn't have the photos to begin with. All of which means that you have to be careful even in dealing with our own people. A few special contacts that Agnes still has, mostly old loyalists, are expecting you. They will be in touch at appropriate times. Probably the bar membership will not be very useful."

"None of this seems very encouraging." Jim refilled Thomas's glass.

"You could find the photographs right away and be back here by Wednesday. Which reminds me." Thomas dug deeper into the carry-on. "Here are some preaddressed, stamped mailers. Stash them in various handy places and always carry one. When you get the pictures, drop them in the mail right away. That way the pictures can't be found on you."

"And once I mail them, I can be thrown to the wolves." Jim picked up the key to Leslie's house, unsnapped his key ring from his left-side belt loop, and began to twist the key onto the ring.

"Not at all. Once Agnes has the photos, she'll be in a position to call the shots. But if you are caught with them, there is little she can do to help you."

"That's nice to know." Jim picked up the stack of mailers. They were brown, padded envelopes, a little taller than legal size and about as long. The address on each of them was "Angus McKinney, 124 8th Street, Austin, TX 78701." "I take it Angus is Agnes's real name."

"That's right." Thomas flipped through the expanding file to see if he had overlooked anything. "Your flight leaves tomorrow at eleven-thirty. You ought to be at the airport at least half an hour early. I can pick you up."

"No thanks. Airport partings make me nervous. I'll take a cab." Jim had his third schnapps. "But what about, you know, incidental expenses?"

"Oh yes." Thomas gulped his schnapps and stood. He pulled out his wallet by its chain. He handed Jim five hundred-dollar bills and five twenties. "With the IDs is a bank card, good in Osage for three times this amount. If any reasonable amount of cash will make the difference, of course, Agnes will pony up. But you'll have to call her to justify it. Don't use the number in the book. We hardly ever answer that one. Use the number on the card with Leslie's address."

Jim put the cash, the bank card, and the card with Leslie's address in his own wallet. Thomas started to sit back down, but Jim took his arm and led him to the living area.

"I really don't think there is much more I can tell you."

"You can tell me about yourself." Jim sat next to Thomas on the sofa.

"There isn't much to tell. I was an air force brat. I finished school, had no idea what to do, knocked around the country for a couple of years, came back to Austin, found Agnes—or she found me. That's all."

"But what are you going to do?"

"Hang on at court as long as I can. Then, I don't know." Thomas shrugged.

"But surely you want to do something, you want to be something besides a houseboy?"

Thomas drew back a bit. "I'm not sure you understand. . . ."

Jim thought perhaps *houseboy* was a poorly chosen word, but he did not know what else to call it. He got up and took Thomas's hand. "Come here."

"Where?"

"To the bathroom. I want to look at our eyes in the mirror."

"What for?"

"Never mind. Just come on."

The bathroom light, reflecting on the tile, seemed especially bright after the dimness of the living area. Jim stood behind Thomas, facing the mirror. "I can't tell whose eyes are the bluer."

"What difference does it make?"

"None, really. Sometimes mine are light. Sometimes they get dark. I guess it really doesn't matter." Jim stared at the mirror. He looked into the eyes of Thomas's reflection. He put his hands on Thomas's shoulders and leaned over so his cheek was against Thomas's. "But tell me what you think anyway."

"I don't see any difference." Thomas seemed annoyed.

This is not the urge to defile, Jim thought. *This time it's lust.* Jim bowed to kiss Thomas's neck. Thomas twisted away.

"I was afraid of that."

"Afraid? C'mon. You're an attractive man. What did you expect?"

Thomas pushed past Jim and went into the living area. He felt in his pockets for the car keys. He found he had put them on his belt loop after all.

"Please don't be that way. Tell me why not. Is it me, or what?"

"No. I guess it's not you. It's me." Thomas's expression turned to sad resignation. "There's something wrong with me."

"What? The clap? Hemorrhoids? Worse?"

"Much worse. I really don't see that you have the right to know, simply because you tried to ravish me—"

"*Ravish* is a hell of a word for a kiss on the neck."

"Well, came on to me or whatever. But since you are about to do something terribly important, I don't want you to . . . I don't want you going off with your confidence shaken." Thomas took his hand off the doorknob.

"Don't put yourself out. I've been turned down before." Jim brought the schnapps to the coffee table and refilled both glasses.

"No, it *is* me." Thomas perched on the edge of the far end of the sofa and drank the shot. "You see, it's hard for me to say this, but I am not much . . . not much of a man."

"Is that all, hon? Look, I'm no size queen. That sort of thing really doesn't matter to me in the least," Jim lied.

"No. That's not the problem. I have a kind of hormone imbalance or something. I'm just not very virile."

"You can't get it up? Hey, there's plenty else we can do."

"That's not it either. Are you going to give me a chance to explain?"

"Sorry. Go ahead."

"Well, you know they say that women work from the

heart and men work from the crotch? I think what it is, is that I got cross-wired. I could go to bed with you without loving you. I would like to. But then if I did, then I *would* love you. I couldn't help it. I mean, I try to trick out like everybody else. But it doesn't work. I'm still crazy about someone I went with once two years ago."

Another weirdo. Why do I always get the neurotics? "Good grief. Have you tried to get professional help?"

"It seems so hopeless. Sometimes I say to myself that everybody else is shallow and superficial—you know, the kind of people who hang out in bars."

"Yes, I've heard of that type of person." Jim filled the glasses again.

"But then I know it's me who's screwed up. If only I could get steroids or hormones or something that would give me a more masculine attitude. But I can't talk to a doctor about it. I'm glad you didn't laugh. The two others I've told did."

"Well, I see that it's a serious problem. I mean if I fell in love with every trick . . ." Jim's eyes glazed over at the thought.

"See? That's it. That's what I mean by cross-wired. I can't even think of them as tricks. I mean, we have sex. And afterwards when they lay there smoking a cigarette, I start thinking of all their good points. I get more and more excited about learning who they are and what their life is all about. That's what I mean. The opposite of the way it is supposed to be."

"So what do you do?"

"Well, at first I would be perfectly honest about my feelings. That was too strange for anybody to deal with. I learned to cover it up. But that ate me up inside. It's driving me crazy. I mean, I get as horny as anyone else. But I know that if I do anything about it, it will be much worse."

30

Jim got up and put his arm around Thomas's shoulder. "Perhaps I can help. Maybe we can desensitize you."

"How?"

"Well, we could fool around a little and, until you get used to it, stop until you get back under control."

Thomas stood. "Don't you ever give up?"

"Hey, I'm only trying to help."

"Yeah. I've met plenty of guys who wanted to help me like you do."

"I'm not like them," Jim lied again.

"Okay, suppose something did happen between us. You don't want a lover, do you?"

"No, of course not. But see, we want to try to cure you of wanting a lover. I'll be very gentle."

"Forget it. It's been tried before. Besides, I love someone else."

"I suppose you Thomases sort of pair off."

"I don't know why I am telling you this. I don't usually drink this much. It's not another Thomas. It's Agnes."

"Wow, you *have* got a problem if tricking with an old gal like that will make you fall in love."

"How it happened is *really* none of your business."

"But she's twice your age and a drag queen to boot."

"These things are unimportant. And you shouldn't be deceived by appearances. Agnes has some fine qualities. You mustn't tell her. She doesn't know."

"I don't understand."

"She doesn't know because she thinks like you do. She thinks like everybody else. I have to face the fact that it's me who's out of step. She thinks she has to hire me as a houseboy. She feels okay about it if she gives me money. She understands that and everybody else understands that. So I work for her and take her money because she can deal with things that way."

"But isn't it hopeless for you? What about Phil and Agnes?"

"That's the one subject I am forbidden to discuss with you."

Thomas was not going to finish his schnapps. Jim downed it. He made a face and slammed the glass down on the coffee table. The day had been too full of surprises, and now both his libido and his curiosity were frustrated.

"I've got to go now," Thomas said. "I don't want your feelings hurt. You really are a very attractive man."

Jim reached for Thomas again, but Thomas caught his hand and squeezed it. "You don't give up."

Jim shook his head and grinned.

"Okay then. Just one kiss to show I'm not stuck up." Thomas kissed Jim quickly.

"Please . . ."

But Thomas opened the door. "Good luck, Jim."

Thomas allowed the T-bird to warm up. While he waited, he looked back at Jim's door. Even one kiss had had some effect. He began to think that Jim had some good points. Thomas put the car in gear, cut the wheel, and drove quietly down Avenue H.

After a minute, the blue MG rolled from its hiding spot in the parking lot behind the Olds and turned south onto the broad, pecan-shaded avenue.

THREE

MONDAY morning comes to Avalon Park with an erudite refinement. Neither Cambridge nor Heidelberg have yet attained quite this effect of stately academe. The directors of the Avalon Park Association have seen to that. No tacky patina of corruption darkens the gleaming bronzes of the residential park. Here stands shiny Newton with his sparkling astrolabe; there, Avon's bard with glistening pate. No expense has been spared to realize the pastoral vision. The association sees that the close-cropped commons flow seamlessly into the private lawns. Deed restrictions explicitly proscribe all but the most elegant of ornaments: a sundial, a faun with pipes, just the number of stones arranged to suggest the ruin of an ancient wall.

Off a drive of imported cobblestone, half hidden by elaborate topiaries worked in both native and exotic flora, reposes a Gothic edifice with ornamental buttresses of reinforced concrete and premoldered façades. It is, since he commissioned it and declared it so, the family seat of Professor Robert Bruce McThacry, Ph.D.

Though Europe had to depend upon age alone to achieve the antiquity of the original, McThacry's architect employed Art in replicating an obscure French abbey. The result, seeming quite the elder of its design, deceives even natural instinct. As dawn breaks, winged animals return to slumber in the bell-less belltower of what would be the chapel, but which serves as garage to the blue MG.

While from a distance even the abbess might mistake it for her own—the present mother being quite myopic—McThacry's passion for accuracy in imitation did not go so far as to preclude extensive acquiescence to the prevailing modes for the interior appointments. The abbess might be perplexed by track lighting or the hot tub or the smart MonoGym which requires such little space. But the cloistered life does not require naïveté; she would know what to think of the waterbed. Not that it often serves its purpose—that of enlightening the distaff undergraduate—but it was there for that.

In fact, McThacry found he could not sleep on the thing. Nor could he get rid of it anymore than he could rid himself of the increasingly impractical MG. True enough, he was the father and sole guardian of an adolescent boy—which contributed, McThacry thought, to the impracticality of entertaining in the waterbed a person more nearly the age of the scion. True, he had achieved a respectable, if undistinguished, scholarly position—more upon repute, he was well aware, than accomplishment. True—yes it was true—he was past his prime. But he was still a vigorous man with all the needs of a vigorous man.

Foremost of the needs of that sort of man is not the urgency of youth itself. The need of a still vigorous man, though past his prime, is the belief in the persistence of youthful urgency. It is not enough to be able, should the opportunity occur. It is not enough to be resonant when a sympathetic note is struck. It is not enough, even, to be ready at the command of will. One must be driven. One must still be seized by forces unbidden. One must be tossed on a rough sea of desire.

A man past his prime but vigorous nonetheless, who believes in himself, has the means, and is again single will drive an MG, however impractically, and recline on a waterbed, however restlessly. But McThacry was beginning to have his doubts. And doubts feed one upon the other paradoxically, increasing in mass and number. McThacry observed with horror the waxing tendency toward self-control, the creeping prudence in every dark corner of his life, and his blossoming regard of consequence.

He was not so narrow in his reflections that the disuse of the waterbed was his only concern. He saw it in other ways: deference to colleagues, consideration before speech, caution in novel enterprise. All part of the same thing, it was merely indexed by one organ, an organ that had led, an organ that had exhorted and inspired, and that at last had abdicated in favor of the mind.

And the mind was unready for the mantle that fell to it.

"Shh!" McThacry brought an index finger to his lips. Sidney thought this strange since he could see that both the inmates of the house were awake. McThacry pointed to the light fixture, set his empty coffee cup on the counter, and led Sidney to the kitchen door.

McThacry was annoyed that their footprints remained as distinct dark green spots on the shimmering, dewy lawn. He walked south until the roadway was obscured by the pyracantha hedge. Then he turned sharply west. Sidney followed this indirect route.

The statue of Niccolò Machiavelli had been something of an embarrassment. Worked as it was in cement and found bottle caps, it produced an effect quite different from that the Avalon Park Association had in mind. The directors found themselves in a difficult position. The commission had been executed by the protégé of the dean of the college of fine arts. Since that dean was also the chairman of the university budget review committee, it was found advisable in judging the statue to apply a more fiscally sound aesthetic than that suggested by simplistic good taste.

The happy, pragmatic resolution had been to display the work in the dimple left from the draining of a small blind lake. This was the spot McThacry favored for discussing sensitive matters because it was virtually invisible from any distance to speak of. Moreover, he supposed it was less susceptible to compromise by parabolic microphones.

Once they had sat on the benches provided for those requiring more than a moment to assess the quality of the art, McThacry explained, "I need to have the house swept again."

"Swept?" asked Sidney.

"Yes. Bobby saw the city electric truck out the other day. You never can be sure what they were doing with the wires."

"A house can't be bugged from the utility lines, can it? You mean you think you're bugged?"

McThacry stood on the bench for a moment and looked around. "God knows what some bourgeois technocrat will invent next. As much time as they spend photographing me—well, when you deal with forces this powerful, you can't be too careful."

"Technocrats?"

"No. The queers. Didn't you read the material for my undergraduate course?"

"Yes I did." Sidney was hurt. "But I don't see what it adds up to."

No, thought McThacry, *he would not see. That is why he is the perfect instrument—earnest skinny little nerd that he is.* McThacry had been careful. He had followed Sidney discreetly. He had searched Sidney's garbage. He had reviewed the academic records. He had questioned Sidney's associates in the New International Proletarian Peace League.

McThacry was used to the platonic admiration of his students. He had observed that not one male scholar in ten was a vigorous man. Most, by far, were like Sidney: pale and bespectacled, weak and soft-spoken, bookish and frankly effeminate. McThacry understood the boyish hero worship he presumed they felt for a vigorous man of letters, even one past his prime. But McThacry had to take care that it was this form of affection and none other. Since he had found his mission, he knew that sooner or later the powerful forces against him would send a spy into his camp.

Evidently, Sidney was not this spy. Sidney was what he appeared to be; a progressive doctoral candidate, with a quiet, uninspired marriage to an appropriately nondescript woman and a record of mild, ineffectual political activity. Sidney would be useful.

"Yes," McThacry reassured Sidney, "the connecting thread in the readings is deliberately obscure. I did not want the administration to see the point of it beforehand. One copy of the syllabus has already disappeared for twenty-four hours. They did not expect that I would count the copies every day. I will draw it all together in my lectures."

"I take it this has something to do with a homosexual underground?" Sidney had been a bit put off by McThacry's use of the word *queer*. Sidney had learned to say *gay* as he had learned to say *black, chicano,* and *woman* rather than *Negro, Mexican,* and *lady*. Sidney selected the word *homosexual* as sufficiently neutral.

"Not an underground at all. Quite the opposite of an underground, in fact. But before I go on, I must warn you. You have been my student long enough to see that the university has consistently tried to thwart me. They never wanted the truth told about the black experience in America. And as you know for yourself, it is not easy being my student. You have seen how they try to get to me through my students. Your thesis, for example."

"Certainly." Sidney's "The Mallet Method: Estate Multiplication for the Estimate of Inequality in Wealth in Bourgeois Society—A Marxist Analysis" had not been warmly received, though Sidney thought the six hundred pages were the equal of many dissertations he had seen.

"And we have become used to discovering that their camera trucks are following us, and all the other petty harassments they devised."

"Certainly we have." Sidney was often amazed at the professor's acuity in spotting the vans, for the photographers apparently had use of many styles and colors of vans, disguised with a variety of counterfeit logos.

"You need to know that what I am about to teach this fall involves issues infinitely more sensitive than racism. If you think that they have opposed me until now, it will surely get much worse—not only for me, but for anyone associated with me. My course will be a deep thrust to the heart of the bourgeois. There is a possibility that it will become physically dangerous."

"They might use violence to suppress your work?"

"Exactly. And my fieldwork has reached the point that I must now make bold moves to continue my research. I will very, very soon—today, if my guess is right—have to apply some unusual and controversial techniques. These may be dangerous in themselves. What I must know is, are you willing to risk everything, even your own safety, to complete this pioneering work with me?"

McThacry knew that Sidney would be thrilled. Any graduate student, once understanding the culs-de-sac of academic advancement, would walk through fire to be on the cutting edge of a major project—any project, but particularly one led by a scholar of McThacry's magnitude. McThacry eschewed false modesty in making this calculation. Sidney quickly indicated that McThacry's judgment on this point was correct.

When Sidney's profession of enthusiasm subsided, McThacry remarked: "We will need to get Connoly off your committee. I've been watching him for some time. There is no doubt that there is something funny about him. Watch the way he holds a teacup. He won't hesitate to sink your dissertation once it's clear what we're onto. But we'll come to that. Now, have you any idea how many children, between say seven and twelve years of age, disappear from their homes each year?"

"I do not. I didn't find anything like that in the readings."

"And you won't. Not in those readings, or any other. The statistic has been deliberately obscured. The figure cannot be less than four hundred thousand."

"I had no idea."

"Few people do. Now, some small part of that, on the order of one percent, is accounted for by kidnapping for ransom, hostage taking, and so forth. A much larger number, maybe ten percent, involves custody disputes, adoption foulups, jurisdictional conflicts involving mostly family, that sort of thing. Many of the remainder turn up missing from the most oppressed, impoverished classes—which is why there is no public outcry. But the really striking thing is that most of the unaccounted for are boys."

"Oh, I think I see. That's the point of the readings: They end up as male prostitutes."

"Many of them do. But that is skipping several steps. Hold on. There's a car passing."

Sidney and the professor sat quietly until the crunch of pebbles faded. McThacry stood on the pedestal with his arm around Machiavelli. He watched the shadows in the hedge by the roadway. "You have to be careful when you think you hear a car pass. Someone can roll out of it while it's moving. A very old trick, but you would be surprised how often they have tried it on me.

"You said you gathered that the course concerned a homosexual underground. But it is not an underground at all. It is an organization of some of the richest and most powerful men in the country. They constitute, in fact, what classic theorists call the ruling class. That's where the missing boys go."

"But you are talking about tens of thousands every year, aren't you? Surely someone would notice."

"Not necessarily. Remember, I said they are mostly from poor families. Some are assumed to have run away. That is what is behind this media campaign to define traditional methods of discipline as abuse. It's to make the running-away explanation seem more plausible. But even if someone with influence takes an interest in the case of one of these missing poor kids, who is it that investigates presumed kidnappings?"

"The NIO?"

"Precisely. It's common knowledge that the National Investigations Office has been in the hands of homosexuals for years. It's still full of them."

"I didn't know that."

"Of course. Remember that Chase B. Martin was a bachelor all his life. And throughout most of its history, Martin *was* the NIO. His proclivities were an open secret in Washington. But no one dared to speak out—"

"Because he kept a dossier on everyone of any importance or potential importance from civil rights leaders to presidents?" Sidney hoped to appear not so very dull after all.

"Good. You are beginning to see. He had almost the perfect organization. Talk about the fox guarding the henhouse. They make a good show of it. And of course they really do make arrests in kidnappings for ransom. Who's going to question the NIO if it can't turn up a lead in the case of a missing poor kid when naturally there is no ransom demand? Local authorities aren't going to presume to attempt cases that appear to baffle the feds."

"But what does happen to the boys?"

"The rich and powerful homosexuals trade them among themselves. They are like collectors."

"Don't the boys try to get away?"

"No doubt they do at first. But a combination of drugs and brainwashing techniques soon brings them into line. The methods a pimp uses with naive girls are crude by comparison. Eventually, of course, the boys get too old to interest the collectors. So the boys are more completely brainwashed. We are dealing with very powerful forces. These forces can wipe out a boy's memory, give him a new identity, and permanently warp his natural procreative drives. The forces can even convince him that he is proud and happy in his barren, perverted, artificial sexuality.

"At first I thought the more resistant boys were killed outright. But this does not seem to be the case. The failures are shipped to the Arabs."

"Well, I don't know much about homosexuals," Sidney said, glad he had not used the term *gay* in the beginning, "but somehow this all seems rather farfetched."

"I realize that." McThacry seemed agitated. "I realize that. That's why it is so difficult to interest the very few remaining uncorrupted authorities in the problem. The first thing they want to know is where is the evidence. Well, I've got some evidence: You will have to hear the tapes. And if I have figured things out correctly, we will get more incontrovertible evidence before the day is out."

"You have some evidence on tape?"

"You know I've been spending my weekends in Houston?"

"Yes. Almost all of them."

"I've been going to Montrose. You know Montrose is a homosexual enclave?"

"No. I'm from Dallas."

"That's what Montrose is, anyway. Homosexuals have been massing there for years in order to capture legitimate elected offices. That is icing on the cake for them; they long since have had the real power. Haven't you noticed how many more homosexuals there are these days?"

"I really hadn't thought about it."

"Well, take my word for it. There are now more homosexuals than ever in recorded history. But I suppose you have noticed that homosexuals are much more aggressive, I mean politically and culturally?"

"Certainly that is so."

"It's the brainwashing process. The old-fashioned homosexuals, the ones who were the result of the ordinary psychopathologies, were more reticent, shy, and—you know—properly aware of the fact that they were ill, that they were perverted. They had shame. And they had the feminine characteristics of their condition. But these new homosexuals are the missing kids, the ones who have been brainwashed. Apparently the brainwashing process is not perfect. It cannot overcome the naturally aggressive, masculine nature of the boys—who had, after all, been developing normally until the collectors got ahold of them. Also, the process does not always completely erase their memories. I've talked to hundreds of male prostitutes in Houston. They are called hustlers, and when I pay them, they tell me exactly what I want to hear. I've got many of these accounts on tape. It was expensive, but the material is priceless. The torture, the degradation, the degeneracy—it is positively fantastic! I promise you, these kids tell an ugly, ugly story."

"And you will use the tapes with your lectures?"

"Yes. But only the milder ones. I've got some really remarkable slides and video from one of their discotheques. I think with the tapes over the right music and, you know, two sets of slides, on either side of the video—maybe a strobe light to give the right impression of the discotheque—I think it will make a striking presentation. But we have an opportunity to get some even more convincing material."

"Yes?"

"I think one of their couriers is being dispatched by the Austin agent of the collectors. This seems to be a new courier. I only overheard a little of his instructions. But I think we ought to be able to break him down and get at the truth."

"Break him down?"

"Interrogate him. I told you this involved unusual and controversial techniques. It could be dangerous. Do you want out?"

"Oh no." Sidney was genuinely excited. "I'm ready."

"Good. I see you brought your taxi."

"It's the only transportation I've got. I have to drive it for my personal use."

McThacry knew that. "And all the cabs in town are centrally dispatched? You hear all of the calls on your radio?"

"That's right."

"Fine. We'll get Bobby and go to the safehouse."

"Safehouse?"

"A place I rented on the east side under an assumed name. I pay the rent in cash so it can't be traced to me. I've got the video equipment there. We are crossing the Rubicon. We must be careful every step of the way. Remember, say nothing in the house. I'll explain the rest on the way."

McThacry stood on the pedestal again and looked around. Then he got down and signaled Sidney to follow the indirect route by which they had come. McThacry was pleased that the dew had dried.

Sidney had been tired from driving the cab all night, but now he felt different. He felt there was a way out of the dead end. He felt he must be about to do something real. The August morning appealed to him in a new way. Vibrant sensations stirred him from every side, and along the way, the primroses were lovely.

Why is there schnapps? Jim asked the coffee maker. The coffee maker gurgled solicitously. *I mean I know better,* Jim explained. *I don't know why I keep that stuff in the house. No. That's not true. I keep it because it goes down potential tricks so good and sort of sneaks up on them. Sometimes. But I don't have to drink so much of that crap myself.*

44

The coffee maker hissed: It was ready. Jim poured out a cup to cool so that the whole dose could be gulped at once.

Where are those pills I had left over from the toothache? he asked. *Oh yeah, the roughneck from Odessa ate them all when he sent me out for cigarettes. Aspirin? Dare I try aspirin?* But the coffee maker's mind seemed elsewhere. *Okay, be that way. Let me rot my stomach out with aspirin and that swill you put out. You'll be sorry when I'm gone.*

But Jim's stomach did not rot out. He checked his wallet and found the money in good order. He replaced his IDs with the phony ones from the pile on the table. Except for the plane ticket and one of the mailers, he repacked the carry-on.

He found the two other pieces of luggage were packed tightly. Everything seemed to be his size, if a bit too preppy for his taste. The shaving kit was complete with small sizes of everything in his own brands and another new straight razor.

Damn. How did Agnes know all of this?

But in a way, the attention to detail seemed reassuring. *Someone who would go to the trouble of packing the right toothpaste must be on top of the big stuff too. Right?* There was even a leather-bound edition of the *New Hip Language Bible,* with Jim's name stamped in gold on the cover.

Jim opened it at random: "No husband? That's right on, chick. You done had five husbands. But that dude you shacked up with now ain't married to you."

Okay. Maybe I'm damned. But I'd much rather be damned in the King James Version. The prospect of becoming a trendy seminarian was too much to deal with before a second cup of coffee.

By kneeling on the suitcase Jim got it closed again. He gulped the coffee and poured a second cup to cool. He had some trouble deciding whether to turn the coffee maker off.

He would remember much later that he had decided to leave it on. The alarm went off. He stubbed his toe on the bedstead. The alarm never managed to wake him, but it contrived to annoy him at intervals. *Shut up, bitch. I hope you're happy now. My toe is going to bleed. Look: You did that.*

It hummed innocently to itself.

Nonetheless, it said it was ten. That ought to be late enough that Jim could have his shower without the interference of the compulsive toilet flushers. He knew, of course, that they did it on purpose. He laid out his own clothes for the trip but found he had to open the suitcase again for clean socks.

Sure enough, a toilet flusher had been waiting to get him. But the flusher had been too early: Jim had not yet stepped under the shower. The foiling of the toilet flusher and the feeling of being clean again encouraged Jim. He looked for the magazine sweepstakes brochure; he could not remember how much he stood to gain. No matter, it had been a substantial figure. Jim had observed that money was a good sign. You get a lot of money and good luck almost always follows.

Time was getting away. Jim called for a taxi. There was a honk from the parking lot almost immediately. Jim could not imagine that it was his cab, but after the third honk, he was convinced.

When Jim brought the luggage out, he was put off that the driver handed him the key to the trunk out the window. Jim stowed the luggage himself in the trunk of the cab. Jim tried to figure out how to avoid giving the driver a tip. The twenties were the smallest bills he had. *Maybe the driver is right: Some guys don't like being helped like little old ladies.* Jim returned the key to the driver and helped himself into the back. "Airport."

"Looks like it's going to be another scorcher," Jim remarked as the cab turned east from Avenue H.

The driver grunted.

Be that way, Jim thought. He looked at his watch. *Plenty of time for breakfast at the airport.* Then he thought again of the few breakfasts he had eaten at airports. *No, maybe not.*

Absentmindedly, he looked at the photograph on the cabbie's license. *Funny: That guy doesn't look so skinny from behind.* The driver's neck was a red color that looked as if it had been shaved too close all over. Jim looked again at the picture of the skinny, pasty-faced guy. *They aren't the same. They must have traded off cabs.*

"Been driving a cab long?" Jim asked.

The driver grunted again.

This time Jim saw the driver's face in the mirror. *It's that guy who was following us. Whatshisname . . . McThacry.*

No. Maybe not. Jim looked for a sign that the driver had noticed Jim's gasp of recognition. Jim looked at the mirror again. He was certain this was bad. *College professors don't drive cabs. A plan. I need a plan.*

Jim thought he would make a jump for it the next time the cab stopped at a traffic signal. Staring forward, trying to present a vaguely abstracted smile, Jim felt slowly along the cab's door. He found the armrest, the window crank, and a strap. The latch handle was missing.

A quick glance at the other door showed it was the same. But Jim knew the outside handle worked. That was how he had let himself in. The air conditioner was on. Jim could not crank the window down without being obvious. He would hope for a stop in heavy traffic, whip the window down, grab the outside handle, and be gone.

The intersection of Manor Road and Airport Boulevard was coming up. Jim noticed that the cab was in the wrong lane to turn to the airport. That no longer mattered. His fist tightened on the knob of the window crank. He would wait until the moment the cab became boxed in at the traffic signal.

The cab slowed and stopped behind a driver-ed training car. Cars stopped to the right and left. A little pickup pulled up behind. Just as Jim began to twist the knob, McThacry turned around.

"Hold it." A nickel-plated gleam in the professor's left hand fixed Jim's attention. There were two big holes in the piece, one over the other.

"This is a thirty-eight two-shot with hollow-point rounds," the professor explained. "I won't need them both. I hit you any place—any place—and it's all over. You understand?"

Jim nodded.

"Now slide over to the other end of the seat." McThacry adjusted the mirror as Jim moved over.

"Sit on your hands. I'll be watching you every second. Don't think about moving. Don't even breathe."

Jim sat on his hands and held as still as he could. The traffic signal changed.

FOUR

PHIL lay on a towel on the deck of the roof garden. The Monday-morning sun was beginning to clear the eastern wall. Agnes was ensconced in the chaise longue with a stack of newspapers.

"Look at this, Phil." Agnes held up the front page of a strange newspaper. The headline read: HOMOSEXUAL RING AT SU.

Phil propped himself on his elbows. "What paper is that?"

"It's the *Osage News-Free Press.* Since Leslie died, we've had it flown in—to keep up with events in the province. Let us read you the story: 'The Reverend Earl Richards, better known as Brother Earl, announced Sunday from the pulpit of Holy Word of God Cathedral that he would present the Oklahoma legislature with documentary evidence that a homosexual ring involving students, faculty, and staff of Sooner University in Norman, Oklahoma, has been operating for at least five years.

"'Richards said he will testify Wednesday before the public education subcommittee, which is considering a bill to provide tax advantages to families with children in religious colleges. Richards claimed that his evidence will show authorities have turned a blind eye to homosexual seduction and recruitment at the state's largest public university . . .' and blah, blah, blah, et cetera." Agnes threw the paper on the deck and let her pince-nez swing from the golden chain attached to her tasteful cameo pin.

"So?" Phil rested his head on the towel. "He's always hated us."

"But this time, don't you see, he's not merely quoting scripture like a pharisee. He's going to do something." Agnes stood and paced around the chaise longue. "He knows Leslie is dead. He either thinks the photos are gone, or he's destroyed them himself. If only we hadn't fought with Leslie. If only we had kept the negatives ourself."

Agnes pinched the spine of the false century plant and spoke into it. "Thomas, you might as well serve breakfast. And bring the telephone."

The first ray of direct sunlight climbed up Phil's right side. "Agnes, you never did tell me why you and Leslie fought."

"Over a man. What else? His name was Thomas."

"That explains a lot," Phil said.

The Japanese Thomas, in his cadet uniform, brushed through the foliage with the silver service. He had been

50

with Agnes the longest. He knew to set the tray down in front of Phil's prone body and to hand Agnes the phone. He plugged it into the jack in the century plant.

Agnes punched the buttons with her knuckle. She placed her hand over the receiver. "Thank you, Thomas. That will be all."

Phil sat up and looked for the marmalade. Seeing Agnes's free hand wave at the tray, he handed her the sidecar. He lifted his Bloody Mary. They clinked glasses. Agnes sipped the sidecar.

"Hello, we're calling Miss Gretta. . . . Tell her it's the Court of the Jade Chimera calling. . . . Well then wake her up. . . . Don't use that snotty tone with us, young man. . . . Have you brought in the morning papers? . . . Get them and open them up and then decide whether you will put us through. . . . Yes, we'll wait." Agnes put her hand over the mouthpiece again. "Gretta's new houseboy thinks he is the perfect butler. Too much British television. Hand us a croissant, if they are still warm."

"Hello, Gretta . . . Gretta . . . Gretta . . . Gretta, getting hysterical will help nothing at all. . . . Yes, the Osage paper had that quote. . . . Well of course, if he actually has such a list, you're bound to be on it. . . . Look, it isn't our fault that Leslie died. . . . Yes, hindsight makes everything seem clearer. . . . There's no point in crying over spilt milk. . . . Yes, you're right. Osage should be in your territory, not ours. . . . Do you want us to cede it to you on the spot? . . . We didn't think so. . . . Yes, Gretta."

Agnes did not bother to cover the mouthpiece this time. "Phil, order us another sidecar. It appears that this is going to be a two-cocktail phone call."

Phil got up and pinched the spine of the century plant.

"Look, Gretta, have a drink and—well have another. And try to pull yourself together. . . . Now, if things get really hot, we'll be happy to receive you at court for a couple of weeks. . . . We know all about Boise. We're almost as old as you are. . . . Screw you too. You know very damned well you were three years ahead of us in school. . . . Have it your own way. The important thing is not to panic. . . . No, you have to hold your head up and weather this out as long as humanly possible. . . . You're the product of a long tradition. You have to show them. You have to set an example."

Phil took another cocktail from Thomas and handed it to Agnes.

"No, we're not asking you to be a martyr to the cause. . . . Suit yourself, Joan of Arc. *Be* a martyr, if it will get you through the day. . . . Don't tell us about your damned career. We happen to know that you have plenty socked away. You won't starve in the streets.

"Gretta . . . Gretta . . . Gretta, this is important. Have they really got anything? Drugs? Chicken? Public lewdness, Heaven forbid? . . . Then tell the senator to stay away for a while. If they had that, they would already be using it. . . . Right. . . . Hold your head up. Speak politely, but firmly. Go on as if nothing were happening. You have a copy of Crisp's book, the first one? . . . Good. Go through it for pointers. . . . Yes, we're working on it. . . . It's our first priority. . . . You ought to know we can't discuss it by telephone. . . . We'll be in touch. . . . Gretta . . . Gretta . . . Gretta, there's someone on the other line. It could be about the project. Gretta . . . Gretta . . . Good-bye, Gretta."

Agnes dropped the receiver into its cradle and collapsed into the chaise longue. Phil looked up from his book.

"What about the other call?" Phil asked.

"What other call?" Agnes said innocently. "What are you reading there? Phil, there aren't enough drugs in the house for Burroughs. There's plenty of nice Mishima and Genet in the library. Look next to the Arno reprints."

52

"Why is Osage attached to the Jade Court?"

"Oh well, as much as it is, all owes to Mary III—or was it IV? We get the dynasty confused because there were three Marys in a row. Anyway, during the Second World War—"

"Then it would have been Mary III."

"Yes, of course. Well, Mary met a bunch of the girls from Osage when she was stationed in Europe. The community in Osage was small and closeted—we mean, even more so than usual for then—and so the girls from Osage would come down here to let their hair down and all after the war."

"I see."

"Yes. One of those accidental arrangements. Lots of other alliances would have been much more practical. The war contributed a lot to—what do they call it now? To the networking, the backbone of the community as we know it now. The war and the Kinsey report. We think sometimes that you could account for almost all of our current situation with just those two facts."

"How was Gretta?"

"You heard. Hard to tell. We've seen her get that way over a run in her hosiery." Agnes got up and walked to the south wall. The Monday-morning rush of traffic was beginning to subside. She looked down to the street for a moment. "Sure, Gretta could lose her job. There don't seem to be any real legal problems. Still, the last time there was a serious disturbance, street gangs killed a couple of dozen people. Not all of them our people. Just whoever seemed effeminate to a bunch of thugs."

"And then there's the Klan," said Phil.

"Yes, and then there's the Klan. That's the other side of the Sunday-morning moralists. Which reminds us, we need to see when the Holy Word of God Broadcast Cathedral comes on. Maybe Brother Earl will tip his hand."

53

"It's not going to be easy for Jim, is it?"

"No, it's not. It certainly appears that the photographs are gone. We're really merely assuming that Brother Earl's character hasn't changed much over the years. We're in big trouble if he really has got righteous religion. But we doubt it. He's been mouthing that hogwash and seducing his proselytes longer than you have been alive. Jim will be able to get new pictures, if he can bring himself to do it."

Phil closed the book. "Agnes, I hate that."

"We know what you mean. It was our Thomas, the one we fought with Leslie over, who posed for the first set."

"You never told me about Thomas."

"Thomas? . . . Well, he had—fiddlesticks, you'll find out anyway. Thomas was Jim's father. Jim is so like him. When Jim walked into the throne room, I . . . I mean, *we* almost lost our composure. The mannerisms. The walk. Those blue, blue eyes."

"I'm always amazed at the number of . . . uh, more mature girls who have been married and had a family."

"You see, Phil, it was often a necessity. It was, what? Protective coloration. And that's not to mention the naive young things who were told that marriage would 'cure' them."

"But," Phil asked, "wasn't it terribly unfair to the women?"

"It seems that way now. What does a woman want? We suppose, like any of us, a woman wants a husband who loves her for herself, a man to share things with, but one who will let her be herself. Someone who thinks she's something special.

"Of course, none of us would feel that way about a woman. But you might be surprised at the number of us who grew to be . . . to have a kind of affection for our wives—nothing romantic, not like love. But the sort of mutual regard that people develop in shared enterprise.

"You have to remember, they were telling women then that if they had a sober husband who didn't beat them and paid the bills and all, well that's a good marriage. And that was all a woman was expected to ask for then. Heaven knows, they never caught any of us with another woman. And some of them who found out didn't really care as long as appearances were kept up."

The university tower chimed ten o'clock.

"This could be dangerous for Jim, right?"

"Well, yes. But who knows how dangerous it could be for all of us if he fails. You never know when some dema-gogue will strike the right chord with the great unwashed. Straights don't care for liberty. A little more fodder and they're happy. You know, today's ranting radio nut can all too easily become tomorrow's führer."

"Come on, Agnes. You exaggerate. Surely this will be unpleasant for Gretta and some people in Oklahoma, but the whole trend of history is toward liberalism."

Agnes frowned. "That's what they thought at the Hirschfeld Institute—before the Nazis burned it. Anyway, we'll just see to Brother Earl and then keep our eyes open for the next one."

Now in the full sun, Phil rolled over and shielded his eyes with his forearm. "I love him."

"You're young."

"Agnes, you act as if it wasn't your idea to get us to-gether."

"Well, yes. We expected you to hit it off with Jim. Our whole plan hinged on that. But look here, Phil, you've got to can the brainy stuff. We don't mean you should act fall-ing-down stupid. We mean, you know, let him have the ideas first. Be a little bit slow. You catch our drift?"

"Agnes, this isn't the fifties!"

"The basic construction of the male ego is timeless. Also, try to appear vulnerable. The brighter ones catch on eventually, but even they appreciate the effort."

"You're kidding."

"We're serious as a heart attack. Men need to feel they are needed. If you have your career, and your friends, and you're all self-actualized, a man thinks he's nothing more than a dildo. They need to feel that they are protecting you from something."

Phil sat up and turned around to face Agnes.

"But what about me, Agnes? I am a man. What about my need to feel protective?"

"You be protective by protecting them from the truth."

"Agnes, you know what you remind me of? You remind me of those straights who always ask which of the gay couple is the man in bed or who can't imagine what lesbians do in bed. I'm sick to death of butch-this and fem-that."

"But child—"

"Hold on, Agnes, I'm not finished. You consider yourself the big mastermind of gay lib and everything. But that means more than stopping the straights from beating and killing us. It means that as things get freer, we change too. It means a lot of other things, but the stinger for you, Agnes, is that one day we will be *ordinary.*"

Agnes sat forward in the chaise longue, but she had to lean back to keep it from tipping over. She took a deep breath. "Have a care, child, before you toss out a culture that has sustained our people for hundreds of years, through some of the most murderous oppression we've ever known. For all you know, this liberal trend is only a backwater."

"Agnes, you're exasperating. I mean . . . I mean, well, there is something to what you say. I don't know."

Agnes smiled. "Phil, there is one thing we know you are right about: Fashion has changed. Whether it's any deeper than fashion, we don't know. We do know that this court is old-fashioned. Something needs to be done about that."

Phil lay back down. "No, I don't mean you should change your own style."

"We don't intend to. Our successor will bring his own style to court."

"*His?* But there's always been a queen on the Jade Throne. Who do you have in mind?"

"You."

"Me? Agnes, this isn't my scene."

"Exactly. Make it over to suit yourself. Make it something that won't seem ridiculous to your own generation. Except for emergencies such as the present one, Court was meant to be amusing. So make it up-to-date amusing."

Phil stood and walked to the century plant. "Coffee?"

"How about some green tea?"

"Sounds good." Phil ordered green tea and some toast to go with the rest of the marmalade. "But Agnes, I'm not going to get up there in leathers any more than a formal gown."

"That's it. Be yourself. Think of it. One day all of this can be yours: the townhouse, the lake place, and, best of all, the card file."

"The girls will never stand for it."

"Leave the girls to us. There are only two to worry about. The Duchess of Waterloo. Her family has been in Austin forever, and no one is allowed to forget it. She was furious when our predecessor sat us on the Jade Throne. She said she thought it should have been a better type of person, but I'm sure she meant 'brighter.' Of course, she was badly in her cups at the time and had never before shown much interest in Court—except to make her annual late entrance at the cotillion.

"Then there's the Baroness DuBastrop. She traces her

chain of partners back to some hero of the Alamo. We've heard the story about a hundred times and can't recall a bit of it. She has no real ambition for herself. She's only a troublemaker. But if things come out okay with Brother Earl, there won't be anything they can do. We'll invest you as our heir at the cotillion, a week after your twenty-first birthday. That seems auspicious."

Tomás brought the tea and began to clear away the remains of breakfast. He almost got the marmalade, but Phil had the presence of mind to grab it.

"Madam, there are some gentlemen from the Homophile Caucus to see you."

"Have them wait a half an hour."

"I took the liberty of doing that already. I hope it was all right."

"Very good, Tomás, we suppose you might as well show them up."

"Yes, madam."

"Phil, you'd best put on some shorts. These respectable girls get scandalized so easily."

When Phil returned from the bedroom, Tomás was holding back a branch to make way for the visitors. They were almost, except for the colors, dressed identically in golf shirts and beltless slacks, and groomed identically with short haircuts and tiny well-trimmed mustaches.

Agnes stood. "Well, gentlemen, what can we do for you today?"

The slightly taller and more slender one in the blue shirt replied, "We have come on a serious matter, Angus."

"Goodness! Would you care for some tea? Something stronger?"

The one in the green shirt looked agreeable, but his companion said, "No thank you, Angus. This is not a social call."

"Indeed? Tomás, bring us the checkbook."

"No, nothing like that. We've come to talk about the Halloween cotillion." The one in the blue shirt was balding, as his short haircut showed too well.

Phil sat cross-legged on the towel and began to apply marmalade to his toast.

"The cotillion?" asked Agnes. "How very coincidental. We were just discussing it. As always, everyone will be welcome. Usually, only members of Court receive formal invitations, but there's no hard-and-fast rule. It is much too early yet, but we will be happy to add you to the list."

As Phil brought the toast to his mouth, he was arrested by the green-shirted man's covetous stare. With a motion toward the tray and a spot on the towel, Phil offered him some toast and a place to sit.

"Angus," said the one in blue, "we are here representing the Caucus. We discussed it completely last night and took a vote. We voted to cancel the cotillion."

"Cancel the cotillion?"

"Or make it very low key. Strictly by invitation only. Not the kind of public display it was last year. Perhaps some kind of quiet gathering at your place on the lake. We didn't vote on that, but I'm sure the Caucus will be reasonable about it." The one in blue glowered at his friend, who had sat on the towel next to Phil. But the one in green seemed oblivious and was, besides, out of nudging range.

"But the cotillion is not a function of the Caucus. It is a function of the Jade Court. You can't vote to cancel it."

"As the responsible voice of community opinion, we have a duty to speak out on issues such as this."

"What issues?" Agnes made a broad gesture of nescience.

"Why in the world do you want us to cancel the cotillion?"

"Because, Angus, it is not politically correct. It tends to reinforce unfortunate stereotypes."

"You mean we are bad for your image?"

"As you know, the election is only a few days after Halloween, and for the first time we have a candidate for mayor—"

"Nonsense. This town has had plenty of gay mayors."

"I mean one who is politically correct." He was still trying to attract the attention of his friend in the green shirt, to no avail.

Phil smiled as the one in the green shirt piled marmalade on a piece of toast to the extent it would bear.

"Politically correct, indeed. Your boy's a closet case."

"No he's not. He doesn't deny being gay."

"He doesn't deny it only because the other side is both too moral and too smart to mention it. I've seen your literature. There's a picture of one of his smiling children on every page."

"Now, if it is the matter of having children, Angus—"

"Of course not. It's the matter of using them like that. We mean, there they are on every TV spot. His kids are the only message of his whole campaign. Then after dark he's creeping around the bars, whispering to us that he's really okay."

Phil folded a piece of toast so that it would fit and wiped the dregs of the marmalade from the pot. Then he tore the toast and offered a part to the one in the green shirt.

The one in blue stepped casually into kicking range of his friend's back. "Frankly, Angus, our lesbian sisters have raised the question of violence toward women."

"Good for them. We are glad to hear that someone in your group is interested in serious issues."

"I'm not sure you understand. They mean the violence

toward women of the Halloween cotillion."

"But there's never been any violence at all at the Halloween cotillion, unless you count a little slapping match between lovers. Granted, it's hell on the crockery. In any event, nothing involving women. The women at the cotillion have always been exceptionally well behaved."

"Angus, we mean the psychic violence that drag represents. Psychologists are agreed that drag represents an outlet of hostility toward women. All effeminacies are based upon an inner hatred of woman. Therefore, you see, whether it seems so or not on the surface, drag is one of the cultural supports of the system of rape." He toed the small of the green-shirted back.

"Nonsense!"

"I'm afraid it's not nonsense. The noted psychologist Dr.—"

"Noted psychologist indeed. Don't you remember what noted psychologists were saying about the sort of thing you do every Wednesday afternoon at the peep shows?"

The one in the green shirt looked up suddenly and sharply.

"Oh, goodness, we forgot you two are married. But then we never see you together. We see Larry at the peep shows and Ben at the tea room in Pease Park. We sluts have such difficulty in keeping up with the doings of you respectable married people."

Larry blushed and cleared his throat. "Whatever. That doesn't deal with the issues."

"Very well. Anyone who can possibly compare our putting on a dress with wife-beating and rape has a screw loose. You can tell those Trotskyites at your meeting that we have never struck a woman in our life. But we are willing to start with whoever intends to dictate our attire."

"Oh no. We don't mean that. What you do in your own

home is no one's problem but your own—although it would do you some good to come to a principled, dialectical relationship with women as Ben and I have. We are saying that when you make your activities public, you are engaging in support of the system of violence against women. That's what has to be stopped."

Agnes folded her arms across her chest. "Let's see if we follow all that. If we do drag at home, that's merely politically incorrect. If we make public what we wear, that is violence. In other words, information concerning the apparel of guests at the cotillion is violence. Information is violence? Then what do you call bricks through windows? Knives? Bullets?"

"Oh, that's violence too, of course."

"Of course," Ben put in.

"So our wearing a sweet little yellow frock out of the house is the same as rape?"

"I realize it seems very different on a subjective level. But objectively, yes. It is the same."

"Gentlemen, this audience is at an end. We have something more meaningful and constructive to do—such as the crossword puzzle."

Ben stood. "Angus, please don't make yourself an enemy of women and the oppressed masses of the third world—"

"And the exploited workers," Larry insisted.

"—and the exploited workers."

"We said we had something better to do than listen to this. It's a shame. We liked you boys much better when you were concerned about the baby fur seals, even though at the time our own people were having their heads broken by the police. But our own people don't concern you as much as the exploited third world working baby fur seals, do they? Tomás, these gentlemen are leaving."

Tomás stood aside and extended his palm in the direction

of the path through the roof garden. Ben started to move, but Larry snagged the sleeve of Ben's green golf shirt and stood facing Agnes.

"If you prefer to stay, we assure you that our remarks concerning the tea rooms and the peep shows were only the beginning. Shall we read your beads in earnest?"

"I see it is true," Larry declared, "you queens do represent reactionary elements."

"Child, you've supped too long on the crumbs from the leftists' table. You actually think they love us. If only there were still a Venceremos Brigade so that you could see for yourselves how the Marxists deal with queers. Now, be gone."

Larry clenched his fists, but Ben took his hand and followed Tomás to the path.

"Well, Phil, is this your brave new gay man?"

Phil's bottom lip curled outward.

"Oh Phil. Don't be that way. We're just kidding. We've always had self-righteous know-it-alls and probably always will."

"Ben didn't seem so bad."

"Neither of them is so bad. Come on, cheer up."

"It isn't that. I'm thinking. The Klan and Brother Earl on the one hand, the reds and Professor McThacry on the other. Looks like we get it from both sides. Isn't there anyone we can trust?"

"Child, it is a hard question. You must keep your own counsel. You must do what you think is right. Dogmatists come. Dogmatists go. Some hate blacks and queers. Some hate capitalists and queers. Some hate Jews and queers. Some hate communists and queers. What they all hate, we think, is to be free, to be free like the truly queer. They hate to make their own choices. They try to believe there aren't any choices for them. Then they can be blameless when things go wrong. No, to answer your question, we don't think we have any permanent allies. What is the saying? Eternal vigilance is the price of liberty." Agnes shrugged and started to recline on the chaise longue when the phone rang.

"Hello? . . . Oh? How curious. Did you check with Monro at the apartments? . . . Hm. What was your impression when you left him last afternoon? . . . Did you call the bars? . . . You're sure? . . . Tell me exactly what Monro said. . . . Red and green cab. Doesn't McThacry's student drive that kind? . . . Well, hold on there until the plane leaves. . . . We're sure you did your best. . . . Probably not. McThacry's never done anything like that before, but he's crazy enough. . . . Worth our looking into, anyway. We're sure Monro knows what McThacry looks like, but not so sure that he could be that sure under the circumstances. Now you better get back to the gate, just in case. . . . Yes. Good-bye."

Agnes held the telephone receiver for a moment.

"Is there something wrong?" Phil asked.

"We aren't sure. Jim left his apartment by cab in plenty of time. But his plane leaves in fifteen minutes, and Thomas says he hasn't shown up at the airport. Probably got cold feet."

"You said something about McThacry?" Phil was alarmed.

"Well, from a distance, Monro says it seemed to him— it's crazy. A wild idea. Probably nothing. But we had better go to the vault and use the card file. Come along. You will need to learn to use the card file anyway."

Phil picked up the shorts that he had removed when the visitors left and followed Agnes into the house.

FIVE

WHAT do you think of the lighting?" McThacry asked, studying the monitor.

"I don't know," Sidney said.

"We need to get that shadow out from under his nose. Get that light over there, Sidney. No, don't touch the reflector with your bare hands. Now move over this way. A little more. Okay. Lower the standard by about a foot."

"How's that?"

"Fine. I wish he hadn't worn plaid. The camera makes it look so . . . so . . ."

"Busy?" Jim asked.

"Yes. You wouldn't mind changing shirts, would you?"

"You would have to untie my hands."

"Okay, we can do that. I'm afraid that shirt would be overpowering on the six-foot screen." McThacry thought it over. His own shirt was plaid. Sidney's was a yellow pastel button-down. It would look all right, except that it would be much too small. He could not remember what Bobby was wearing.

"Bobby, come in here a minute," McThacry shouted toward the door to the kitchen.

"What is it now?" Bobby hollered back.

"Get on in here!"

Though Bobby trudged to the door with the exaggerated weariness that adolescents reserve for demonstrating exasperation with stupid parental demands, all Jim noticed were the deltoids. Bobby was wearing a terry-cloth shirt with three broad horizontal stripes.

"Good." *Colorful,* McThacry thought, *without being . . . busy.* "Take off your shirt, Bobby."

By all means, Jim thought, *take off your shirt, Bobby.*

"What for?"

"I want him to wear it for the taping."

"Oh, gawd . . ."

McThacry's lecture began with: "One day, young man, you will realize the importance of this work and it's a lucky thing. . . ." Bobby looked at Jim, rolled his eyes toward the ceiling, and flopped against the door frame. Bobby planted his left wrist on his hip with a flourish. That made Jim wonder. Maybe it was a boy's gesture of disgust, but it seemed to Jim to be a tad girlish. Jim raised an eyebrow and looked sidelong at McThacry as if to say, Might as well get on with it and shut the old fart up.

McThacry concluded his remarks. Bobby stood away from the door frame, peeled the shirt over his head, and handed it to his father. The display was better than Jim had hoped: *abs 8, pecs 10, delts 9.* Bobby noticed, a little too well, Jim's mental scoring process—or so it seemed to Jim. *And doesn't he seem a bit too self-conscious about standing around bare chested?*

No, I'm letting my imagination run away with me. A beauty like that would be the talk of the town if he was available. On the other hand, Bobby is too young to make the bar scene. Of course, one hears of action on the running trails, and perhaps, since he is too top heavy to be a runner, there is action at the springs and swimming pools too.

Jim resolved, if he ever got the chance again, to look into the matter of a healthier lifestyle.

McThacry reached for the derringer on the mantelpiece. "Okay Sidney, loosen one wrist at a time."

The change of shirts proceeded awkwardly, but Jim was just as happy he did not have to expose his whole chest at once to the boy. As it was, Jim thought he detected a sneer of disdain when Bobby assessed him. Sidney secured Jim's wrists again. McThacry put the derringer down and slurped the rest of the scotch from his coffee cup. Bobby put Jim's shirt on, sniffed the armpits, and buttoned it. McThacry handed the coffee cup to Bobby.

"Get me a little more, will you, son."

"It's still real early."

"Damn it, Bobby, do as I say." McThacry swung his arm in Bobby's direction, and Bobby took the cup back to the kitchen.

I suppose, thought Jim, *that every family has its ups and downs.*

McThacry looked at the monitor and nodded to himself.

He touched a button on the video recorder. The machine whirred as it pulled the tape up to engage the head. "Okay, let's start the interrogation."

"What's that?" Phil thought it sounded like an avalanche bearing down.

"Oh. You haven't spent much time in the vault. That's what the hot tub upstairs sounds like when you turn on the whirlpool. We suppose Thomas is entertaining the mailman again."

Agnes sat down at the console of the automatic file. "Now, we know McThacry has a place on the east side. So first we punch him up on the alphabetic file." Agnes touched the dimple marked *Mc* on the board in front of her. The automatic file squealed. Six layers of bins rolled past the console before the automatic file clunked to a stop. "We should find the address of McThacry's other place here, as well as something about his student. Then you see what you can do to locate the cab while we go to the geographic file—that's the one over there by the terminal. Tommy's trying to computerize all of this, but he seems to be having a technical problem. Are you listening to us, Phil?"

"What's the flashing light?"

"Goodness, it's the red line. Thomas can't hear it in the hot tub. We better pick it up." Agnes reached under the console and came up with a headset. She held the earpiece with one hand and pressed the red dimple on the board.

"Hello? . . . We see. We only this minute sat down at the card file. . . . No, you best stay put until we get some more information. We will want you to drive through Avalon Park if nothing pans out here. . . . We doubt it too. He's too paranoid. Go ahead and book every flight leaving today that has connections for Osage. . . . Keep us informed. . . . Thank you, Thomas." Agnes pressed another dimple and replaced the headset on the console. "Jim missed his flight," she said to Phil as she wedged a fingernail into one of the drawers of index cards.

"How long have you known McKinney?"

"I only met her yesterday."

" 'Her'?"

"Him. By 'her,' I mean 'him.' I only met him yesterday."

McThacry gave Sidney a significant look and continued. "How long have you been working for them?"

"Who?"

"The boy kidnappers."

"I don't know anything about any boy kidnappers."

"No? Then why are you flying to Osage today?"

"To go to grad school."

"Okay, that's your cover story. Don't deny it. I overheard part of your instructions."

"Well, if you had heard it all, you'd know it has nothing to do with little boys."

McThacry's cup was already empty again. He looked into it. "Then what is it to do with?"

"Agnes has an old feud with Brother Earl. That's all."

"By 'Agnes,' you mean Mr. McKinney?"

"Yes." Jim braced himself. Sure enough, there was the significant look again, passed from McThacry to Sidney.

"God, Sidney. Stay on the right side of him. If you get on the left the reflection off your glasses makes flares on the screen. As for you, I don't know what they are paying you, but I'm sure we can match it. You know I'll get to the bottom of this sooner or later. It will be a hell of a lot easier on you if you come clean now."

"First, there's nothing to come clean about. And second, you aren't a cop. In fact, I'd be happy to see a cop right now."

"Okay. I bet you would. But you people cannot possibly have corrupted all of the cops in the country." McThacry looked again into the empty cup. "I'm going to the kitchen, Sidney. You question him awhile."

Sidney moved away from the chair in which Jim was tied. "But what if he tries something?"

"You are the one that tied him up. Are you very sure you did a good job of it?"

"Yes."

"Then what is he going to do?"

"Something. *You know.*"

"Ha. Just keep your fly zipped. You'll be all right." McThacry walked out of the room.

Sidney moved behind Jim and tugged on the ropes binding Jim's wrists. The bonds seemed secure. The chair seemed safely bolted to the floor. Sidney sat on the floor, wiped his glasses on the tail of his pale yellow shirt, and looked Jim up and down carefully. "You aren't going to tell us anything about the boys, are you?"

"I don't know anything about any boys. And neither does he. It's all lies." Jim realized, because of the way Sidney drew back, that the answer had been rather too sharp. It would be better to be less hostile toward Sidney. It might be possible to play Sidney off against the professor.

"There certainly is something to it." Sidney was indignant. "Professor McThacry has it all very well documented."

"Really? Then maybe so. But this is the first I've heard of it."

"But you are one of them."

"I have nothing to do with any kidnappers or boys."

"I mean, you *are* gay."

"Well, yes. But that doesn't mean I know everything that goes on. You all have the wrong person."

70

Sidney seemed for a fleeting moment to be the least un-
certain. He looked toward the kitchen door. He couldn't
hear anything stir in the kitchen. Then he whispered,
"What is it you guys do, anyway?"

"I told you I don't know anything about boy kidnappers."

"No, I mean you guys, what you do. *You know.*"

Humor him, humor him, Jim reminded himself. "I like to
screw."

"I thought you were gay!"

"I am. I like to screw guys."

"Screw guys?"

Jim nodded. "Surely you've heard of that."

"I thought it was a figure of speech." Sidney's glasses
made it appear that his eyes had got even bigger than they
had. "You mean guys actually, you know, put . . . stick the
Staff of Life into the body's sewer?"

Jim blinked. "I never heard it put that way before. But
yes, yes, I guess we do."

"Ooh!" Sidney squeaked, suddenly very much ani-
mated. "You've done that yourself?"

"Every chance I get." Jim smirked.

"Ooh. Isn't it terribly icky?"

Icky? "I never thought so until just now."

"And you spill your Vital Life Fluid in there with all that
refuse?"

"That or use a condom. You see, that is rather the point
of the whole thing."

"Wow, I've met gay—" A noise came from the kitchen.
Sidney looked nervously at the door. "I mean, I've met
queers at political rallies. Do you think they really do stuff
like that?"

*Little wonder McThacry keeps this guy around. He must
be an endless source of amusement.* "Well, being gay and

going to bed with men are highly correlated phenomena."

"Highly correlated phenomena. You've been to college?"

"I told you. I was going to Osage to enroll in grad school."

"Did you go to college before or after they brainwashed you?"

"During, I think. What's this brainwashing stuff?"

"When you changed your shirt, I saw that you had a lot of hair on your chest."

"Yes." Jim expanded his chest as much as the ropes would allow.

"Then you aren't one of the natural, hormonal queers. You must be one of the changed ones."

"Oh?"

"Yes. Robert—that is, Professor McThacry—explained it all to me."

"I see."

"Yes. It's perfectly obvious that you were born normal."

"How so?"

"You call men by women's names. You say 'her' when you mean 'him.' The brainwashing isn't perfect. Deep inside you really want women, and it shows up in the artifacts in your speech."

"Ah, what an ingenious deduction," Jim said, genuinely awestruck.

"Don't you remember any of it?"

Sidney looked sympathetic. Jim thought he must have found the right line to take with Sidney, but he wasn't sure what line he had taken. "No, I don't think I remember any of it."

"It must be terribly sad for your real parents."

"Mother didn't take it well. She stayed drunk for a week when she found out. She blamed my father."

"You remember your real parents?"

"Yes, of course. It was a mistake to tell them over Christmas with all that brandy in the kitchen. She kept brandying everything, including herself, and saying that my psychiatrist would blame her. I mean, have you ever tasted brandied potato salad?"

"Psychiatrist?"

"Dad was dead set against it. But she made me go for a while. The psychiatrist was in the middle of his sixth divorce, so I don't think he paid much attention to me or anything I said."

McThacry crashed into the door frame as he returned from the kitchen, and a splash of scotch sloshed out of his cup. "Did you get anything out of him?" he asked Sidney.

"He remembers his real parents."

"I mean about his mission."

"No, I am afraid not."

McThacry took the derringer from the mantel. "Now we're going to start getting some answers from you."

"I don't know what you are talking about."

McThacry cocked the derringer with his thumb. "Start by telling us where you are going to pick up the boys."

"I don't know anything about boys. I really was going to Osage to go to school."

"I'll give you thirty seconds."

"Look, tell me what to say. I'll say anything you want. But I don't know anything about any boys."

Sidney did not know either. McThacry himself had said he had not heard all of Jim's instructions. Jim could be telling the truth. It did not seem right, the way McThacry was treating Jim. After all, wasn't Jim as much a victim as any of the others?

McThacry slurped at the coffee cup. "Goddamnit, I'm not kidding." McThacry flung his right arm across his chest and back, as if he might pistolwhip Jim with the little derringer. The derringer slipped out of McThacry's hand and flew toward the wall.

Over her shoulder, Agnes saw Phil put the headset down on the console. "Did you find out anything from Charlie at the cab company?"

"Oh Agnes, I'm afraid you were right. They must have got him."

"Come here, hon, and tell us about it."

"None of Charlie's cabs picked up Jim this morning." Agnes had turned back to the geographic file, and Phil hung his head over Agnes's shoulder. "That Sidney drives for them, all right. But he owns his own cab. And he hasn't hired any relief, so he takes the cab with him. He's off duty. Charlie has no idea where the cab is when Sidney is off duty, like now."

"Oh hon, we'll find him." Agnes pointed to the index card that she had lifted almost out of the file. "Now see, here is the card for the block on which McThacry has his other house. Anything on the same block on the same street would show up here directly. But there's nothing. However, we have a cross-reference. That means we have something on the same block, but facing another street. Then you would look up the cross-reference. But in this case, we recognize that it is Miss Mona's address. Miss Mona— that's good. Now we will go back to the alphabetic file to get Mona's phone number. Got that?"

"It all seems so complex." Phil leaned against various parts of Agnes as she got up, went to the console of the alphabetic file, and sat down.

"Yes, it's complicated. But it's second nature once you get used to it. And how could a girl get by without her card file?" Agnes pressed the dimple marked *Mo.* "Fortunately, this file has complete double entries for drag names. Otherwise it would be almost useless to us. Aha! Here we are. Miss Mona's number." Agnes put the headset to her ear and poked the numbered dimples with her index fingernail.

"Miss Mona? This is Agnes. . . . Yes, it's been a long time. . . . We were wondering if you would do us a small favor and look out your back door at the house behind yours, two doors to the west. We're looking especially for one of those red and green taxis, or anything else that seems unusual. . . . No, we'll hang on if it's no imposition for you to go look right now. . . . Thanks, hon."

Agnes said to Phil, "She's going to check." The whirlpool above them stopped making the avalanche noise. The vault was silent. "We suppose the rest of the mail will be delivered after all." But Phil did not crack a smile. "Oh Phil, it will be all right. If they aren't on the east side, we'll have Thomas drive to Avalon Park. And we better call the bars again. We mean, we don't even know for sure that they—

"Mona? Yes, we're still here. . . . Goodness! How very alarming. . . . Are you sure—oh of course you are, you were in the infantry. . . . Would you keep your eyes open? We've got to ring off. . . . Thanks. Bye." Agnes lowered the headset.

"What is it?"

"Uhm, probably nothing. Just a coincidence."

"It's not nothing. You said 'alarming.' What's that about 'infantry'?"

"It seems . . . it seems that at McThacry's place a shot has been fired."

"Oh no." Phil laid his head on Agnes's shoulder.

SIX

AIWOH!'' McThacry shrieked. "The faggots, the fascists killed me! Queers got me!"

Sidney, who had been sitting cross-legged on the floor, drew his legs up to his chest, hugged his legs, and rested his chin on his knees. "Oh no. Oh no. Oh no." Sidney began to rock himself, forward and back.

"Fairies! Faggots! Queers!" Then McThacry stopped writhing on the floor and lay limp and still.

"Gawd . . ." Bobby said when he looked through the door. He knelt on the floor and placed his ear against his father's chest.

"Oh no. All dead. Oh no." Sidney rocked.

Bobby ripped open his father's shirt. "What happened?"

Jim deferred to Sidney for the answer. But Sidney only rocked faster and faster and began to sing the words: "All dead. Oh no. All dead."

Bobby turned around and glared at Jim. "What the hell happened?"

"He threw the gun at the wall and it went off."

"Gawd . . ."

"Is it bad?"

"He winged himself. Not much blood. I think he fainted. Or more likely passed out. He usually doesn't get this way this early in the day."

"You sure he's okay? He said it was hollow-point rounds."

Bobby lifted the tatters of the shirt from his father's upper arm again and inspected it again. "It's okay. Another eighth of an inch and he would have missed himself altogether."

"Dead. Oh no. All."

"He's not dead, Mr. Potter," Bobby said. After a considerable struggle, Bobby managed to turn his father over onto the uninjured arm. Then he looked up at Sidney.

Sidney was still rocking. "All dead. Oh no."

"He's not dead, Mr. Potter. He's not even hurt bad."

Sidney was rocking so vigorously that his glasses had slipped down and now bounced on the tip of his nose with each oscillation. "Fairies and faggots and queers, oh my. Fairies and faggots and queers, oh my."

"Gawd . . ." Bobby glanced at Jim. Jim shrugged as well as he could. "I expect my father is going to puke. Tell me if he starts to heave, okay?"

"Yeah."

Bobby circled Sidney several times. The rocking had

become quite violent. At last Bobby stopped behind Sidney and grabbed his shoulders.

"All dead. Oh—" The singsong stopped as Bobby held Sidney's shoulders still.

"Mr. Potter?" Bobby asked softly.

"Yes?" Sidney answered in a squeaky cartoon voice.

"I need you to go call an ambulance."

"Call an ambulance?" Sidney giggled.

"Yes. There's a phone at the store on the corner. Have you got a quarter?"

"Got a quarter."

"Good. Now what are you going to do?"

Sidney appeared puzzled. He stared at a light rectangle over the mantel where a picture had hung for many years, as if he expected the answer to be written there. "Call an ambulance?" he guessed.

"That's right." Bobby lifted his hands from Sidney's shoulders but waited a moment to see if the rocking would begin again. "Get up, Mr. Potter." Bobby wedged his hands under Sidney's arms and lifted him up. Jim watched Bobby's biceps and thighs strain against the dead weight. Bobby noticed. "I asked you to keep an eye on my father." Jim looked away quickly.

Sidney stood more or less upright.

"Are you okay, Mr. Potter?"

"Yes."

"And you can go to the corner and call an ambulance for my father?"

"Yes."

"Then do it."

Sidney pushed his glasses back up on his nose and went to the front door. He turned back to the room as he opened the door. "Did you hear? Did you hear what they do with the Staff of Life? Bourgeois! It's totally bourgeois!"

"The ambulance."

"Yes. The ambulance indeed!" Sidney slammed the door as he left. Bobby went to the front window and watched until Sidney reached the sidewalk.

"Gawd, what a twit."

McThacry snorted. Bobby scrambled back into Jim's view and knelt next to his father. McThacry snorted again. Bobby watched his father's breathing for a moment more. "Snoring," Bobby said, half aloud.

"Bobby?" Jim tried the name.

Bobby sounded very tired. "Okay, yeah, I'll let you go."

The boy squatted in front of Jim and began working on the knot at Jim's ankles. Bobby's fingers were thick and stubby, and the knot was tight. Bobby pulled Jim's legs one way and the other, trying to gain a bit of slack in the knot. Suddenly Bobby sat up and slapped himself across the forehead. He reached into his pocket and pulled out a folding knife. But its little blade was dull. Bobby sawed fiercely at the ropes. When the rope fell slack around Jim's feet, Bobby moved around to the back of the chair and began to saw the ropes on Jim's wrists.

"You handled Sidney very well," Jim said.

"Someone has to manage."

Jim could feel the heat of the boy's muscles at work. One of Jim's wrists snapped free.

"You are, aren't you?" Jim asked.

"Am what?"

"One of us."

"I love my father. I want you out of here before he gets in more trouble than he's already in."

"But you are."

The pocketknife popped through the last rope holding Jim to the chair.

"Go out the back way. The fence is low. Even you can jump it."

"Aren't you?" Jim turned in the chair, unprepared to find tears on Bobby's cheeks.

"*He's* my father. Can you imagine what that is? You're loose. Get out!" The boy shouted and waved the pocket-knife at the kitchen door.

Jim went.

The fence was low, but Bobby had overestimated Jim's abilities. The toe of Jim's shoe caught the top wicket of the wire. He fell face first into the caliche dust of the alley.

Jim's ears rang, which is why he did not hear the cycle turn into the alley. *Stupid.* Mostly it bothered Jim that he had been so stupid as to try to jump the fence on the run. *It is an interesting type of pain, the nauseating pressure that comes after a deep visceral whump. Remarkable, really, how much it hurts. Do you suppose,* Jim wondered, *that I have ruptured anything? Broken my nose at least? Pain like this ought to indicate some serious and spectacular form of injury. Probably not. I get the pain and have nothing to show for it. As usual.*

Jim lifted his face feebly out of its impression in the caliche dust. He found himself looking at a fun-house image of his face, reflected in the spit shine of the cop's black leather boot.

"Where do you think you are going, boy?"

"Nowhere, Officer." Jim slumped back into the dust.

The cop poked Jim's ribs with the tip of his long, hard, shiny nightstick. "Up on your knees, scum," he snarled.

"Yes sir." Jim drew himself back on his knees and sat up. He found himself eye-to-zipper with the cop's blue-gray jodhpurs. The cop unsnapped his holster.

"Now all the way up and against the wall."

Jim stood quickly and looked around. "There isn't any wall."

"The Dumpster," the cop ordered from behind his mirrored glasses. "Up against the Dumpster."

Jim laid his palms on the hot metal of the Dumpster and leaned against it. He discovered inside the Dumpster the site of a fly orgy: fuzzy, green, half-eaten pizza and stacked rotting watermelon rind. Then he saw the maggots crawling in the pizza. "Oh ick."

The cop slapped one meaty hand down Jim's loins and patted up his legs. Each side, the hand slid too quickly and too high up the inseam of Jim's jeans. "Oof!"

"What was that?"

"Oof, sir."

"Now son, you just turn around real slow-like and see if you can tell me why you were laying in this alley behind the scene of a shooting."

"I was only taking a shortcut. I tripped on the fence."

"Oh yeah? And how come you're in such a hurry?"

"I just wanted to get home."

"And where is it you live, boy?"

"Avenue H."

The square-jawed cop's lip curled in a victorious sneer. "Then how come you were facing the wrong way?"

"I guess I got confused."

"Yeah. Maybe you are confused. Are you confused, boy? Tell me what that blue bandanna in your hip pocket means."

"Means? Oh, it means I think I might have to blow my nose."

"That all you planning on blowing, boy? Your nose? And what about those keys on your belt loop? What's them for?" The cop leered menacingly.

"I put them there to keep from wearing out my pockets."

"A likely story. What's that in your hand?" The cop showed his teeth in anticipation.

"Nothing." Jim could not understand what the cop meant. Jim did not have anything in his hand.

"Don't lie to me, son. I saw something shiny."

Jim looked down at his hands. There was something shiny on the right one: Agnes's ring. He held out his hand so that only the plain side showed. "Oh, it's only a ring. I'd forgotten I was wearing it."

"Well I'll just bet you did. I believe I'll have a look at it. Take it off."

Jim grasped the ring with his left hand and began twisting the ring to pull it over his knuckle. The gem was exposed for an instant.

"Hold it!"

Jim froze at the sudden command.

"Turn your hand over, boy," the cop growled.

Jim turned his right palm upward. The tigereye in the chimera's claw caught the sunlight and glinted yellow fire.

The cop's jaw muscles went slack and the superior sneer evaporated from his face. "In Her Majesty's service?" he asked in a reverent whisper.

"What?"

The cop spoke up: "Are you in Her Majesty's service? Sir!"

"Well, yeah, I guess so."

"How can I be of assistance, sir?" The cop replaced his revolver in its holster.

Jim looked at his wrist, but his watch was not there. He could not remember whether he had been wearing it. "I suppose I missed my flight."

"Not if I can help it, sir!"

As the three-wheeled cycle turned out of the alley, the cop switched on the siren and lights. Jim found the sensation of the tight turns exhilarating. The cycle sped toward the airport, around stopped cars and through red lights.

If he had thought of it, Jim would have asked to ride to Agnes's, or home, or—even better—to Sleazy Sue's for an afternoon bracer. But he had not thought of it and he was happy to be going anywhere, so long as he went quickly and far from McThacry and the investigation of the shooting.

The third time the cop scooted back in the saddle, Jim did not try to give him more room. He had finally realized that the cop was only being friendly.

Phil lay in bed, watching the shadow on the snowy egret. The shadow had crept halfway up the stained-glass window when Phil's green and white stuffed bear spoke to him in Agnes's voice: "Good news, Phil! Thomas just put Jim on a plane for Osage. Now cheer up and come help us in the closet."

Phil sat up and hugged the bear.

When Phil reached Agnes's closet, he found the door ajar. "Agnes, are you in there?" he shouted.

"Yes," came Agnes's distant voice, "we are back here in gentlemen's costumes."

"Where's that?"

"Come ahead until you get to the cocktail dresses. Then turn right."

In the dimness, Phil felt his way along the central aisle until he came to a rack whose foremost garment was a garish thing of mustard rayon and lemon chiffon. *No doubt something left by one of the Marys,* Phil thought. He turned right and rustled through the racks of dresses. He found Agnes in something of a clearing, under a bare bulb, in front of a triptych mirror. Agnes was struggling to wrap an olive aba over a perfectly white, flowing dishdasha.

"What are you doing?"

"We're getting up Arab drag. What do you think so far?"

"So far, so good. Whatever are you doing this for?"

"As it turns out, Jim did have a brush with McThacry, and McThacry is the worse for it. But in the process, Jim left his luggage in whatshisname's cab. We are going to fetch it." Agnes stood back from the mirror and folded one of its wings forward. She began rummaging through the shelves behind the mirror.

"But why bother with the luggage? I mean, is it wise?"

"What do you think? The fez?" Agnes asked, trying it on. "Or the turban?"

"I don't know. The fez looks like something out of *Amos and Andy*. The turban, on the other hand, looks like you are carrying your laundry on your head. What kind of Arab are you supposed to be?"

"The very wealthy kind."

"Then I think not the fez or the turban. A headband thing with a piece of checkered cloth."

"Oh, we know what you mean. Yes, that can be approximated. It doesn't have to be exactly authentic. We only mean to fool the locals. We wouldn't bother with the luggage except that his documents are in it. It would be very difficult to replace them in time for them to serve their purpose. There now. What do you think?"

"Agnes, your nails."

"Goodness, you're right. We mean to pass them off as a religious custom if necessary. But the emerald polish won't do, we suppose. Remind us again in a minute. And we'll need a number of things. Where do Arabs keep their money? It's bad enough doing without a handbag, but this costume has no pockets. Haven't you ever seen an Arab with a handbag? Don't you think—"

"Agnes! Don't even think of it."

"We guess not." Agnes pouted.

SEVEN

W HY did you do it?" Sidney asked quietly.

"Gawd . . ."

"Why did you do it?" Sidney insisted.

"Look, there's going to be enough problems when the cops get here—Gawd, look, they're here already."

"Queers shot me," McThacry groaned.

"No." Bobby turned his father's face and stared hard at the slit-open eyes. "It was an accident. That's our story. It was an accident."

"The queer? The subject?" McThacry asked.

"Escaped," said Bobby. "But the story is he never was here. No one here. The shooting was an accident."

Sidney had been examining the ropes. He held up a ragged end. "He didn't escape. You cut him loose. Why did you do it?"

"Gawd..."

But the first of the cops was pounding at the open door, and men in orange jumpsuits were wheeling a green-sheeted gurney up the walk.

The first cop through the door took Sidney for the responsible adult. McThacry mumbled "Faggots" as the paramedics pasted electrodes to his chest, and one of them seemed to take it personally. For a moment Bobby was ignored. In that moment Bobby realized that the video recorder was still running. He walked around the tubes and wires attached to his father and casually pressed the rewind button on the VCR. Then he stood by the kitchen door, hoping to overhear what Sidney might be saying to the first cop.

Soon the room was awash with cops. The derringer was discovered, chalk-marked around, and gingerly prodded into a plastic bag. The paramedics lifted McThacry onto the gurney, and a chalk outline took his place on the floor. Radios crackled from the cops' belts and the paramedics' instruments and the PAs of the blue and white cruisers in the street. But Bobby listened for the little click of the tape machine, the little click that would mean he could slither around to press the record button and erase the record of the interrogation.

The monitor rolled the picture of the empty chair. Someone would figure it out at any moment.

They found the hole in the ceiling, and the steel tapes and little notepads came out. The ambulance pulled away from the curb, its lights flashing but its siren silent. On hands and knees, a cop sniffed at the shards of the coffee cup, nodded his head knowingly, and began pushing the pieces into a bag with the eraser end of a pencil.

Bobby told a cop about the drinking and the accident. The awkward question was, What were they doing with the derringer and these lights and all this equipment? Bobby heard the tape machine click. *Why haven't they thought of it? Why haven't they played it back?*

"Whose cab is that?"

Bobby pretended to be distracted by the booming question and turned toward the fat cop at the front door. Bobby pointed at the kitchen door, and from the kitchen came Sidney's mewling voice: "Mine. It's my cab."

Then in a small flurry, Sidney was escorted out the front door by two chuckling cops, and Bobby saw a wad of greenbacks in the fat cop's fist.

"So you'll take the sheikh to his meeting and come right back here, Mr. Potter?" the fat cop asked.

"Oh yes. Right back here." Sidney nodded.

"Good." The cop turned to the even more enormous Arab. "It's all arranged. I hope you will be in time for your meeting."

"Thank you, my good man. I have always relied upon the kindness of strangers." The Arab thrust another wad of bills at the cop, too obviously for the cop's sensibilities. But the bills were whisked out of the Arab's long-nailed hand, and the cop stepped back to open the door of the cab with a little bow.

The gross Arab in the passenger seat, Sidney's cab scraped bottom backing out of the drive. "Where to?" Sidney asked.

"The Society of Petroleum Resource Research Engineers Convention," the Arab said. It seemed to Sidney that the Arab had a strangely Hindi accent.

"I'm afraid I don't know where that is."

"Oh no? Let me see." The Arab extracted a card from his aba. "Aha. The Thompson Conference Center. That is written here. Do you know it?"

"Yes. I know where that is." For the first time in many hours, Sidney knew where he was going. He turned the cab toward the highway.

The shot. The escaped queer. The unspeakable bourgeois sex practices. The kidnappers. The cops. The questions. Too much, too much indeed to think about. Then there was the great inhaling, wheezing snort behind his head. At the stoplight Sidney looked into the mirror. The Arab held up a small vial and made the vacuuming noise again with his nose over the bottle.

"Sir, I wish you wouldn't use drugs in my cab," Sidney said, afraid that it would cost him a big tip.

"Please do not misunderstand. This is not contraband. Oh no, the traveler must not contravene the local customs. Not contraband at all." The Arab took another whiff at the little bottle.

"Medicine?" asked Sidney.

"Yes. Yes." The Arab giggled. "Medicine. Very good. Very funny. It is medicine. The medicine of love."

The cab stopped in the access lane. At the head of the line of cars was a timid soul, unready to dart into the afternoon traffic on the highway.

"Medicine of love?"

"Oh yes, ho ho." The Arab seemed scarcely able to contain his amusement. "I will explain." The Arab inhaled at the little bottle again and struggled to compose himself.

"Our customs are very different. You know that the Prophet allows a man to have four wives-women?"

"Yes."

"But it is written that the husband-man must treat them all the same, the four wives-women. Aha! For a young man this is well. Young bull-man, it is well. Four wives seem scarcely enough, ha-ha."

Sidney recognized the pause here. It was a pause for sharing the bourgeois, male-supremacist humor. Sidney forced himself. "Yes. Ha-ha." The line of cars moved up the access ramp.

"But for a man of greater years, it is not so good. One wife may be too many. There is suspicion. The wives-women think another is favored. They think he does not do all his duty. Very bad. Inharmonious." The Arab snorted over the amber vial. "For that, then it is. Hee-hee. Medicine, you call it. And it is. Medicine for love. Ha-ha."

The cab jumped into a hole in the stream of traffic on the highway. The Arab continued to whiff and chuckle.

"But . . ." Sidney felt uneasy. "But your wives are not here. Why do you need the medicine now?"

"Ah. Yes. That is the sad thing. At first the medicine is very good. A little sniff and for days a man is like a bull again. All the wives are happy. Harmony and love return to the dwelling place. But alas! It is not always so. After many years, a little sniff does no good. A man must have his love medicine all the time. Not only to make love. It is necessary at all times. Very sad."

"A little sniff works for days?"

"Yes. At first. At first. Very sad."

It was a bourgeois impulse. Sidney recognized that it was. Whatever would he say when he explained it at a self-criticism session of the New International Proletarian

Peace League? He would tell them, of course. He would have to tell them because he knew he was going to yield to the bourgeois impulse.

He took the redheaded woman, passionately.

Sidney had read that line; and reading it in a novel supposed to be a model of socialist realism, Sidney had first experienced the bourgeois impulse. Well, it wasn't really rape, was it? It had not said she protested. It had not suggested that she struggled. In fact, it implied that she enjoyed it.

But the swarthy peoples' cadre hadn't asked permission either. He took her. "Took." He didn't ask her permission. He didn't take her to dinner. He didn't marry her. He did not even at that point in the novel know her politics. He just took her.

Sidney wondered about that. He thought surely one of the women would bring it up when they discussed the novel at the New International Proletarian Peace League. But none of them did. Instead they discussed whether the nationalist leader might have turned into a progressive force and whether possibly it was an error when the swarthy cadre disemboweled him.

Contrary to instructions, Sidney had already read the following chapter, wherein it was revealed that the nationalist leader had been a Trotskyite agent. So Sidney knew that disemboweling, at the very least, was called for. But no one said anything at all about this "taking" of women. And that was the first time Sidney felt uneasy and bourgeois.

The last time Sidney had felt that way was when Jim told him about the bourgeois sex practices. Nothing Sidney would think of doing. But still it proved, as Sidney had come to suspect, that there was a parallel universe, another world, a whole dimension of things beyond his experience. It was a dimension in which queers screwed guys, on the one hand, and swarthy cadres took redheaded women, on the other.

Perhaps, after all, the discussion group had not remarked on the taking of the redheaded woman because none of the others in the collective found it remarkable. Perhaps Dick and Carlos and Charlie and Frank were accustomed to taking women, and Becky and Donna and Rachel were accustomed to being taken.

So Sidney had tried taking Linda, but that had not worked out and better not to think of it. Better not to think of it because, although Linda seemed pleased to be about to be taken, Sidney had discovered that he could not take women.

For a couple of weeks he'd resisted Linda's advances. But that had not increased his taking powers. Neither had any of a half-dozen potions he had sent for from the two-inch ads in the back of bourgeois male-supremacist magazines. Sidney went so far as to horde quarters from the laundry money so that once a week he could throw away his sprout sandwich and have lunch at the steak house. Even defiled with the flesh of dead animals, the temple of his body seemed no better prepared for the taking of women.

When the discussion group reached the penultimate chapter of the novel, there was the taking of the redheaded woman again. Sidney had fewer questions this time. The politics of the redheaded woman were known and they were correct. The swarthy cadre and the villagers had vanquished the landlord. The redheaded woman knew—somehow knew, by chapter's end—that she had conceived a new socialist. All of that was in order. But the swarthy cadre had still taken her, not only passionately, this time, but manfully as well.

Sidney directed the cab off the highway at the LBJ Library exit. He took the chance, again, to look at the little amber bottle.

"Can I try some?" he blurted out.

"Try some?" the Arab asked.

"Try some of the love medicine."

"Ooh, no-no-no, no. It is too strong for you. Very bad. You would rage like a bull."

"Oh please. I only want a little. Just a little sniff."

"Oh my, oh my. Young man, you do not know what you are asking." The Arab sat back in his seat, clutching the bottle against his chest.

"I'll be careful. I just want a little. I'll just smell it."

"Our customs do not allow me to refuse you. But think, young man, think. Do not ask for it unless you want it."

"Yes. Yes, I do want it."

"Very well then. But you must arrest the vehicle first."

Sidney stopped the cab in the parking lot of the Thompson Conference Center and switched off the ignition. He turned around in the seat of the cab. "Now, please."

"I fear this is the wrong thing to do." The Arab offered the bottle tentatively. Eagerly, Sidney snatched it.

Sidney raised the vial to his nose, forced it half up his right nostril, and inhaled deeply.

Then, very slowly, he slumped over on his side.

Agnes rolled down the window of the cab, used the outside handle to open the door, and extracted herself. She removed her headdress and waved it over her head. The titty-pink T-bird pulled abreast of the red and green cab. Agnes reached into the front of the cab.

"Hand us our bag, Phil. Here are the keys. Jim's luggage is supposed to be in the trunk."

"What are you going to do?"

"We are going to give him the impression that he has had

a good time." Agnes opened her handbag. "Let's see now. Lipstick on the collar. Splash of cheap perfume. Lower his zipper to half-mast. Eyeglasses akimbo. On the mirror, a pair of raunchy panty hose. For the turn-indicator lever, we have something here. Yes, boy's underpants, size six, ripped and stained. A few chicken feathers here and there and miscellaneous clumps of fur. All the physical evidence. Did you get the luggage, Phil? Come and see what you think."

"Looks like a hell of a party."

"Good." Agnes smiled sweetly. "Exactly what it is supposed to look like."

"Gee, Agnes, isn't that unnecessarily cruel?"

"He wanted to have a good time. Now you tell us, what is the difference between giving a man a good time and giving him the impression he's had a good time?"

Phil shrugged.

"Exactly. There is no difference whatever. And that's a lesson worth remembering."

"Agnes, isn't that Jim's watch?"

"Where?"

"On his wrist."

"We don't know. Is it?"

"I'm pretty sure it is. It scratched me the other morning."

"Well what do you know." Agnes bent into the cab again and removed the watch. "A petty thief as well as a repressed sex maniac."

Phil took the watch from Agnes and put it on his own wrist.

"Phil, you'd best drive. It's almost time for Brother Earl's afternoon program. We'll see if we can't find it on the radio."

Phil directed the T-bird toward the airport while Agnes

twisted the knob on the radio slowly and carefully. In the middle of a ball of static, Agnes found Brother Earl's voice:

". . . to clean up our colleges and universities. Why, brothers and sisters in Christ, do you suffer this abomination to fester among our youth? Isn't it high time we cleaned up our cities and towns? Ask yourself, what have I done to get the perverts and sodomites out of the sight of our children, away from our young people? Are you going to clean up your town? Or are you waiting until it rains fire on your hometown?

"The choice is yours, brothers. . . ."

The voice faded as Phil turned onto Airport Boulevard. Agnes touched the knob gently but could not coax the voice out of the ball of static again. She switched the radio off.

"Well, Agnes?"

"Well, we've never heard him getting this bad before."

"Not good?"

"Not good."

Thomas was sprawled across two lobby chairs when he recognized Phil coming toward him with the luggage. Thomas jumped up, adjusted his shirt, and to little avail ran a comb through his short black hair. "Isn't Madam Agnes with you?"

"She was just behind me in Arab drag."

"Oh good, I see her."

"Thomas," Phil asked, "is there still a seat reserved on the next flight to Osage?"

"Damn. I forgot to cancel it. I hope Agnes won't be upset."

"And when does it leave?"

"In thirty minutes."

"Good. I just have time."

"Just have time for what?" Agnes asked, out of breath.

"Agnes, I'm taking the next flight to Osage."

"Absolutely not. We forbid it. Jim and our people in Osage are perfectly capable of dealing with the situation, if it can be dealt with at all."

"I'm not going through again what I went through this afternoon. I'm going to help Jim."

"Child, you will only be in the way. How can you possibly help?"

"I don't know. But I intend to be there and not wondering who's got him or what they are doing to him."

"But he's not expecting you. How will you find him?"

"He's expecting to pick up his luggage, isn't he, Thomas?"

Thomas looked to Agnes for a cue. "Well . . ."

"The answer isn't written on Agnes's face. Tell me, Thomas."

Agnes nodded.

"Well," Thomas said tentatively, "I did tell him to check the later flights for his luggage or whatever we could send."

"Then I'll find him one way or another."

"But dear, it could be dangerous. Thomas, tell Phil it could be dangerous."

"Now look here, Phil—" Thomas began.

"You stay out of this, Thomas. It could be just as dangerous for Jim. And I've got as much of a stake—more of a stake—in this than he does."

Agnes put her arm on Phil's shoulder. "Now don't be rash."

Phil ducked from under Agnes's arm. "Look Agnes, it may be your style to fan yourself on the veranda while the men do all the dirty work—"

"Phil! You know that's not true!"

"Okay, that's not true. But why shouldn't I help too?

Why should I be trapped here in a gilded cage to worry about him? I'm going, Agnes, with your blessing or without it."

Agnes opened her mouth and closed it again and swallowed. Then she spoke softly: "You mean it, don't you?"

"Yes, Agnes. I do."

Agnes reached into the aba. "Here, child." She sighed. "Our blessing and our charge card."

Phil stood on tiptoe to kiss Agnes's neck. "Bye, hon, I'm off!"

As Phil ran down the corridor to the check-in counter with Jim's luggage, Agnes called after him: "Remember! Play dumb! Let him protect you from something!"

Agnes stood on the observation deck and waved at the plane while it sat at the terminal, while the jetway telescoped away from the hatch, while the ground crew tugged away the blocks around its tires, while it taxied to the line at the end of the runway, while it waited in line, while it raced down the runway and was airborne; and she waved until the plane disappeared far to the north.

"So hard to know if we've done the right thing."

Blue-eyed Thomas took Agnes's hand, and with his bandanna he dabbed at her cheeks. Agnes looked down at him and Thomas had to look away. He looked in the direction the plane had gone.

"Thank you, Thomas. That's quite above and beyond the call of duty."

Thomas squeezed Agnes's hand and sighed.

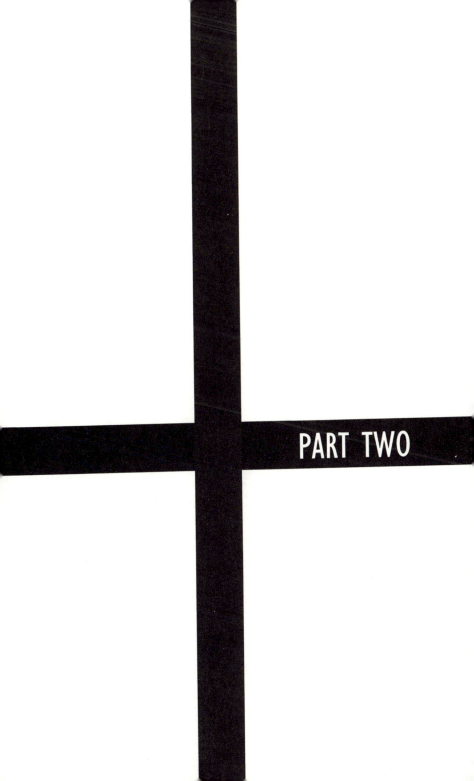

PART TWO

GLENN waited by the door while Jack paid the check. The beveled edges of the lead glass cast dozens of swimming rainbows as the passing headlights shone through the door. The cashier recognized Jack and looked around for Glenn. Glenn nodded at the cashier and opened the door. Armand's was always a bit chilly. Glenn rolled up his sleeves in the warm September evening.

Jack stepped out of Armand's and looked slowly up and down the street.

"Let's take your car home," Glenn suggested. "I'll catch the bus to work in the morning."

"No. I don't think that's such a good idea."

"Big bear, what is bothering you?"

"Let's walk awhile. Somewhere less crowded." Jack turned toward the warehouses. Armand's stood on the frontier between fashionable restoration and frank commerce.

Jack kicked a stone in front of them. Glenn noticed Jack's increasing stoop as the streetlights faded behind them. *Not good,* Glenn thought. Glenn thought it had not been good for days, maybe weeks. Jack was big and strong and smart, but not smart enough to hide whatever it was. The shadows were deeper among the tall, naked security lights of the warehouses. Glenn drew a breath to speak just as Jack began.

"You know I was never sure."

Glenn swallowed. "You used to say that."

"Well, now I'm sure. . . ." Jack lowered his head and kicked the stone again.

"No. Not yet."

"It's too late." Jack looked up again. "You know there is a girl?"

"Yes, I know." Glenn could not help but know.

Jack tensed the corners of his mouth, rolled his lips against his teeth, and made the clucking sound that some people make when, for good or ill, done is done. "I've asked her to marry me."

Worse—it was worse than Glenn had guessed. "But why? Things have been so good."

"I've asked myself why. It's the way I was brought up, I think. Things have been good. But the bars . . . your friends . . . the others. They make me sick. They disgust me."

"We don't have to go out."

"We can't live all to ourselves."

"We could move, make new friends."

"You're right. It's an excuse. The real reason is that I

don't like sex with men. I like women and I want a family."

"You liked it well enough—what is it now? Three years?"

Jack picked up a flat stone and sailed it onto the corrugated tin roof of a warehouse. It clunked and rattled down and scattered the loose pebbles in the street under the eaves. Jack stepped toward the sound. He stopped, his back to Glenn. "Because I love you."

"But if you love me . . ."

"I never liked the sex. I mean, I do like it. But only because it's you. I never wanted, I never had another man." Jack crouched to look for the flat stone.

"What about New Year's?"

"I couldn't. Whatshisname was too drunk to know the difference. He thought it was so wonderful . . . so I let him think so."

"Really?"

"Really."

"But why didn't you tell me?"

"You had a good time. I thought you would feel guilty if you knew."

"I would have. Forgive me, Jack. I'll never trick with another man."

"That's not it, and you know it." Jack had not found the flat stone. He tossed aside a handful of pebbles and stood. "Don't you see? None of this was supposed to happen. It wasn't in the cards."

"And all this time we've been together means nothing?"

"No, it's not nothing. It seemed so . . . what? Heroic? Romantic? You and me against the world."

Jack walked. Glenn followed.

"Does she know?"

"Sort of. She doesn't know what it is. I mean it's just words to her. She doesn't think it was serious."

They passed the last of the truck docks and crossed a railroad spur. Glenn reached for Jack's hand.

"Look, I'm not denying you, I mean that it happened. I don't want people to find out. As a practical matter. But I'm not ashamed. It's something I tried. But it's not for me."

"So all of a sudden . . ."

"You know that's not true. You knew this was coming. You knew I was lying about the nights I stayed out. I could see it in your face."

"But you always dated women some. I never objected."

"No. Not when it was a football banquet or something to do with my job, or when I had a date with some whore you knew I wasn't really interested in. But you've known it was more than that lately."

Glenn knew. He knew it was not like the college girls. He knew it was not like Martha, who would show up on Saturday morning with a sly wink and carry Jack away for the weekend. This was not like the nights Jack went to dinner at the house of some meddling matchmaker. "Yes, I knew."

The crescent moon stood over the decorative arch of the old redbrick factory. Glenn thought the abandoned building looked like a palace—not a fairy-tale castle, but like the real palaces of Europe that come right up to the sidewalks, disappointing, not so grand. The tall windows began far up the wall and reached almost to the scrollwork. Each window was crowned with a semicircular arch, glazed in pie-shaped pieces. Glenn wondered what had been made here.

"Okay. Say I'm a selfish bastard. I won't go on sacrificing my chance for happiness."

"Has it been that bad?"

"No. Of course it hasn't been bad. But don't you see, sooner or later I'd be bitter. I'd blame you for losing my chance at true happiness."

"And you think you'll find true happiness with her?"

"I don't know. It's my one chance."

"You were my one chance." Standing in the right spot, Glenn could see a star through the factory's skylight and the tall windows.

"You'll find someone else. That's why it's better now. While we're both young. You'll find someone who is right for it. Someone who's less of an accident."

"An accident?"

"An accident. It wasn't meant to be. I can't go on fighting it the rest of our lives."

"I'll wait. You'll come back. You'll see."

"Don't. I won't let you make me feel guilty if you do. Maybe years from now, when we both have new lives, we'll see each other again. But you have to understand, we will never be lovers again."

"You'll get enough of it. You'll be back."

"No. It's this I've had enough of. Sometimes even now—I thought it would stop—sometimes when we're having breakfast, or when I wake up in the night, or even when we're making love, I forget who you are and all that has happened. It's like I'm in a strange place. It's like a sickening smell. All I've ever had to do with a man has been with you.

"You started playing with other boys when you were, what? Nine? I started three years ago. Don't you remember how difficult it was for me? How I tried? How sometimes I couldn't do some things? You were very sweet and patient. But I wasn't kidding: I really didn't know how.

"They had me the twenty years before that. They were teaching me. You've ridden in a car with my dad. All it is, is a play-by-play of every pair of tits we pass. And he expects you to say something too. They were teaching me that when a man reaches for your crotch, he's planning to rack you. Remember how I used to jump when we first started sleeping together? That was reflex—one of the ones that showed. Maybe I could unlearn all of that if I tried hard enough for long enough. But I won't unlearn wanting a woman and a family. You can't understand any more than I can understand how you get turned on looking at those pictures of guys you don't know in those magazines."

"You got turned on."

"Only because it was you."

"I don't understand."

"Neither do I."

Glenn sat on the curb in front of the old factory door. He thought he might sit there forever.

"Glenn, I moved out today."

"Just gone?"

"I was going to do that. I was just going to be gone. But I didn't want you to just come home like that."

"Where are you going?"

"Better that you don't know for a while. You've got to realize that it's over. Go out Friday night. Cut loose. Your friends tell me you used to be good at that—don't bother to deny it, I don't care if it's true."

"Then this is good-bye?"

"Yes. No. Don't cry. You've been very good so far."

"Jack, kiss me good-bye."

"You're determined to make this as painful as possible, aren't you?"

"You're afraid to kiss me again."

Jack offered Glenn a hand and pulled him up. "Okay, little bear. This is good-bye."

They kissed.

For a moment it was like it had been. For Glenn it was the sense of rightness and completion of the symmetry of their bodies in embrace. For Jack it was the sense of a thing so beautiful that it ought to be, but too fine, too fragile to survive. Then Jack's resolve returned. He lifted his head and rested his chin on Glenn's hair. Jack saw the star through the factory windows. He thought he was about to say something beautiful and comforting.

When the brick clunked onto the sidewalk Jack looked up, thinking it had fallen from the old factory. Glenn stepped into the street.

"Get 'em!"

Glenn could not see where the voice had come from. Jack crouched and spun around. They came from both ends of the block and from the shadows across the street. They came steadily, deliberately, forming a rough semicircle, closed by the factory wall. Glenn saw a knife.

"We saw you, cocksuckers. We saw you, cocksuckers." It was a single voice in the singsong of schoolyard taunts.

Jack glanced at Glenn. The ranks were closing around them. Jack could see a dozen of them, in white, greasy T-shirts and also shirtless. Glenn backed against the factory wall. In a moment it would be too late. Jack sprang head-first, obliquely into the street. He charged without looking up.

Two of them grabbed Jack's collar. The swinging pipe caught Jack behind the left knee. They folded him backward at the knees. A pointed boot jabbed at his crotch.

Glenn flipped his wallet onto the sidewalk. "Look, we've only got a couple of bucks."

"You can't buy your way out, faggot!"

Glenn's arms were pinned against the wall. He could see them lifting Jack up by the collar. Then there was the face, the twisted, mocking face. The face showed its teeth. The voice came from it: "No way, sissy. We're cleaning up this town."

"You're wrong. He's Jack Pickard. He played football here."

"We ain't wrong. We followed you from that fairy restaurant. We saw what you was doing just now."

The open ring of fingers extended toward Glenn's face. He had seen that before. It was a gesture that meant "Eat me, faggot!" but of course it does not mean that at all. The gesture stopped for a moment in front of Glenn's lips. The hand opened, and Glenn was slapped one way and backhanded the other. The open hand clenched into a fist. Glenn's head sagged.

When the next fist came at Jack's gut, he shrank back, bending over it. He touched the ground with one hand and found his footing. They did not expect it. It was second nature for Jack to bull his way forward from a three-point stance. He ran free from the clump of them.

Jack was in the clear and knew it by the time he reached the corner. He was almost into the street again when he saw the red box on the pole. He did not really decide. He flung his arm at the pole and stopped himself. Jack pulled the levered door of the red box. It revealed a little peg. He pressed the peg, but it did not give. Then he saw that the peg was fitted into a slot. He pulled the peg down. It only went halfway. He could not be sure that was enough. The feet were behind him. He yanked on the peg. Then it was too late. They had him again.

Glenn raised his head. The mocking face was turned toward the corner. Glenn tried to move his arm, but the shadow pinning the arm against the wall only grunted and held tighter.

They pulled Jack into the street again. The glinting pipe thwacked down on Jack's shoulders. He staggered. The pipe reversed its arc and slammed across Jack's chest. He fell backward stiffly. His head thumped against the curb.

The dark wet spot spread from his crotch, down the legs of Jack's tan jeans.

At the plump thud of skull and concrete, a universe mapped in neurons unraveled. The horror, spreading horror, occulted the shimmering stars, the distant streetlights, the warm air, the nightmares and dreams. The petty embarrassments, the last embrace, the plans, the calculus, the Camus, the silly free verse, the first downs in the Cotton Bowl, and the last bloody view of his little bear dissolved.

When Jack could not hear them, there came the sound of distant sirens.

"Jesus, I think this one is dead." The sirens grew nearer: the long, wailing ones, the whooping ones. The warehouse dogs howled.

"Let's get out of here." Glenn's arms fell slack.

"No. Hold on. This one saw me. Let's finish him off."

Pebbles scattered in the darkness. "Hey, come back and help me."

"Damn." The last flurry of fists swept over Glenn's face. Glenn sank down, his back to the wall, not knowing where to look for Jack. The flashing lights came and more sirens.

After a while Glenn found himself standing with his cheek flattened against the red bricks.

"Spread 'em."

Glenn shrugged his shoulders, lifting his head from the wall. "Jack . . . where's Jack? . . . They are getting away."

"I said spread 'em." The nightstick tapped the insides of Glenn's thighs. "Oh Christ you fucking fairy."

It spilled against the wall: the stilton, the chablis, the filet, the espresso and amaretto. It gushed like the fire hydrants they open on a summer afternoon; the splattering stink bounced off the brick and pooled at Glenn's feet.

The cop released Glenn's belt and stood back. Glenn lowered himself to the sidewalk again, thinking it was soft down there, thinking he would just have a little rest, heaving again, shuddering, sobbing—weary, sick, sore.

The cop brushed his boot on Glenn's shirttail to remove a splash of vomit.

Much later, it was the cold room with the light. The coarse wool blanket. The light and the scratch of the drab blanket and the questions.

There was the light and the angry rough cop and the smooth quiet man in the three-piece suit. The rough cop yelled. The smooth man spoke softly and gently. Another cop at the door handed the smooth man a piece of paper. The rough cop shook Glenn by the shoulders. The blanket scratched. The smooth man sent the rough cop away.

"Now Glenn, there wasn't really any gang, was there?" the smooth man asked. The smooth man glanced again at the piece of paper and put it in his breast pocket. "He told you he was leaving you for a woman. We found the note he left for you. But he met you downtown and told you instead."

Glenn remembered that. He nodded slowly.

"You fought," the smooth man went on. "You didn't mean it. It just got you so angry. You didn't mean to kill Jack. He hit his head on the curb. That's what killed him. You didn't mean it. That's not murder. That's manslaughter. You'll get a lawyer. If you behave, you'll be out in less than five years."

Glenn shook his head.

The light. And the room was cold. The cold light and no clothes. Just the blanket, the blanket that scratched and stuck to the oozing blood of the scrapes. The smooth man smiled at him. The smooth man had warm, understanding eyes.

The rough cop appeared in the doorway again.

"Just tell me about it. Tell me about it and we can send

the officer away. I'm doing my best to help you."

The smooth man looked helpful.

Glenn shook his head.

"Look, if we have to send the stenographer home, we'll have to put you in the tank for the night. You know what can happen in there."

Glenn nodded vaguely.

"You tell me what you can. Then we can charge you and send you to the county."

The room was cold.

The radio sat on the forty-eight-point sorts. Brother Earl's voice sounded tinny in the little speaker.

"An abomination!" Brother Earl's voice rose in all the pews of the Holy Word of God Broadcast Cathedral: the highballing pews loaded with grain and furniture and sows, the nursing home pews where parishioners listened in the dark with full bedpans and waited for the stoned attendants to feel like doing something, in the white-framed porch pews of Knoxville and Phoenix.

"Open the Word of God for yourselves! It's not Brother Earl's law, it's God's law: You shall put them to death! Read for yourself. The Book says, they who lie with a man as they lie with a woman shall be put to death."

The compositor squinted at the copy on the clip below Brother Earl's voice. His stick grew heavy with lead as his hand flew over the sorts, picking the ones he needed.

Homosexual Killing:
Ex-SU Grid Star Dies
In Love Triangle

NINE

WHEN the floodlights crackled on, Jim dove into the shrubs.

Osage was dark by the time the taxi let Jim out, several doors away from the address on the card Thomas had given him. The houses around were low, squat rectangles, with little tufts of dying grass spotting the yards, and here and there a spindly, bald sapling. But one, set farther back from the street, was a massive, cube-shaped structure of porticoes and colonades, surrounded by juniper and flanked by two symmetrical magnolias. Before he checked the number on the mailbox, Jim knew it must have been Leslie's.

Jim found the key on his ring. But he saw a light from a small window in the rear. He left the horseshoe drive and approached the house obliquely. Then the crackle and the blinding light.

Jim did not land in the juniper. He landed among the bodkins of a pyracantha. Looking at the house, all Jim could see was the blue-white wash of light. He heard nothing until, with a pop, the floodlights went out. When the burned-in spots on his retinas cleared, he could see the shapes of the windows and the shutters. Another light was burning in the interior.

Missing his watch, Jim tried to count chimpanzees to estimate the passage of time, but he kept losing count. Still, he thought it better to lie among the briars he knew than to risk having to jump into the unknown again. He watched the cusp of the moon rise above the roof. By the time he could see the second horn of the moon, the floodlights had crackled on and popped off three times and the interior lights had closed a cycle.

Timed, he thought.

Jim stood up and released his socks from the pyracantha. As expected, the floodlights crackled on again. He was ninety percent certain it was only a notch in a mindless clock, but Jim flinched.

He walked directly to the front door and pressed the button. The house chimed eight bars of Tara's theme and then was perfectly silent. Jim looked through his ring again for the key, found it, and tried it in the ornate lock. It worked.

The entryway was marble-floored, and by the light through the open door, Jim could perceive the lines of a broad, scarlet-carpeted, gracefully curved staircase. Jim kicked the door shut behind him.

* * *

The logical place to look for the photos, if they were hot at all, would be the master bedroom. But Jim decided instead to follow the automatic cycle of the lights until he had got the layout of the place. The clicking of the little timers led him first to the laundry room, then to an upstairs hall, to the powder room beneath the staircase, the dining room, back upstairs to a guest bedroom with an empty closet and an empty chest of drawers, and downstairs to the parlor. *Nothing.*

From the exterior, Jim had assumed that the late Leslie had been a belle of the old school. Yet the interior was furnished with an eclectic—no, a decidedly peculiar—taste. When the lights took him to the kitchen and he opened the cupboards, he realized what it was. No two pieces of china were of the same set. There was crystal, perhaps for twelve, and a like complement of sterling tableware—no two of anything in the same pattern. Very like Jim's own kitchen, except that it was real china, crystal, and sterling: Leslie had done it on purpose. That was it: mismatched bulbs in the chandeliers; an assortment of chairs in the dining room; the scones on either side of the mantel, not a pair. Everything— everything was different.

The kitchen light went out.

Jim wondered what the point was. Well, the point was that everything was different. But what had Leslie meant by that? Or had Leslie been seriously unbalanced? God, would this mean thumping around for secret panels and revolving bookcases?

At last the light came on in the master bedroom.

The room was dominated by the projection TV and the stack of tapes by the VCR. Nothing under the bed. Nothing between the mattress and the springs. Liquor in the cabinet in the headboard. In the commode by the bed: an asthma inhaler, a mound of pennies mixed with various small foreign coins, a box of tissues, assorted small pins and beads and machine screws. Top drawer of the dresser: socks—Leslie hadn't taken the one-of-a-kind theme as far as apparel, at least not so far as to mismate socks—and a stack of folded handkerchiefs. Second drawer—

Jim felt the whoosh of the change in air pressure as the front door of Leslie's house was opened. He heard the voices echo off the marble. He froze. The voices and the soft footfalls on the carpet moved up the stairs. Jim ran into the closet.

It was a walk-in closet with a light of its own. Jim could not find a place to hide. He pulled a bedspread from a stack of linen and crouched under it in the corner. Jim realized that he looked like a guy hiding under a bedspread. He got up and pulled down the whole stack of linen. He unfolded the sheets and wadded them up in a corner: a tangerine silk sheet; a fitted bottom sheet in a green bamboo pattern; one plain white; leather?—yes, the black sheet was real leather; a stunning paisley print; and a picture sheet of a mountain lake with hemlocks. Jim crawled into the pile.

"Wail, Gary Lee, this is what I wanted you to see."

"It's one of em humongous TV sets."

"That's right. What do you reckon it's worth?"

"New, I guess they're three or four thousand. Used, maybe fifteen hundred. Does it work?"

"Don't know. It can't be very old if you ain't seen it."

"Anythang else?"

"The chandeliers. I was in a junk store last—sh! D'ya hear somethang?"

"Someone pulled up outside."

"Kin we git out of here? Kin we hide?"

"Sh! No. Ah'm Leslie's own brother. We have as much raht to be here as anyone."

"They're comin in."

"Relax. We got a perfect raht to be here."

"Oh, lookie, lookie, Jonny Bill. It's Allie Jean and Gary Lee, got here afore us."

"Apprizing everthang that ain't tied down, Ah'll bet."

"Don't mind him. How are y'all, Allie Jean?"

"Tolerable. Tolerable well, Joanie Sue. And y'all?"

"Peachy. Jes peachy."

"Gary Lee, you gonna speak to Joanie Sue and your own brother Jonny Bill?"

"Find out what the vultures want first."

"Oh men! Y'know how it is, Joanie Sue."

"Do I ever! Why, y'know what Jonny Bill was sayin to me whiles we was drivin over?"

"Why no, Joanie Sue. What'd he say?"

"He said we best git ours before those marauders grab everythin. Now ain't that jes like a man?"

"No! He didn't, did he?"

"His very words. Ain't it a hoot?"

"Jes like a man. Oh, let me tell you what Gary Lee said. Jes slays me. Sometimes Gary Lee jes slays me."

"What's Gary Lee say? Ah bet it's rich."

"Wail, Gary Lee says, he says, wait 'til the estate gits settled. He says all those relations who never had nothin to do with Leslie while he was alive—y'know, on account of Leslie being sensitive, y'know—he says them that would call Leslie a flit to his face will be the first ones there with their hands out, spectin somethin."

"No! Gary Lee says that?"

"Deed he does. But you know Gary Lee. He's always wondered what became of his mama's china. D'ya know Gary Lee's always wondered what became of his mama's china, Joanie Sue?"

"No. No, Ah didn't know that."

"Wail, he has. He's always wondered. But Ah reckon Leslie's fixed their wagon—whoevert was."

"What do you mean, Allie Jean?"

"Oh. I forgit. You never was in Leslie's home whiles he was alive, was you? You'll see, Joanie Sue. You'll see soon enough. Leslie's had a joke on folks that like to furnish their houses with the leavins of their dead relations."

"Wail, Ah guess Gary Lee's always felt protective of the sensitive types—what with that partner of his, that Roger."

"Aw Joanie Sue, you're wrong. Roger's not one bit sensitive. He jes likes his freedom. That's all. Roger's a regular stallion. But Ah guess, y'know, you wouldn't recognize such a thang, livin all your life with Jonny Bill an all."

"Maybe not. Ah suppose you know all there is to know about stallions, Allie Jean. You spendin your senior year at your granddad's ranch. That's where you spent your senior year, isn't it? Your granddad's ranch. That's what you said at the time."

"Hey! Joanie Sue. Allie Jean. Why don't y'gals see if you kin rustle us up some coffee?"

"Gary Lee's right. You girls run along now."

"Wail, Ah guess we better, Allie Jean. Man talk, y'know."

"Aw god, Gary Lee. You're not gonna take any of that stuff the girls said serious, are ya?"

"Naw. Naw, of course not. Ah do wonder about Mama's china. And still . . . still Ah think it's a shame Leslie didn't have the comfort of all his family when he died."

"Cut me some slack, Gary Lee. I've still got young kids, y'know. Not everyone got an early start on their child-rearin."

"Fair enough. You still worried bout little Kenny Bill?"

"Aw hell, Gary Lee, he won't go out for football. Sits in his room drawin pitchures alla time. Kin you blame me? Ah mean, if you was me, would you be bringin him over to see his Uncle Leslie?"

"Naw, Ah reckon not. You got my sympathy, Jonny Bill."

"Hell, Ah don't know what to do. Ah beat the tar out of him, worse than Paw ever laid it on us. It jes don't do no good. Christ, Ah'd settle for soccer. Y'know, some of em play soccer now. Even a chickenshit kin play soccer. But no. An y'know what he wants for Christmas?"

"No."

"Guess."

"Ah hain't got a clue."

"He wants pastels."

"Naw. No shit?"

"Wail, it's not as bad as it sounds. It's jes a fancy kind of crayons. But y'know what it does to a man when his only boy wants pastels for Christmas?"

"There there, Jonny Bill. Ah think Leslie keeps somethin around here for snakebite."

When the closet door opened Jim could see the light through the sheets over his head. The door closed again.

"Not in there. Oh yeah. Behind the bed. . . . What's this? 'Amy . . . maretto.' What in the hell is that? No. Wait. Here's some Jack Daniel's."

"Gary Lee, you jes never knowed trouble like mine."

"Lookit. Here's the bottle. Oh god, stop it, Jonny Bill. No wonder the kid's a fairy, his old man goes around slobberin like that alla time."

"Ah'll kill him. Ah'll kill him if he's a fairy. My kid's not gonna be no fairy."

"Okay, okay. Hey, Jonny Bill, come on. Lookit, you ever see this machine of Leslie's?"

"What of it?"

"Allie Jean says it's a TV set."

"Yeah. Ah seen one of em in a bar once."

"An what's this?"

"That's one of em TV motion pitchure machines."

"Think so?"

"Yeah. They had one of em in the bar too."

"How's it work?"

"Wail, you turn it on first. Like that. Now, here, let me see it. You take one of these out of the box and you jes sortta nudge it up here. See? It swallows the whole thang all by itself."

"Nothin happenin."

"You gotta turn on the TV set too."

"Oh. Now what?"

"It's on some special channel of its own. Two or three, Ah think."

"Oh my god."

"You menfolk through talkin? We brung ya'll some hot coffee—Jesus H. Christ! What the hell is it?"

"Joanie Sue, you spilt coffee all over this rug!"

"That can't be done, kin it? What the hell is it?"

"It's jes Leslie's machine. Ah'll shut it off."

"My god, Allie Jean, d'ya ever see anythang like that?"

"Oh, that's nothin. You should've seen some of the magazines and pitchures Ah found up here last week."

"How horrible!"

"What'd ya do with the stuff, Allie Jean?"

"Burnt it. Ah couldn't put that stuff out. What if the can came open and one of the garbage men saw it? What would they say?"

"Good! Good for you."

"An some of em magazines, on the cover, they said they cost upwarts of thirty dollars. Must of burnt up a thousand dollars worth. Ah hope that executer don't spect me to make it up."

"Oh no, Allie Jean. Our lips are sealed. No one'll be the wiser."

"An not jes magazines. He had a bunch of real pitchures. An folks in em—men, Ah mean—you'd probably recognized some of em."

"Who? Doin stuff like on the TV? Oh tell us, Allie Jean. We'll never breathe a word of it."

"Joanie Sue, you know Ah'm terrible on faces. Ah recognized a lot of em. Not recognized like Ah know em, but recognized like they was famous men. Ah jes can't tell you who they was because Ah don't know myself."

"An you burnt up all the pitchures?"

"Every last one. All that stuff cept the dirty books cause y'know ya had to read the words and all to know they're dirty."

"Wail, should we do somethin with these TV motion pitchures?"

"Ah don't know. Isn't there some way to wipe em off? Y'know, erase them?"

"Could be."

"Wail, let's leave em for now."

"Yeah. Ah think that's only raht."

"We kin figure it out when the estate is settled."

"If there's anythang left by the time the estate's settled."

"Huh-uh, honey. Drop it."

"If you say so."

"Hey! I've got an idear! Let's all go out for supper!"

"Ah don't know. Ah've got to go by the plant."

"Oh come on, Jonny Bill, don't be such a stick in the mud."

"Ah don't know. New safety engineer at the plant. Ah really need to check by."

"Tell you what. We'll all go to supper—there's this new Chinese place near the Welfred Center—and afterwards, we'll drive Joanie Sue home sos you kin go to the plant. How bout it?"

"Ah guess. Okay."

"Wail, what's keepin us?"

Jim lay with the pile of sheets for a long time after the voices had gone. *"Burnt up the pitchures."* Well, *that's that, isn't it? If the pitchures—if the* pictures—*are burned up, someone will have to go to bed with Brother Earl. Someone,* Jim thought, *like me.*

Nothing, nothing really to do now but look for secret panels. Allie Jean did not sound like the kind of woman who would have missed anything obvious. Knock on the walls. Look behind the wall hangings. What else? Oh yeah, under the carpets for trap doors. Look for stuff taped under drawers. Fiddle with the mantel. The secret lever is always in the mantel. If it's not behind a book.

Then after all that fails, which it will, maybe to the bar to have a few drinks and think about things.

Jim got up.

The studs in the walls were depressingly regular. Jim knocked. It was thunk, thock, thock, thunk every time. None of the paintings or mirrors were hinged, except of course the mirror in the bathroom.

Box of shaving soap, ancient. Underneath it, a Raid roach bait. Revlon Moon Drops almond masque. I wonder about anyone who would put something that shade of purple on his face. Neosporin ointment. Half book of matches, heads all stuck together. Empty tube of Tronolane. Murine ear drops. Coty Peel-Away apricot facial mask. Icy Hot balm. For godsake don't put that on the wrong place. Vick's Vapo-Rub. Ditto. Three boxes of Avon Tracy deep clean cream

samples. *Tinactin cream. Ear plugs. Five—yes, five—differ-*
ent razor handles. One Bic disposable razor. Aristocort
cream. Shaving mug. Oil of cloves. Shaving brush. Pramo-
sone Lotion 1%. Band-Aids. The tin is totally full. Monoject
syringe. No needle. Curved tip. What in the world is this
for? Three thermometers in a glass. Another thermometer in
a case. What is the deal? All oral anyway. Amorous brand
roll-on deodorant. Goody trimming razor. Now for the
drugs.

Valium 10s. Empty, naturally. Motrin. Empty. Dara-
prim25. Don't know what that is. Terfonyl. Sounds like an
antidepressant. Like Elavil or Triavil, maybe. They're no
fun. Something called an antidepressant ought to be at least
a little cheery, but they're not. A shitload of Erythromycin.
Tagamet. Guess Leslie had an ulcer. Orinase? Deconges-
tant, I guess. That's it. No amusing drugs. And no photo-
graphs of Brother Earl.

All of it was hopeless.

Jim had his hand on the knob, about to let himself out of
Leslie's house, when he thought he'd look just once more
in the bedroom. *They just have to be there.* He knew it was
the kind of delusion the victim clings to, the first few mo-
ments after the disaster. But he gave in to it and he padded
up the scarlet carpet for the last time.

Jim ran his fingers between the mattress and the box
spring. He didn't expect to find anything between the mattress and the springs, any more than he had found anything
the first three or four times he had looked. He felt the
seams: They felt perfectly regular, like all the other seams
and crevices and buttings he had felt in Leslie's house. He
sat back on his heels. Now what?

He recognized the whoosh. Someone had come in. He
glanced at the closet and thought better of it. He squeezed
under the bed and tried to pull the dust ruffle down the way

that it had been. The muffled steps came directly to the bedroom. There was the rustle of a grocery bag. Someone plopped down on the bed and pinned Jim's skull against the carpet. He heard the ratcheting of a dial telephone.

"Joanie Sue, honey? . . . You git home okay? . . . Lookit, Ah'm gonna be tied up at the plant for a while. . . . No, don't wait up. This new engineer, he's made a mess of thangs. . . . It'll probably be after midnight, if nothing else goes wrong. . . . Jes put the kids to bed and lock up tight. . . . Ah will. Bye-bye now, hon."

When the weight was off his skull, Jim wiggled to a spot under the far part of the bed.

Flick-flak. Flick-flak. *What is that sound?* Flick-flak. *Surely not.* Flick-flak. *Yes. It is. It's the sound of someone flipping down the stack of Leslie's videotapes.* Flick-flak. *No doubt.*

A little jangle, then a heavy buffered thump with a trace of a jingle. *Well,* Jim thought, *that's a sound I know for sure. A man with a pocket full of change just dropped his pants.* Clicks and whirs. *Must be the VCR.* Loud, spacey theme music. Plop of man-sized body on the bed. More rustle of grocery bag.

—Plebe-scum, you done with my boots?
—Yes.
    (Twak.)
—Yes what?
—Yes sir!
    (Twak.)
—You call that a shine, mullet?
—Yes sir!
—Well I don't. *(Twak. Twak.)* Give me ten, slime.
—Yes sir! *(Pant-grunt, pant-grunt, pant-grunt, pant-grunt, pant-grunt, pant-grunt, pant-grunt.)*

—I said ten, roadapple. I only count seven.

—Please sir! I can't go on.

   (*Twak.*)

—On your feet, turdblossom! Assume the position.

—God no, sir! Have mercy! No! Oh no!

   (*Sh-thwack.*)

—Ugh-aww!

   (*Sh-thwack.*)

—Ugh-awwoh, sir! Not the cat-o'-nine-tails! Anything, anything else, please sir!

   (*Sh-thwack, sh-thwack, sh-thwack.*)

—Anything, Maxipad? Anything?

   (*Sh-thwack.*)

—Ughh-ouawghough! Yes, anything, sir!

—Then how about taking this on, spawnbreath?

—Gosh sir! I've never seen one that big.

—Beg for it, maggot!

—Oh no, sir! I could never take all of that.

   (*Sh-thwack, sh-thwack, sh-thwack.*)

—It's this or the lash, zitsucker!

—Urgarawigckoohuemarhgeh! Then please, sir, split me with that log! Tear my guts with your manhood! Drive your Lincoln up my chocolate highway! Ram it into me, sir!

—That's better, snotbucket.

—Oh god. Oh GOD! Oh sir! Yes, yes, yes, give me more of it! I love it! I want it all, oh sir, oh wonderful!

—Aah! Aah! Great!   —Eeyow! Don't stop.

—Grr. Grr. Oh! Oh!   —Ah-ah-ah-ah-ah-ah

—I'm getting it! Oh!   —Ah-ah-ah-ah-ah-ah

—Take it! Take it!   —Ah-ah-ah-ah-ah-ah

   (*Squish, squish.*)   (*Splat, splatter, splat.*)

—Gee, Biff, that was great!

—Great, Marty. Next time you're the pledge, right?
—Sure, Biff.

At last the mattress was still above Jim's head. *I may be old fashioned,* Jim thought, *but I'll never get used to talkies.* The TV buzzed a fuzzy snow-sound. And, barely perceptible, a distant-sounding, tiny, mesmerized moan: "Oh oh   oh   oh."

Jim lifted the dust ruffle a little bit. Over a dustbunny, he could see the reflection of a digital clock. Jim watched the numerals flip over for ten minutes. Still, the little minimal vocal sound: "Oh   oh   oh   oh."

Five reels of high-test video. The guy must be out. It's got to be a kind of snoring.

Gone! The pictures burned up by that stupid hillbilly slut! Now I've got to go to bed with Brother Earl if I want the sweepstakes money. I hope, Jim thought, *that Agnes has plenty of those zebra pills. Anyway, there is no point in looking around Leslie's house anymore.*

Jim listened. "Oh   oh   oh   oh."

No time like the present. Sidewinder-like, Jim slipped from under the bed and sat up.

Jim gasped. He was staring into an open, bloodshot pair of green eyes. But that wasn't why he gasped.

"Sorry," Jim said, and he scurried to the bedroom door.

On the curved staircase, Jim could hear the bare feet after him. Jim skidded on the gravel in the horseshoe drive and cut across the lawn to the street. Still the man came after him.

My God, Jim wondered, *how long can he chase me, barefoot, naked, and with a quart bottle of cooking oil hanging out his tail?*

TEN

THE stooped old man walked.

He had walked a long way with the little ragged case. The case was the shape of a stringed instrument. The handle of the case was a piece of clothesline, doubled and redoubled on itself and wrapped with masking tape. Scuffs and scrapes on the case showed that, under the thin tissue of black vinyl, it was cardboard.

Gusts of twilight breezes stirred bits of paper and cigarette butts and dust across the sticky, dirty stains on the sidewalk. Once or twice in a block, an island of glass bricks appeared in the sidewalk, but these were dark and murky

124

and slowly being reclaimed by urban soil.

The old man's jacket was too long for him in the sleeves, and around the collar the sizing had worn through the dusty gray material. When Crumbelly raised his head or looked around, the sizing pricked his neck and scratched.

Crumbelly did not raise his head or look around. He kept his eyes on the dirty sidewalk.

He plodded on, past the three-balled pawn shops, past the barred storefronts, past the alarm-striped windows of the credit jewelry store. Past the hanging-out guys supporting their boomboxes with hypertrophied arms, the early hookers still yawning and stretching, the old paddy snoozing in his cherrytop, the cluttering of dishes and the smell of burning grease, the barking dog stationed for the night in the gun shop—Crumbelly walked on.

Headlights of passing cars were flicked on. The last of the day people hurried along the streets in the ruddy light, hoping to get away before those certain parts of town became completely dark.

Crumbelly walked on the sidewalk until he came to a clear stretch of concrete along a plain gray, drab, windowless wall where a rose-colored security light warmed and flickered. Here it was clean only by comparison. Pinstripes of soil showed the brush strokes where the washwater had been swept.

Then Crumbelly did look up; he knew well where he was.

He let himself down from the curb, slowly and carefully. He turned and walked up the alley. When he reached the wooden steps, under the unmarked awning, he climbed, a step at a time, pulling himself up by the gray drab two-by-four that was the handrail. At last he stood in the dimly lit doorwell, facing a gray drab wall.

He clamped the cardboard case between his knees and

removed a folded poster from the breast pocket of the prickly jacket. He bit pieces of masking tape off a roll with his good tooth. He flattened the poster against the wall.

"Limited Engagement—One Night Only," it said.

And there he was, the way that he had been. A lavender jacket trimmed in black velvet. A white carnation in his lapel. All his own teeth in his head and sparkling. A black bow tie.

"The Original Lavender Bluesman," it said in script.

Then there was his name in block letters and the blank space that was supposed to be overprinted with the name of the place he was appearing and the date. And finally, below that, in smaller script: "Singing his blues hit: 'I Left My Mojo in My Other Bag.' " Except it did not really say that anymore. He read it that way because he knew how it was supposed to be. But a corner of the poster had been torn away and it really said: "nging his blues hit: 'I Left My Mojo in My Other Bag.' "

Crumbelly stooped again to get the handle of the case. Then he turned to his right and grasped the knob of the drab gray door and pulled with all his weight.

In the Reservation, behind the counter at the door, Jerry was amusing himself by flexing his left forearm and watching the wiggles in his eagle-and-anchor tattoo.

The first time the door opened, Jerry glimpsed a bit of tattered jacket. Jerry stiffened his back and pumped his biceps. Hardly anyone but the right people found the door to the Reservation. Jerry did not mind being kept for his decorative value, but he thought that if there was any doorkeeping to do, he as doorkeeper ought to do it.

The second time the door opened, the old man made it through. Jerry saw who it was and relaxed.

"What are you doing, Crumbelly?"

"Not much, Mister Jerry. I just make my music for my people. But they don't care. Don't matter to me if they don't. It's all I know, making music for my people."

"Are you going to play here tonight?"

"I will if it would be all right, please. That old fleabag hotel, they say they're about to put old Crumbelly on the street again."

"Sure. I'm sure it'll be all right."

"You still got my old tip jar back there?"

Jerry scooted off the stool and looked under the counter. Under someone's forgotten gym bag, next to the bank bag with the bribe money for the commissioner, Jerry found an old crock. It was heavier than he thought. With both hands he picked it up, blew the dust out of it, and set it on the counter. "This it?"

"That's the one." The old man reached for the crock.

"I'll set it on the stage for you."

The stage at the Reservation was just a triangular platform across a dim corner of the lounge. The lighting was controlled by a foot switch—dark, click, white, click, red, click, blue, click, dark. And so it was for everything that the Reservation called a show.

Crumbelly boosted himself on a low chair twice before he lurched onto the stage. The speaker hummed until Crumbelly clicked the ukelele lead into the amplifier. He sat on an upturned washtub in the dark until he imagined that a hush came over the bar. He tapped the foot switch with his toe.

"Git down, sisters!" Crumbelly shouted at the bar.

"What happened to the jukebox?" Donald asked Ellenor.

I got em two bit blues again.
I got em two bit blues again.

Oh please, Mistah Peep-show Man,
I got em two bit blues again.

Sistah Mary went down to that peep show,
Mussa been bout half pas ten.
Lawdy, Lawdy, save dem quarters,
Cause it's too late to save de men.

"Are you listening to me, Donny?" Ellenor asked.

"Of course." Of course Donald was listening, because Donald certainly wanted to be on Ellenor's list.

"As I was saying. He's really quite scattered. About a week ago he had a few drinks and quoted me a price. He had forgotten that I had it while it was free—and it was hardly worth it then."

Donald smiled but could not quite manage the giggle he knew was required.

Don't sell my sistah mo' quarters,
Oh please, Mistah Peep-show Man.
I's late for a three o'clock fittin
And her car's got me blocked in.

Osage is an early town. By the time Crumbelly had finished his first set, all of the regulars were in attendance. Indeed, the Reservation seldom serves anyone but a regular. Crumbelly crawled off the stage and found only the dollar Jerry had slipped into the crock when he'd put it on the stage.

Ellenor merely looked sharply at the bartender with the big pecs; she forgot his name—not that it mattered, because she was certain he would be leaving Osage soon. The bartender made a scotch and water and set it on the corner of the bar nearest to Crumbelly.

Monday is the big night at the Reservation. Weekends, people show up for eye-openers at three in the afternoon, but shortly after dusk, anyone who can, leaves the bar for one of the private parties. That is why Donald was eager to get onto Ellenor's list. He did not realize that he was too dull to remain on Ellenor's list once he had been passed around. But if you aren't on someone's list you have to stay at the Reservation after dark on Saturday night and then go home with someone poor and ugly.

Monday is the big night. Mondays, one must attend or be talked about. Mondays, one must confront one's sisters and pretend that nothing happened, you know. Monday is taking census, mending fences, and, according to one's list, planning the next weekend's gala: who will give it, what is the theme, and what occasion will serve as an excuse.

Strangers are rare in the Reservation. Mondays they seem stranger still. Ellenor saw him immediately: the tall dark man at the door, showing his card to Jerry. Jerry appeared to be puzzled, but he sat back on his stool at the counter by the door and nodded. The stranger walked into the bar. Ellenor lost sight of him behind the mirrored column in the center of the bar.

Donald stopped talking. Ellenor realized it was her turn to say something, but she hadn't noticed any of what Donald had said. Not that it mattered: Donald was seldom very amusing.

"Why don't we move down the bar a bit, dear?" Ellenor asked.

"Oh, I see." Donald peeked around the mirrored column.

"Sh! No. Don't be so obvious." Ellenor moved her stool half the distance she thought necessary. After two slow sips, she moved the rest of the way. "There," she said when the stranger was in view.

Donald saw that it was pointless to try to talk to Ellenor for a while. So Donald looked at the stranger too.

The stranger downed the drink he was holding and set the empty glass on the bar. Immediately the empty glass was replaced with a full one. A clean, full glass, Donald noticed, with fresh ice.

"He wasn't here Saturday night?" Ellenor asked, without thinking that it was tactless to imply that Donald had nowhere else to go on a Saturday night.

"No." Donald swallowed the humiliation of being able to answer Ellenor's question.

"Something very peculiar . . ." Ellenor said, mostly to herself.

Donald did not see anything peculiar about the stranger, except of course that outside of the staff the stranger was the only competition Donald had for Most Attractive Unaffiliated Young Man in Attendance.

"Aha!" said Ellenor. She put on her spectacles to be sure.

"What? Is he some kind of cop?" Donald spoke the question that always occurred first when a stranger appeared in the Reservation.

"No. Nothing of the sort. Did you see the ring?"

"What ring?"

"There, on his finger."

"What about it?"

"It looks ordinary enough from this side. But when he turns his hand, on the other side is a chimera."

"So?"

"So, that young man is an imperial tribune." Ellenor tapped the bar with the earpiece of her spectacles. The bartender with the big pecs mistook the absentminded tapping for a signal and appeared so quickly across the bar that Ellenor was startled.

"Yes ma'am?" he said.

"Oh! Oh yes. Won't you please send that young man a drink from me."

"I'll be happy to put you on the list."

"The list?"

"Fresh meat, you know. He hasn't bought a drink since he came in. There are about a half dozen ahead of you."

"Right you are. Well then, never mind."

The time was not so long past since Donald himself had been fresh meat. "Imperial tribune. Big damned deal," Donald said.

"No," said Ellenor, "I think possibly it is a big damned deal."

"Why? The Jade Court, I mean. It's all ancient history, isn't it?"

"Well that's it. Don't you see, Agnes—of course you are much too young to have known Agnes, and I don't know what you may have heard—Agnes, whatever they say, is very shrewd. She knows very well that the Jade Court is nothing anymore in Osage. So she wouldn't, you see. She wouldn't send an imperial tribune here unless something momentous was going on."

Donald watched the bartender with the big pecs pour good call whiskey over ice, add a splash of water, and place the drink in front of the fresh meat. No one had ever bought call whiskey for Donald.

"He doesn't look so hot to me."

"Gracious, Donny, one might think you were envious. Not a very attractive sentiment in one as young as yourself, envy isn't."

"Who, me? Oh, nothing like that. I only think it is silly

for everybody to get all excited simply because a stranger walks into the bar."

"You mean a stranger who diverts attention from yourself."

"What of it? I could have him anyway."

"Oh, you think so?" asked Ellenor, embellishing the evil tone in her voice with a sneer of her right eyebrow.

"Dare me."

Crumbelly had drunk three-fourths of the scotch and water when he asked the bartender for a fluff.

"Okay this once. But you know it's not allowed."

"Sorry. It's only that Crumbelly's voice, you know, his old voice needs a little more priming these days."

"I'm sure," said Charlie, which was the name of the bartender with the big pecs. He fluffed Crumbelly's drink with scotch all the way up, not so much because Crumbelly was old and poor and not so much because Charlie liked Crumbelly's music, but because Crumbelly was the first person all evening who had looked at Charlie above the neck.

"Oh, thank you very much, sir," Crumbelly said, so that Charlie would know that Crumbelly had been watching the whiskey bottle. "I dedicate my next set to you."

"Thanks," said Charlie. "I like jazz a lot."

Crumbelly kept smiling and showing his one own yellow tooth, but inside he said sternly: *Ain't no jazz. It's the blues. It's my original, the lavender blues. But you got to keep on the good side of your bartender even if he don't know nothing.*

"Nurse!" Someone who had forgotten Charlie's name, if he had ever bothered to learn it, called from down the bar. Charlie turned away. Crumbelly returned to the stage and set the drink down carefully where it would be safe while he lurched and boosted himself up again.

Jim had perched on the first free stool he had encountered when he entered the bar. Thus Willard was sitting to the left of Jim, and Willard is furniture.

Each afternoon at four-thirty Willard enters the Reservation and occupies Willard's stool. Everybody knows it is Willard's stool. Some of the day customers, the nightshift workers and the true alcoholics, dare to sit in Willard's stool.

But it is not done to be in Willard's stool when Willard comes in. Although Willard had never entered the Reservation more than five minutes before or after four-thirty, it is better to be safe than sorry. By three-forty-five even the very intoxicated steer clear.

Willard occupies his stool and drinks Orange Blossoms, which is what he calls gin screwdrivers with a splash of Triple Sec. Precisely an hour before closing Willard stands and leaves.

Alone. Always alone.

Willard never speaks unless spoken to and then only if spoken to by a person entitled to speak to Willard. Very few are entitled to speak to Willard: Ellenor is one. Those who are passing at the moment for the younger clientele occasionally debate whether Willard is, or ever has been, gay. Sometimes from sheer boredom a young hot item throws himself at Willard in the attempt to discover whether Willard will.

After all, Willard does not look really bad and Osage is a small, dull town in very many ways. Willard does not look really good either. Willard looks correct and merely that.

Another moot question is that of Willard's age. The reverse of a cheap insult: Willard will never look as old as he must be by now.

Ellenor says that Willard has become fashionable again.

What she means by that is that Willard first appeared at the Reservation in 1955. He was correct for 1955. His fine brown hair was neatly combed, just long enough to comb neatly and well trimmed above his ears and collar. In 1955 he was cleanly shaven, and he wore a double-knit golf shirt, beltless slacks, leather boat shoes, and no jewelry save a tank watch. In 1955 he was smooth-skinned and lean, without being thin. And so, altogether, Willard has remained.

Willard remained through crew cuts, through madras, through paisley, through long hair and the emaciated look, through wide lapels, through Nehru jackets, through pre-faded jeans, through designer jeans, through the cowboy revival, through the muscle-bound look, through slogan T-shirts, and through camouflage prints. That's what Ellenor means when she says that Willard has become fashionable again, but when asked what she means, Ellenor only smiles.

They say Willard has a trust fund. They say Willard is retired from the light company. They say Willard is still a virgin and no one admits to being certain of the contrary. They say Willard was once a big-city hustler who saved his money. They say there was a great love affair and the other party is now high in politics. They say much and know little.

Sooner or later even the very curious and the very bored learn that Willard is just there, like a piece of furniture. And Willard was in the stool to Jim's left, so Donny knew there was no hope of getting that place until an hour before closing.

At Jim's right, however, was George.

George had latched onto that stool as soon as Jim sat down. But unlike Willard, George could be counted on to have functioning kidneys. Moreover, it would be feasible to take George's place when the pressure of urine in George's bladder overcame the flow of testosterone in George's mind.

Donald orbited until the moment came.

George took all the precautions. He left the change of a twenty-dollar bill on the bar under a pack of his cigarettes and his lighter. That was a sufficient sign, were the game played fairly, that George was planning to return to this place at the bar.

But Donald did not reckon he had to play fair with George. As soon as the men's room door closed behind George, Donald slid George's money, cigarettes, and lighter down the bar and hopped onto the empty stool. Barely in time, as it was, for few of the Reservation's patrons reckoned that they had to play fair with George, and Jim had attracted satellites other than Donald.

"Hello, my name is Donald. Call me Donny. Can I buy you a drink?"

"What, George? Oh, you're not George."

"No. May I buy you a drink anyway?"

"I'm afraid someone is ahead of you. They won't take my money in this bar."

"No wonder. You have such beautiful blue eyes."

"Do you think so?" Jim reflected. "Sometimes they are light. Sometimes they are dark. Do you think they are really all that blue?"

"Oh yes. A really deep, true blue."

"Yes?"

"Yes."

"Nice of you to say so. My name's Jim. I didn't get yours."

"Donald. Call me Donny."

George inserted his face between Jim's and Donald's. "Pardon me."

How tiresome, thought Donald.

"I hope I'm not interrupting."

Of course you are interrupting, you old fart. Donald almost said it audibly.

"I'll just get the things I left here when I went to the men's room for only a second." George reached in front of Donald and retrieved his money, cigarettes, and lighter. "We'll meet again soon, I hope," George said sweetly to Jim.

"That would be nice," said Jim abstractedly.

"And I'll see you again for sure," George hissed at Donald.

"Oh my, I guess I must have inadvertently taken his seat," Donald said as George did his best to stomp away on the padded gold carpet. "You know how touchy the *older gals* can be about things like that."

"I suppose queens are the same all over. Tell me, do you come here often, Danny?"

"Donny. Yes, it's the only place to go in Osage. If you'll be here awhile, I'll get you on one of the party lists."

"Party lists?"

"Yes. Private parties is where all the fun is. I'll just have Ellenor put you on her list. Ellenor has the most exclusive list."

"I don't know that I'll be here that long."

"Where are you from?"

"Austin."

"Oh." *Well,* Donald thought, *maybe Ellenor is right about that imperial tribune stuff. Better, then, to avoid discussing politics.* "Where are you staying?"

"Nowhere yet."

A place, Donald thought. *Where? Can't ask him to try to sneak into the dorm. Maybe he's got a car. No, not in the car. Not in a motel. Best not ask right away. Glenn and Jack have that spare room they keep for show in case Jack's par-*

ents show up. That's it, if I can get away to call Glenn and Jack.

Jim interrupted Donald's thoughts. "Can I ask you a personal question?"

"Of course."

"Are you a kept boy?"

"A kept boy?"

"You know, a houseboy. A live-in . . . Well, you know what I mean."

"I know what you mean. Of course not! Whatever would make you ask such a question?"

"I'm sorry. It was a rude question. Only it seems every time I meet someone I like lately, someone I could . . . well, they turn out to be somebody's houseboy or something."

"How awful."

"Tell me, Donny, everybody's being so nice. I mean, I'm not used to Osage. They don't expect something for buying me a drink, do they?"

"Of course not! What terrible people you must be used to. But your glass is almost empty. I insist on buying the next one. Then you won't owe anyone but me. You won't mind that, will you?" Donald turned toward Charlie and yelled "Nurse!" because Donald pretended not to remember Charlie's name.

Watching from across the bar, Ellenor thought Donald was doing very well after all. Donald had not been so very nice to George. *But George should have abdicated with better grace once he saw the young people were hitting it off. Besides, if the new one is around for long everyone who's interested will have his chance.* Osage is a small, dull town in so very many ways. *And if he's not around for long, well, it's appropriate that the young people have their fun.*

A stranger in the bar and Donald has picked up on him.

The issue is settled. See, the others are motioning to the bar-tender and taking their names off the list. Oh how sweet. That one is having the drink sent to the singer instead. What a good sport. On with the business of Monday night.

—Ellenor, it's your turn to host the entertainment. Isn't it —Let's see, too early for Harvest Moon. —And too late for Sun and Surf. —A Pledge Party. —Pledge Party theme. Just the thing! —And how about let's ask Donald. —Yes, Donald. Maybe he'll bring his new friend. —If not, we've been meaning to get to know Donald better anyway. —He does seem to handle himself well after all.

—I wonder where George is pouting. —On the patio I'm sure. —That's right, I haven't seen the barback lately. —And what is that supposed to mean? —I thought everyone knew. The barback turns tricks on the patio. —Goodness, what does the management say? —Are you kidding? Her Nibs doesn't bother with the bar since she hired that new doorkeeper. Get this mary, she trusts him!

—What a shame. —You know I think what the help does on their own time is their business and a young person needs to supplement his income. —But one does not want one's bar to become an open brothel. —My sentiments exactly. —After all, they could do that business any-where. But we only have one bar in this town.

—Look, Donald's friend seems a little bit tipsy. —Small wonder. I bought him four cocktails, just myself.

—Pledge party? Does that mean no drag? —Right. No drag. —But Edwina! —I suppose we have to let Ed-wina come as the housemother. —Right. —Otherwise Edwina won't attend at all.

※　※　※

If outsiders are always unexpected at the Reservation and on a Monday one stranger is a sensation, then Jerry was better prepared for the Second Coming than he was for the second new face at the door: the slim, blond, gray-eyed boy. Jerry was caught off balance as he leaned his stool against the wall, flexing his arms and considering his offers.

"I'm sorry, this is a private membership club," Jerry said, trying to right himself and the stool.

"I know," the boy said softly. "I want to speak to someone who may be here."

"I'm sorry, but that is impossible."

"But I see him. He's right over there at the bar." Phil waved at Jim, but Jim did not see him.

"Do you have an ID? You have to be over twenty-one to enter this club at all."

"But I've entered it already. Really, I'll only be a minute." Phil walked past the counter.

"Maybe you didn't hear me." Jerry grabbed Phil's wrist.

"I heard you well enough. I'll be right back." Phil pulled away from Jerry, but Jerry's grip tightened.

"I told you, I can't let you go in there."

"But you must."

"No I don't." Jerry stepped free of the counter, stood between Phil and the bar, and grabbed Phil's other wrist.

"I'm in a hurry. Sorry," Phil said. With a cricket-flick Phil was free.

Jerry melted slowly to his knees. As he cringed on the gold carpet, Jerry barked like a seal: "Hurts!"

"Doesn't it just. You'll get over it. I didn't break anything. Be back in a minute."

Jim found it a curious sensation. He had been looking at this Danny-Donny-Whatyoumaycallit person. Then the whole room rotated. Well, it seemed that way. A fast panning effect, like the change of scene in an old-time movie.

Then there were the gray eyes. *Ish the angel,* Jim said to himself and then aloud: "Ish the angel. Hiya, angel! How's it hanging?"

"You're drunk," said the angel.

"Yesh, ish twue, how twue."

"You're coming with me." Phil picked Jim up by the collar and began hauling him to the door.

"Gosh to go wid dish angel now. Bye-bye, Danny boy, bye-bye."

After an awkward moment in which Jim's foot tangled in Jerry's crumpled body, Phil and Jim were gone. Donny stood, took three steps toward the door, recovered himself, circled the bar twice, and threw himself onto the stool next to Ellenor. "Well, I suppose you saw that?"

"I did," said Ellenor.

"That little queen waltzed in here and stole my trick."

"I'd guess, Donny, that he was only reclaiming his husband."

"Husband? You said it wasn't a wedding ring."

"No, it wasn't a wedding ring and it was on the wrong hand besides. But that surely looked married to me. Or as good as." Ellenor rotated the ice in her glass and decided to have another.

"But he said—well, he implied he was single."

"Men have said stranger things."

"Two watches! Did you see that little bitch had two watches?"

"A few years ago I read that was fashionable. Something to do with the Princess of Wales."

"I'll snatch that little bitch bald-headed."

"Now Donny. These things happen. When you get to a place with a real nightlife where everybody doesn't know everybody else anyway, you'll see that such little misunderstandings are commonplace."

"Little misunderstandings? That chicken queen took my trick."

"I said I thought they were married." Ellenor counted silently as she watched the bartender pour her new drink.

"Then he shouldn't have led me on. How humiliating. I owe them both one. And I won't forget it." Donald rested his chin on his arms, which were folded on the bar.

"But Donny, wasn't it that you were trying to pick him up on a dare?"

"Irregardless, I'll get even if it's the last thing I do."

"Donny! That's very rash if he is an imperial tribune."

"I'm not afraid of old Agnes. Agnes-bagnes, she's only an old has-been."

"That too is a rash statement. But if it has to do with the Jade Court, we are unlikely to see either of them again."

"Then they'll both be very, very lucky."

Ellenor clucked and shook her head sadly. "Dear, dear, I'll tell you what, Donny: How would you like to join myself and a few of my friends for a small entertainment I am giving this weekend?"

"You mean . . ." Donald sat up on his stool.

"I mean perhaps you would enjoy visiting our little group a time or two. We'll see how things work out, you know."

"Oh." *She means,* thought Donald, *that I am not really on the list. I'm on probation.* "I see. Why yes. I *am* free this weekend."

Willard's stool was empty. Crumbelly peeked into the tip jar. There wasn't nearly enough. *No matter,* Crumbelly thought, *I just make my music for my people.*

Crumbelly found he could not boost himself onto the stage. He stood on a stool and crawled on his belly onto the stage. In the darkness on the stage, Crumbelly regained his dignity. He sat in the chair and poised his toe over the foot switch.

No one noticed when the white light washed down on Crumbelly and he pretended to be surprised, his right index finger stuck far into his nostril.

"Heh, heh." He chuckled to his imaginary audience. "You know, children, when you get caught with your finger up your nose, ain't nothing you can do about it. You best be going for the big booger!

"Heh, heh."

ELEVEN

J IM opened one eye. "Vibra," it said.

Yes. How true. Vibra.

Jim opened the other eye. It said: "Vibra-Soothe 25¢," And also: "Insert coin, twist timer past 10."

No, Jim thought, *I won't. I won't insert coin and twist timer past ten.* From the lampshade and the little bit of carpet he could see, Jim guessed this was a blue room.

There would be two molded plastic, white pedestal chairs with thin blue cushions, cream drapes printed over with blue and green interlocking circles, and a not exactly the right shade of blue dial-less telephone with a little red plastic lens to light up if there were any messages. Of course there never would be any messages.

There would be a color TV chained to a shelf near the ceiling on the wall that faced the foot of the bed, glasses wrapped in wax paper, and in the drawer of the plastic writing desk would be elaborate-looking ballpoint pens that would spill indelible ink all over any pocket they were put in.

The shower was running.

Now's my chance. Jim felt along the floor for his pants. They were not there. He felt under the mattress for his wallet. It was not there. He sat up too suddenly and had to lean back against the gold-embossed blue and aqua padded headboard, which was attached to the wall, not the bed. The pain was exquisite.

Trapped.

Next to the Vibra-Soothe on the bedside table was a glass of something burgundy on the rocks. And something else. Jim squinted. It was a little white and black striped capsule. *Yes.*

I remember this one. I think.

He picked up the pill and held it in the flat of his palm, close to the eye that seemed to be working better. *I could be wrong. What if it is poison?*

The valve squeaked as the shower was turned off and the white noise of the spray turned into dripping thuds. *So what if it is poison? All the better if it is fast-working.* He put the capsule in his mouth. The burgundy stuff turned out to be a Cape Cod.

"Oh, I see you are awake," said the moist angel, stark naked and ruffling a tiny towel through his snow-blond hair.

"Ullgar," Jim said.

"Perhaps you'd best just read the paper while you wait

for the pill to take effect. I'll just finish getting myself together."

In the vacant spot on the bed, Jim found the morning edition of the *Osage News-Free Press*. Halfway through the first section, Jim realized what kind of paper the *Osage News-Free Press* was. It was the kind of paper that did not have charcoal sketches of ladies modeling the lingerie in ads, but instead had sketches of the undergarments suspended in space, as if they were worn by the transparent kind of ghosts. The lifestyles section was still called the "Women's Page," although it was much more than a page and was by far the largest section of the paper.

There was a rather lengthy article about penny-wise ways to reuse the plastic bags that newspapers come in on rainy days. *Condoms for elephants. They left out condoms for elephants.*

The sports section was rather full of tire and gun ads. Jim thought the basketball action photograph was the most erotic thing he had ever seen. Hardly in keeping with the tone of a family newspaper: the incredibly long muscular legs, the bush of hair under the player's arm, hinting of the animal musk, the spread legs of the opponent and the straining bulges at the crotches of all the players, the orgasmic grimace on the shooter's face, the feather touch of the player's fingers caressing the ball even as he released it—the symbolism, the heat, the fleshy sexuality.

But then Jim realized: It was only the pill taking effect.

"Oh, uh, Phil? Would you mind coming in here this instant. Don't bother to dress." It was not right, of course. After all, wasn't Phil Agnes's party boy? However sweet he seemed, wasn't he allowing himself to be kept by a big old fat ugly queen. And was he too dumb to know any better? *He doesn't have any choice. He has to keep me happy to further Agnes's plot.*

But a zebra-striped capsule has no conscience. "Oh, Phil, please do hurry."

"Sorry, honey," Phil called back from the bathroom. "I know what you want. But we are expecting company."

"Company?"

"Yes. Mack is coming to set up the camera."

"Camera?" Jim tried to arrange the tent in the sheets so that it would not seem such a spectacle. "I thought we wanted pictures of Brother Earl."

"That's right." Phil came out of the bathroom wearing a little pair of white running shorts that made his golden legs seem to go on forever and a T-shirt that made his torso appear positively muscular. "But from what I could understand of all you said last night, the pictures—the original photographs—are not at Leslie's house and there is every reason to believe they are 'burnt up,' I believe you said."

"Yeah."

"Then we need to get more photographs made. Unfortunately."

"Unfortunately. That's easy enough for you to say." *After all,* thought Jim, *it probably is easy for him to say, considering his profession.*

"No. It's not really. If I could think of any other way . . ." Phil saw a shadow move across the drape. He went to the door. "I think this is Mack now." Phil opened the door.

It was Mack, Jim guessed. He was not a young man. He was half a head shorter than Phil. He was shirtless and wearing coveralls. Smoky puffs of gray hair billowed up from his shoulders and delts. He looked weathered but solid; not the ballooned-up chest of a bodybuilder, but the hard tone of muscles built of practical work; not tanned by an act of tanning, but from exposure to the elements. Jim's immediate impulse was to throw himself at the man's knees, to kiss the scuffed black workboots, and to try to unbutton the coveralls with his tongue.

Knowing it was an effect of the drug, knowing that he would not give Mack a second look, might even give Mack an unpleasant first look if it were not for the effect of drug, knowing that the pill would wear off and he would be embarrassed did not much help Jim in his efforts to resist the impulse.

"Mack," Phil said, "I would have known you anywhere."

"Can't say the same for you," Mack said. "The last time I saw you, why you . . ." Mack began to indicate a level only a bit lower than his hips, but Phil grabbed his hand and began to shake it.

"We can discuss that later." Phil winked at Mack with a clear expression of warning.

Mack raised an eyebrow. "You haven't introduced me to your friend."

"Oh, of course." Phil took the wooden tool box from Mack's left hand. "Mack, allow me to present Jim, who has been specially selected for this mission by Agnes herself."

With the door closed and his eyes becoming accustomed to the dimness, Mack saw Jim clearly for the first time. "Golly, I see why. He looks just like—"

Phil carefully tread on Mack's toes.

"I mean, he looks like just the man for the job." Mack extended his hand.

Forgetting for a moment the physical effects of the zebra-striped capsule, Jim stood up and took Mack's hand. "I am very pleased to meet you."

"Yes," Mack said, "I can see that you are."

Jim grabbed the corner of the sheet and wrapped it half

around his waist, not in any effective way managing to conceal his condition.

Phil set the tool box on the molded plastic motel desk. "Jim is glad to meet anyone this morning. If you would like, I could step out for some breakfast. Or I can assist Jim in the shower."

Mack chuckled. "Oh, thank you for the thought. But you young people go ahead and, uh, get cleaned up. I'll get to work."

"Kiss me!" Jim said.

"Jim!"

"I think you better get him in the shower in a hurry," Mack said.

"You're right. Jim, just behave yourself for an instant."

"Can't help it."

"I know. Come on into the shower."

When Phil and Jim returned from the bathroom there was a fourteen-and-a-half-by-eight-inch hole just under the shelf with the television in the wall that faced the foot of the double bed.

"Goodness," Phil said, "I haven't heard a thing."

"Small wonder," Mack said. "No, really. If you didn't mind disturbing the folks in the next room and if you didn't care whether it showed or not, anyone could do this. For quiet and an exact fit, there is nothing like handwork."

"That is a pun, isn't it?" Jim asked, only the edge taken off his pill-induced appetites.

"Didn't mean it as one. But now that you mention it, there is something to be said for that. Quiet and an exact fit. That's witty in a way. I believe I'll tell my friends that I said that."

"Well, you did. In a way."

Phil dropped his towel and stepped into a pair of bone-colored cords that had been folded over the back of a molded plastic chair. Jim asked for his clothes. Phil told him there was a clean change in the luggage stashed under the vanity. Jim put on his clothes in the bathroom. Then the boys sat at the foot of the unmade bed and watched Mack work.

When he had finished making holes in the studs with a hand drill, cranking it a half turn at a time, Mack blew the holes out and fitted pegs into each of them. Satisfied that each fit was correct, he shot glue into each of the holes with a hypodermic needle and tapped each of the pegs soundly with a rubber mallet. While the glue took hold, Mack fit the phony thermostat into the piece of wallboard he had removed.

"The dial is the camera lens," he explained. "Sooner or later, of course, someone will notice that this room has two thermostats and that this one doesn't work. Course, the real one doesn't do anything either. The management just puts them in so people have something to play with."

"How do you control the camera?" Jim asked.

"The TV's remote control, when I finish modifying it, will arm the camera. *You* hit the mute and the off button at the same time. *You* actually take pictures by pressing back on the headboard on the right side—as soon as I put the contact in. If *you* don't start taking pictures within ten minutes, the camera will turn itself off again."

"Do you have to point the TV control at the camera?"

"No, *you* don't. The TV control does work on infrared. But the camera is radio-controlled." Mack laid a piece of particleboard across the pegs, snapped the camera into the back of the wallboard he had removed, and slid the piece of gypsum back over the hole in the wall. The cracks where the wallboard had been removed were almost invisible.

"It almost doesn't show," Jim said.

"It won't show at all with a little putty and paint."

"The fresh paint won't show?"

"No, it won't. I've been told I'm pretty good at this sort of thing."

"And you are, Mack," Phil said quickly. "Agnes says you are the very best."

"Thank you, Your Highness."

Phil winced.

"Your Highness? What's this 'Your Highness' stuff?" Jim asked.

"Oh," Mack said. He pretended to rummage through his tool box for a moment. "It's just a figure of speech. I forget these old-timey expressions are not always understood by younger people."

When the putty was in the cracks, Mack began painting with an artist's brush. "The key, you see, is to do a little bit at a time, sort of pointillist-like. It's the sharp lines that call attention to things. No sharp lines. Just blend and blend. See?"

"Well yes, I guess so," Jim said, although he was not really listening and was watching more the effects of the movements on Mack's musculature than their effects on the wall.

The wall was soon restored to perfection. Jim was slashed out of his reverie by the noise and light when Mack opened the drapes. Evidently the light was necessary for the operation on the TV's remote control.

Once Mack had removed the cover of the control, Jim got up and went over to the window to have a look. Jim expected to see something very complicated-looking. But in fact, the interior of the remote control looked very simple. There were four or five things-from-inside-a-transistor-radio–looking things.

Mack produced something about the size of a push pin

that had three tiny colored wires at its base.

"The transmitter," Jim deduced, from what Mack had said he was going to do with the control.

"Yes. This one's about four times as big as the modern ones. Fortunately there's plenty of space in the remote control for it: They make them a lot bigger than they have to so people will be able to find them." Mack stuck the transmitter to the wall of the remote unit with some white gummy substance. With three tiny balls of a gray sticky substance, he affixed the tiny colored wires, each to a different pin of the chip.

Mack picked up the remote control's cover and the single screw that had held it in place.

"That's it?" Jim asked.

"That's it. All these units are pretty much the same."

"Tell me, Mack, how far away will this transmitter work?"

"I'll tell you, Jim," Mack said, "I've trimmed this one down. That wasn't really necessary. We only want it to work once. Oh, I guess, given what motel construction is, it would work from any room in this wing or from out in the parking lot."

"But it's not a bug?"

"You mean it won't transmit voices? Well, yeah, it would if we were going to use it for that. But you're just going to press the buttons for a second. That will be long enough to arm the camera. Not long enough for anyone to overhear anything intelligible, even if they were tuned in on it—which is literally a million-to-one shot." Mack produced something from his tool box that looked like the button of a pea jacket. "This is what will actually take the pictures." He handed it to Jim and tightened the screw on the remote control.

"It seems so much bigger than the other one."

"That's for what they call mechanical interface. It's what makes calculators so large. They have to have buttons big enough for human fingers to hit and numbers big enough for human eyes to read. In this case, it's so you can press anywhere in the general area on the headboard and not try to find an exact spot."

Mack took the button back from Jim and went to the bed. Mack knelt on the head of bed, exposing the bottom of the headboard, reached behind the headboard with the button, and stood off the bed. "There. That does it."

"But what if you miss the button?" Jim asked.

"*You* don't have to hit the button. It's constantly comparing the stresses all over its surface. Just press anywhere on the right side of the headboard. The padding will convey the force to the button and the button will do the rest."

"What else?"

"That's it. Mute and off together to arm the camera. Press the headboard to shoot. You've got thirty-two frames, so take as many as you can."

"Wonderful."

"Jim doesn't seem to be as thrilled about all this as he might be," Mack said to Phil.

"Oh Mack, it's not funny. Do you blame him?"

"No, I guess not. I guess it was thoughtless of me. I'll just be running along."

"No Mack, we really are very grateful for your help."

"I know. But I do have to go. No, don't get up."

When the door was closed behind Mack, Jim plopped down on the bed next to Phil. Despite the residual effect of the zebra-striped capsule on Jim, they lay quietly and looked at the bumpy white ceiling for a long time. Jim had not had breakfast, and the other effects of the pill began to assert themselves. Jim's stomach spoke to them.

"Oh, it must be me," Jim said. And a moment later: "You know, I have an idea."

"The same old idea?" Phil asked.

"No, no. I mean, how to get pictures of Brother Earl."

"Well, we know how. The disgusting thing is doing it. Jim, you haven't eaten. Let me call room service."

"Room service?"

"Yeah, you know. Room service."

"Well, yeah, I know what it is. I've just never used it before."

"Oh. Then you're in for an experience. What would you like?"

"Later. Listen to me first. Now first, tell me why this motel. This is a motel? Why this room in this motel?" Jim sat up.

"Because this motel is where Brother Earl takes his tricks, those he doesn't do right away in his office. Or so we hear. He thinks this place is safe and we're pretty sure he tips the staff to keep it that way."

"What if he picks another place?"

"Then develop a sudden headache or something. But he won't pick another place. He's been coming here awhile and nothing bad has happened. He'll come here."

"And why this room?"

Phil sat up. "Yeah. This is important. You have to insist on getting the room. We have compromised the desk clerk. He'll give you this room every time you come in."

"But then you could get him to give this room to Brother Earl whether I was here or not."

"No. Like I said, we think he's paying them too. They will work for us because they think that's all they are doing: working for us. I don't think they would work against Brother Earl."

"But sooner or later he'd get this room by chance."

"Jim, what are you driving at? Spill it."

"Okay. He's going to be seducing his students anyway."

"Right."

"And he's going to be bringing some of them to this motel."

"Right."

"And one way or another, sooner or later, he'll get this room."

"I suppose so. So what?"

"So. Mack said that transmitter could work as a bug. And all we would have to do would be to wait and to listen. And if we are listening we can figure out pretty well when to snap the camera, and with thirty-two shots one of them is bound to be the one we want. So we just wait until he brings one of his students up here, snap away, voilà, our pictures." Jim was bouncing on the bed. "And. And I don't have to go to bed with Brother Earl!" Jim seemed so happy and excited.

Phil shook his head and looked very sad. "No."

"What do you mean, no?"

"First, we don't have all the time in the world. But more importantly because—"

"Because why not?" Jim glowered.

"Because the whole idea of getting the photographs is to threaten to make them public."

"Yeah. Of course. So what?"

"So what about Brother Earl's partner? I mean, what about whomever he brought up here?"

Jim thought he saw but tried not to show it. "What about him?"

"Or her. Once in a while it's a her. But don't you see, he's just as likely to be a relatively innocent hayseed. Maybe even a virgin. If he has to go to Holy Word of God he probably already has two strikes against him. If we ever had to use the photos it would probably ruin his life."

"You mean I have to go to bed with Brother Earl to save some undergraduate closet case from a little embarrassment?"

"More than a little embarrassment. Did you read the newspaper this morning?" Phil began to look for the newspaper in the bed.

"I looked at it."

"In the city and state section. That killing last night."

"Homosexual killing?"

"Yes. That's the one."

"Love triangle. Jealous lover. So what? When I was younger—I mean, there was a time I almost did the same thing myself."

"No. Not a love triangle. Do you just read a newspaper without trying to figure out what it means? Get up. I think you're on the part I'm looking for."

Jim stood. Phil shuffled through the pile of newsprint Jim had been sitting on.

"Here. Look. It says: 'Police Detective Lukes said that the accused first claimed that the homosexual couple had been the victim of an attack by a street gang. . . . Three hours of interrogation were required before the confession was obtained. The suspect was then treated at Municipal Hospital for injuries he obtained in the fatal struggle.

" 'Detective Lukes denied any history of gang activity in the warehouse district. . . .'" Really, Jim, did you take that story at face value? Do you really think that's the truth of it?"

"Well, yeah, it's in the paper. . . . I mean, I'm very under the weather. I was when I read it, anyway."

"It's not a little embarrassment. Whether whoever came with Brother Earl was a closet case or not, exposure means death in many parts of this state. If the gangs used rope it would be called lynching. Lynching. That's what it amounts to."

"What about me? I don't want to be lynched."

"Well, by the time we have to use the photos—if we ever have to use them, which is very unlikely—you'll be back in Austin. Not that Austin is the safest place in the world. But face it, in Austin the news that you go to bed with men is hardly a lead story."

"Are you implying that I'm indiscreet?"

"Perish the thought."

Tomás stood at the door of the vault until Agnes looked up from the geographic card file. "We are ready for the briefing," he said.

Agnes sighed and pushed away from the file. She followed Tomás through the narrow corridor to the conference room and took her place at the head of the conference table.

Tomás cleared his throat and squared a stack of papers against the table. "We'll begin with Austin, if that is all right."

"Quite."

"Tommy has the report on McThacry."

The redheaded young man stood. "McThacry was treated and released at the emergency room, as you know. His wound was extremely superficial, calling only for a little cleaning and a large adhesive bandage. McThacry, however, believes his wound was serious, nearly mortal in fact, and he has been rebandaging the wound himself in a more elaborate way and has taken to wearing his arm in a sling."

"We are not surprised," Agnes said. "This is after all his war wound and he is going to make the most of it and the bloody shirt."

"So it seems. Tomás has been following the police angle of this."

"I have. As best we can ascertain McThacry believes we are responsible for the shooting and for Jim's escape, and—"

"One moment," Agnes interrupted. "Wouldn't Sidney, we mean Sidney would know what happened. Didn't he tell McThacry?"

"I was coming to Sidney. Agnes, you have really overdone it this time."

"Why whatever do you mean—no, never mind. Finish with McThacry first."

"McThacry thinks we somehow arranged the shooting and provided for Jim's escape. The son, however, called McThacry's lawyer to the emergency room and together they convinced McThacry that it was better if the affair was put down to an accident, as in fact it was. McThacry was not convinced it was an accident, but he wanted the police out of the situation as much as we did. The principal investigator for the police is suspicious that there was more to it, but all the physical evidence pointed to an alcohol-involved, self-inflicted, accidental shooting on private property and the injured party, after consulting with his attorney, made a statement consistent with the physical evidence. The police have more pressing business. It's been what—four days—the matter is forgotten."

Agnes stood and walked to the large Austin map. She found the red pin that marked McThacry's residence. "What about the son? Thomas talked to Jim at the airport, and Jim rather thought . . ."

"Tom was supposed to follow up on that. Tom what have you got?"

If Tom was not asleep, he was the next thing to it. He had

to be nudged into action and informed of the subject.

"I looked into the possibility that McThacry's son was gay. That was what I was asked to do. I think Jim was just, what's the word?"

"Engaging in some wishful thinking?" Agnes suggested.

"Yes, that. He is hetero and very enthusiastic about it. But he is very good looking."

"Are you sure?"

"I have eyes."

"We mean are you sure he is straight?"

"Oh yes. As sure as I can be."

"Tomás, do you concur?"

"I do. Besides the girlfriends and such, we arranged for Tom to run in the opposite direction where the son runs in the morning. Tom was shirtless and wearing those tiny shorts."

"You mean the teal ones?"

"Yes, the teal ones. The son did not look back at Tom."

"Didn't look back?"

"No. And also when they met on the trail again, we had Tom retying his shoelaces. The younger McThacry did not stare at Tom's ass."

"Well, we suppose that is as conclusive as it gets."

"Yes. The son is fair-minded, progressive, and free of his father's delusions. Naturally, having any cool head near McThacry is likely to be an asset to us. But it seems very unlikely that he would consciously work with us against his father."

"Now, what was the thing about Sidney?"

"He's out of touch with McThacry for the moment. He's . . . well, I have a copy of a personal ad he submitted to *The Austin Grackle*. Shall I read it to you?"

"Please."

"It's an ad for the 'variations' section. It reads 'All purpose stud. Ever ready. All scenes considered. Available for parties. Sid. Voice mail box 6763.' He faxed it to *The Grackle* the same evening you removed Jim's luggage from his cab. We are having difficulty keeping up with him. He has been seen in most of the sleazy straight pickup bars in town. He has completely broken out of his usual orbit, and it will be a while before we are able to keep up with him completely. Agnes, how could you do such a thing?"

"Do what?"

"We think he is trying to become a gigolo."

"Goodness. Does he have the physique for it?"

"Oh Agnes, evidently, Sidney has assets that do not necessarily meet the eye. You know what they say, it is always the tall, slender, quiet ones."

"You mean . . ."

"You know Marlee? The woman with the male dance troop?"

"Oh, the heavyset woman with the hats. Yes, but she only has use for the most muscular studs."

"Sidney applied to dance for Marlee."

"No."

"Yes. Evidently he was not aware that her dancers mainly appear in gay bars. Anyway she gave him an audition just for yuks. Now hold on to your garter belt. They couldn't find a dancing strap to fit him."

"Oh don't be silly. He's skinny as a rail."

"Agnes, you are not listening to me. His waist size was not the problem. They couldn't find a dancing strap he could fit into."

"Surely they could take one of them up a bit."

"Agnes, it wasn't a matter of taking them up. He's hung like Godzilla. They couldn't find a strap to stuff all that meat into."

"What? Why haven't we had a report of this before?"

"It was Sidney. We never thought of looking into it. But now the genie is out of the bottle, so to speak. Agnes, was that the only way of getting Jim's luggage back? Didn't you have some kind of backup plan?"

"It never occurred to us he wouldn't go for the bait. I suppose if he hadn't taken a whiff, we would have offered him a generous tip to show us to some nonexistent room in the conference center and surely Phil would have the presence of mind to pick the lock of the trunk of the cab. But we were sure he would fall for it, and he did."

"But Agnes, now he thinks he is a major stud of the Western world."

"Well, he's not the first man to have such aspirations. And sometimes, you know, if they do believe it, they do become it. Besides, if what you just told us is true, he's well equipped for the role."

"Agnes!"

"*Que sera, sera.* Next case."

"Well there is the mess of the Caucus and the Cotillion and all."

"Vital issues indeed. But for now let's move on to the Oklahoma situation. Delegate, delegate, delegate."

"As we're all aware, there was a killing in Norman the other night. In spite of her making quite a few hysterical phone calls to Agnes; Gretta seems to be on top of the situation."

"Yes. That is quite like her. Frantic, but muddling through somehow. The question is, was this an organized attack?

"Our best intelligence is it was a street gang. Gretta obtained an attorney for the young man who was charged. His reputed confession was, of course, coerced. His description of the actual assault as he related to his attorney doesn't suggest the Klan or any of the various vigilante and neo-

Nazi groups we know of. Evidently it was just some street punks who decided to beat up some queers."

"And the young man's legal situation?"

"Well, there is some evidence that suggests multiple assailants. If the confession can be set aside, there is a fair chance of an acquittal. There is very little chance of the prosecution withdrawing, for to do so they would have to admit that there was something irregular in the confession and such admissions by law enforcement officers are not very common in this part of the country."

"Heavens. Well, this seems to be out of our hands. Now about Osage."

"Yes, Osage. Thomas, what have you got?"

"Brother Earl's activities appear to be relatively normal. The rhetoric of his new homophobic campaign has become very alarming. Clearly his immediate object is to obtain public funding for tuitions at his college. He seems very likely to obtain that objective—at least to pass his bill through the legislature. Whether it would withstand judicial scrutiny is quite another question. But it seems likely he could have passed the bill quietly, without the present campaign. There is no principled opposition, only questions as to where the money might come from. For this reason I doubt whether he will let up on his campaign once his bill passes. Perhaps he has some other, more far-reaching objective in mind. He draws some rather pointed parallels between public university dormitories and military barracks. Could this be the start of something bigger?"

"A good question. We talked to Phil this morning. There is good reason to suspect that the photos have been destroyed, but if so, it is not at all clear how Earl might know for certain that they had been destroyed. Phil has activated the motel plan. The problem with it . . . well, there are several problems with it. Tom, we have been going through the card file this morning. What is the state of our resources in Osage?"

"We have no reserves in Osage."

"None?"

"Nothing to speak of. We've got a locksmith, a plumber, the people involved with the motel plan, Her Nibs who is as always out of town, several retired persons with no relevant skills, absolutely no models. The locksmith might prove useful if we had been able to penetrate the college security staff—we do have someone well placed in the personnel office and could probably place some on the security staff if there ever were an opening, but there simply is no turnover in the security staff."

"We do have someone in the personnel office?"

"Yes we do."

"Hmm . . ." Agnes tapped her long nails on the conference table.

TWELVE

THE highway rises as it approaches the campus of Holy Word of God University and Technical Institute. Some say it is no accident that the overpass, having cleared the railroad switching yard, continues upward until at its crest it presents a dramatic panorama of the campus. No one doubts that Brother Earl would have had the will and the influence with the highway commission to have arranged it thus. The only question is whether he had the vision.

The Worshiptorium is the shape of a crown roast with ruffled pantaloons. It cannot be confused with the Chapel, which resembles an upturned colander, or with the Cathedral, which looks like a public address horn. The college conforms to the first rule of religious architecture: the more reactionary the theology, the more revolutionary the structure, and vice versa.

The Cathedral, of course, is a cathedral only in the fundamentalist sense of a very grand impressive church. There is neither a dean nor a bishop, only the Reverend Brother Earl Richards, who, they say, was ordained directly by God and commissioned by a vision of a seven-hundred-foot-tall lamb to use AM radio transmissions to solicit the funds to construct Holy Word of God University and Technical Institute and to perform various other things as one or another vision from time to time communicated with Brother Earl.

The Worshiptorium receives the overflow of the faithful on Sunday morning and is used for sacred services of a smaller size—those expected to attract less than two thousand attendees, since so small a congregation would be lost in the Cathedral—and also for various types of college assemblies, because, as the saying goes, at Holy Word of God University and Technical Institute there are no secular activities.

So it was that Jim had scarcely the time to take it all in before the taxi took the HWOG & TI exit from the highway, was waved past the guardhouse at the entrance to Gospel Drive, and came to a stop in front of the reinforced-concrete crown roast. The driver got out and unloaded Jim's bags into a pile on the sidewalk, while Jim fumbled with his currency to ensure he was giving the driver the smallest feasible tip.

Jim would just as soon have bypassed the orientation assembly and evidently Jim was not alone in that sentiment, for the registration instructions were very clear on the point: Key information necessary to the registration process would be made available only at the orientation assembly, with no exceptions.

Jim had delayed his arrival on campus until the last possible moment. He could see he was the only one of the students who was still encumbered with luggage. He did not have time before the assembly to determine which of the twin towers was the men's dormitory, to go to it, and to check in. Indeed, the cheerleaders were already beginning to warm up the crowd for Brother Earl's appearance by teaching the new students the traditional cheers:

> *Whogutti Woo!*
> *With an aitch!*
> *And a double-you!*
> *And an oh-gee-you!*
> *With a tech-eye, tech-eye, tech-eye too!*
> *Whogutti, whogutti!*
> *Woo! Woo! Woo!*
> *Word of God, Word of God,*
> *Smite them down!*
> *Holy, Holy,*
> *Gain some ground!*
> *Whogutti woo! Whogutti woo!*
> *Whogutti, whogutti,*
> *Woo, woo, woo!*

While everyone was standing, Jim took the opportunity to squeeze down a row of seats, bearing his luggage on his head, to a point where he had seen three vacant seats. When he reached that point a young woman informed him that all of the seats were saved. Jim set his luggage on one of the vacant seats and sat in another, although everyone else remained standing.

"I just want you to know you are just about the most inconsiderate and irreverent person I've ever seen!" the young woman said as if she were delivering the most crushing, unanswerable, cruelly accurate personal insult. Then she flounced away, or flounced as well as one could flounce, squeezing past the bodies and the auditorium seats until she reached the aisle, where she performed an additional flounce, giving Jim an idea of how she could flounce when she had working room.

Once she seemed safely gone, Jim stood and alternately folded his arms across his chest and put his hands in his pockets, failing to reveal the least excitement for the acrobatics of the cheerleaders or to betray the least response to their exhortations. In this, he noticed, he was not alone.

The reassuring thing, Jim thought, *is that some of them seem to think this is as silly as I do.* Of course many of them were carried away with the frenzy, a few were moved to tears for love of their new alma mater, and some were visibly affected with prenostalgia, the belief that someday they would be nostalgic about this moment. But almost as many accepted the hubbub impassively. In some cases, maybe, it was only a masculine reluctance to display strong emotion. Perhaps some of the quiet ones secretly shared the excitement and the sentiments that the others showed with tears. But, yes, it certainly looked as if some of them expressed a certain skepticism.

They all looked so young.

At last Brother Earl made his appearance. Although most of the others remained standing throughout the ovation, Jim sat the first time that Brother Earl made a weak gesture for quiet.

Jim did not look at Brother Earl and he made every effort to ignore Brother Earl's remarks. What he heard of the remarks assured him that all such addresses are very much the same and that he had heard it all, except for the numerous references to the Divine, when he was welcomed to elementary school, to middle school, to high school, and to Hogg University.

New beginnings, the unpredictability of success, but the assurance that success will come to all who work earnestly, the usual platitudes designed to assist the young in confusing power and prominence in the world with virtue: Brother Earl went on and on. While Jim knew the speech was a sham, Brother Earl was a sham, Holy Word of God University and Technical Institute was a sham, and Jim's attendance was a sham; still Jim could not help feeling a little younger, a little like it was a new beginning, and a little like he really was starting college afresh. As Brother Earl spoke on and on, Jim felt he shared the eager enthusiasm, the restless youthful urge, the magic of bold enterprise at its outset, and, with the skeptics, he shared the thought: *I wish the old fart would shut up so we can get on with it.* Perhaps to inspire that thought is the reason all such addresses go on too long.

When Brother Earl finished his remarks the sincerity of the ovation from all quarters could not be doubted. The registrar took the microphone and began to read in a monotone the code numbers associated with the registration process. Jim found that he, like many of the others, had not brought a pencil and paper to record the numbers, though the numbers were what he came for and he was sure the same could be said for many of the other students.

The resulting confusion caused the registrar to stop and deliver a small lecture on the importance of carrying the essential tools of scholarship. Jim realized that he had heard this lecture too somewhere before. But he had forgotten. He was just like the others. He had to borrow a pen to write the key numbers on the back of his hand.

This going back to college, it is like a fountain of youth. It is like becoming one of these beautiful young people again. I am, after all, one of them again.

The elevator looked clean enough but seemed to Jim to smell distinctly of vomit and stale urine. Half the numbers on the control panel were missing. Jim pressed the button above 16. The elevator moved very swiftly. When the doors opened, two six-foot numerals on the revealed wall confirmed that the button above 16 had indeed been 17. The doors began to close again almost immediately and continued to bump against Jim's foot while he shoved his luggage onto the landing and got out.

The odor of the elevator was immediately replaced by another smell. The smell of a men's dormitory. It was, to Jim, intoxicating. The effect was much like that of a zebra-striped capsule, only more so.

Jim picked up his luggage and stepped into the corridor. He was almost upset by a muscular young man who was wearing only a towel and his pursuer, a darker young man wearing only a jock. Wet bare feet squeaked on the polished floor. The two young men crashed into the snack machine at the end of the corridor. Then the pursuer and the pursued changed roles and the chase continued in the opposite direction. The slender dark man slid past Jim. The muscular one seized Jim by the hips and set Jim aside.

The contact electrified Jim. Stunned, he could only sigh as he watched the two shrink far down the corridor and skid around a corner. Jim composed himself and looked at the key he had been given at the desk. "17.451," it said.

Once it had been explained to him, the system seemed easy enough to understand. But the look of a fractional room number, especially one so precise, would take some getting used to. The nearest door said "17.237," so Jim picked up his luggage and began his trek down the corridor.

Many of the doors were open. And many of the doors that were open revealed young men languishing in various states of undress. Some revealed young men still abed, embracing their pillows or sprawled on their bellies, sheets thrown off a nude body altogether or sheets revealing a thigh or a shoulder or covering the head and revealing everything else. All of them were beautiful. And young.

Surely, surely, Jim thought, *some of them must be too young to be in college. After all, I am young enough to pass for a student. Some of these boys hardly look thirteen. Where are the scrawny nerds and fat boys, the pizza faces and geeks that were so common when I was in school?*

He came to a room without a door. It was a bathroom. There was a row of standard public restroom stalls, a row of lavatories, and a row of urinals. He set his luggage down and stepped into the room. There was a common shower area, not individual stalls.

Too much, really, to have hoped for. I'll really have to try to control myself. But Jim realized it might be very frustrating. How many students who would come to a school like Holy Word would be doable? *I must be very careful. Brother Earl obviously considers this his private preserve. No doubt he takes a dim view of poaching.*

When Jim turned back toward the corridor he found a young man in the way, leaning against the frame of the entrance to the bathroom. The young man was wearing baggy drawstring shorts and a chrome-yellow tank top. He had coffee-with-cream-colored hair with many sun-gilded streaks, a nose he was bound to hate because everyone would call it cute, and a square jaw. His head was set on the pinnacle of a triangle of muscle. He had delts the size of cantaloupes, biceps that seemed as if they might burst although they were relaxed, snaky thick blue veins, hard pecs with tight erect nipples visible through the tank top, diamond-shaped calves: All in all he was the picture of an off-duty surfer, although the nearest sea was five hundred miles away and it was more than twice as far to the surf.

"Can I help you, sir?" he asked, without sounding very helpful.

"I'm looking for my room," Jim said.

"Well you won't find it in here, sir." This time the suspicion was mixed with a little amusement, but what Jim noticed was the "sir."

"Yeah, I can see that."

"What is the room number, sir?"

"Seventeen point four five one."

The expression on the surfer's face changed. "Why that's my room. Then you must be . . . I mean, sir, they asked me if I minded having an older roommate, but I didn't think . . ."

Jim could very clearly see what the surfer didn't think. He didn't think anything quite so old as Jim could live. "My name's Jim. I wish you wouldn't call me sir." Jim extended his hand.

"Oh, my name is Tad, sir—I mean, *Jim.* Forgive me if I forget. It's just the way I was brought up."

I know, Jim thought, *you were brought up to respect your elders. Damnit, it's only been . . . well, only a very few years since I was in college myself.*

"I'll help you with your bags and show you to the room," Tad said, "as soon as I drain ol' Derrick here."

Evidently, Jim thought, *the young man means to imply that in dimension or in action there is some similarity between his male member and an oil well.* Jim adjusted his position relative to the row of urinals, but Tad stepped into one of the partitioned stalls. When he stepped out, Tad made a display of washing his hands.

Tad pried Jim's fingers off the handle of the biggest, heaviest-looking piece of luggage and led the way to a door with a number that matched that on Jim's key.

"Sir—uh, *Jim*—it's a good idea to keep the door locked. This is supposed to be a Christian college, but . . ."

Jim used his key to open the door. The room was hardly six feet wide and was, perhaps, ten feet deep. There were two tiny desks just inside the door, and beyond them were two things that could only be described as racks, each furnished with a thin piece of rubber foam, which, being covered with striped ticking, Jim assumed they were meant to be taken for mattresses. A folded set of linens was lying on the bed Jim took for his own. Another set of linens was clumped at the foot of the other bed, on the side of the room that was obviously occupied. Jim observed that the distance between the beds was so slight that a person lying in one of them could easily touch a person lying in the other one. This observation Jim greeted with mixed emotions.

Jim's luggage was set down on his bed. "You won't have to worry about me, Jim. I'm not here a lot. And if we start getting rowdy around here, I'll see to it that we go somewhere else."

"Don't bother," Jim said. "I get rowdy a lot myself."

Tad received this statement as some kind of unfathomable koan. "Whatever. Anyway, this came for you." Tad picked up an envelope from the unoccupied desk and handed it to Jim. "Things that look like that usually are invitations to meet Brother Earl."

Jim opened the envelope. "Yes," said Jim, "I'm supposed to meet Brother Earl on Monday afternoon."

"Wow, he's getting started early this semester." Tad seemed almost to snicker.

"What's so funny?"

"Oh, it's just about Brother Earl's interviews."

"Yes?" Jim asked.

"I shouldn't have said anything. I'm sure *you* have nothing to worry about."

"No, I want to know."

A half-naked young man skidded into the room. "Tad, hurry up, it's almost—Oh, I'm sorry. I didn't know you had company." The young man turned to Jim. "Hi, I'm Ike. And you must be Tad's father. I'm so pleased to meet you, sir."

THIRTEEN

THE administration building of Holy Word of God University and Technical Institute is the single concession to tradition of all the structures on campus. It is a four-story rectangular prism with a brown brick façade and an arched entrance with two real columns and two suggested columns. The arched entrance is in the middle of a long side of the building and is supposed to be the front. In fact, owing to the natural traffic patterns, the front is the front only for ceremonial and photographic purposes. With its arched entrance—which some Holy Word of God University and Technical Institute graduates have seen only in photographs in the annual—the ad building is an entirely plain American institutional building and would seem appropriately placed in any American prison, lunatic asylum, military reservation, public hospital, or junior college.

The ad building fits endways against Trinity Mall, where all paths at Holy Word of God University and Technical Institute cross—or would cross, save for Trinity Mall's being a pedestrian traffic circus of fifty yards diameter. To defeat the natural tendency to expedience found in undergraduates who are late for class, the center of Trinity Mall is occupied by a garden where through the year a succession of hothouse flowers are set out in geometric patterns to die.

And so almost every day, as the business of the college swirls around, one old gardener or another stoops in Trinity Garden in Trinity Mall, replacing the dead plants with the doomed and hoeing to bits any native species that raises its Osage-hardy head above the much-turned, much-modified soil.

Brother Earl has several grander offices, but his favorite is in the ad building on the second floor, straddling the door of the ad building that faces Trinity Mall. In this office he is not rector of the Holy Word of God Broadcast Cathedral, not chairman of the Holy Word of God Foundation, nor trustee of the Holy Word of God Hospital. Standing at his window, watching the young people circle Trinity Garden, Brother Earl is chancellor of Holy Word of God University and Technical Institute, a title that impresses even its author, Brother Earl.

The spoke of sidewalk from Trinity Garden to the door beneath Brother Earl's window is generally traversed with foreboding and anguish. Generally a walk to the ad building is not a good thing. The bursar's office is there. That generally costs money. The command post of the university police is there in a Plexiglas cube. Those who must go there usually must pay money, but worse, they are in peril of losing their parking permits. The central records office is also in the ad building. A trip to central records in the attempt to reclaim a summer credit or a lifetime of study is a forlorn and fruitless errand that is completed only to confirm an impression of hopelessness. Indeed, between matriculation and graduation, the only kind of visit to the ad building that is not in itself a bad thing is a trip to the chancellor's office. A student is not already in trouble if he is called to the chancellor's office.

If he were in trouble already he would be summoned to see, according to the degree of his transgression, a spiritual peer counselor, a pastoral associate, the dean of students, or in the worst case the psychologist. This last implies that psychology could do little harm for the student, who is thought to have no future at Holy Word of God University and Technical Institute and little prospect of a future among the elect.

It is not a bad thing in itself to be called to the chancellor's office, yet Brother Earl, standing at his window watching the frantic vortex of students between classes, could sometimes guess—when he did not know already—which of the students on the mall was bound for his office and an introductory meeting with the chancellor. This afternoon Brother Earl did know from the application photograph which of the students beneath his window was coming to his office. The application photograph was the reason the student had been summoned so hastily and so early in the semester.

Usually Brother Earl thought it better to wait a few weeks to let the summer wear off, let the home influences seem more distant, and let the deadly boredom of college life in Osage set in. Let the boys get really restless, frustrated, and horny. A few weeks on campus, or so Brother

Earl thought, and the young men become much more receptive to ministry. But the application photograph had shown this one's blue, blue eyes and dark hair. It was a combination Brother Earl could hardly resist.

As the old gardener hoed in the center of Trinity Garden, Brother Earl looked down on Trinity Mall, looking for today's appointment. And there he was: the tall, dark-haired one, taking the little shuffling steps and talking to the slender blond. A few more words to his friend and then they parted on the hub of Trinity Mall. The dark-haired one walked very slowly up the spoke of sidewalk toward the ad building and the door below Brother Earl's feet.

Jim could hardly see in the dimness of the ad building. It had an institutional interior: green, glazed bricks; basically gray vinyl floor tiles, sealed and polished until they shimmered; at intervals, blond wood doors with frosted glass panels and, painted on the glass, black decimal-fraction room numbers. Jim walked slowly down the corridor until he spotted the fire alarm box that Phil had mentioned.

That was the plan. If things got out of hand in Brother Earl's office, Jim was supposed to signal Phil in some way. Some way, it had not been determined how; and since as he walked to the ad building Jim had seen that Brother Earl's window was the kind of glass that appears smoky, dark, and opaque from the outside, Jim thought it unlikely he could find a way to signal Phil at all. But if Phil did get a signal, Phil was supposed to run into the ad building and set off the fire alarm.

That was supposed to disrupt the interview with Brother Earl. After all, there was no camera in Brother Earl's office. So the idea, according to Phil, was to encourage Brother Earl enough that Brother Earl would invite Jim to the motel, but not encourage him so much that he would insist on consummating his ministry right there in the office.

Phil was very irritating when he explained it. First it was irritating that Phil moved around campus so freely while Jim was challenged to produce his ID at every turn. That rather rubbed Jim's nose in the fact that he did not so much look like a college student anymore. So it was that Phil was able to produce a sketch of the ad building complete with a red *X* to mark the location of the fire alarm box.

And of course, rather to drive the message home, Phil seemed to be able to talk to the students, and he even became familiar enough with a few of them as to obtain some information on the present state of Brother Earl's ministry.

Phil had explained it in his irritating way as he sat with Jim in the student union while Jim regretted having the chicken salad.

"Now, there are three types of students here."

"Yeah," Jim said, "but I've noticed they are all pretty rednecky. How in the world did Agnes get admitted here?"

"Agnes didn't go to college here. Whatever gave you that idea?"

"I don't know." Jim was thinking that maybe if he sent a milk shake after the chicken salad the two would fight it out in short order.

"Agnes is a Morehouse graduate. I thought everyone could tell."

"Oh."

"Okay, the three types of students here are called the Hicks, the True Believers, and the Beats."

"The Beats?"

"Yes. Osage has just now entered the 1950s. Of course, at the college they don't wear berets or beards or black turtlenecks. They just call themselves Beats, although what it is, is that they are aware, hip, with it, know the score, whatever you may call it."

" 'Beats' as in 'beatniks'? That's even before my time."

"Really? Well anyway, yes, 'Beats' as in 'beatniks.' They smuggle around copies of Kerouac and Ginsberg, that kind of stuff. They think they are very advanced. Which when you consider that it is still controversial for the biology department to teach that men and women have the same number of ribs . . ."

"If there are beatniks, why don't I see any?"

"But they are all around you. Your floor of the dormitory is notorious for its number of free thinkers. Nonconformists, I think they call it. They just don't give any visual clues. You have to talk to them. Their major theorist—Donald is his name—is supposed to be staying two doors down from you. I've not had a chance to talk to him. He's a sociology major, which at Holy Word is about the same thing as admitting you are a communist."

The chicken salad repeated again. "Ginsberg? *The* Ginsberg?"

"Yes. *The* Ginsberg. What other Ginsberg is there? Anyway, I got most of the lowdown from the Beats. You come to Holy Word for one of three reasons: You are a Hick who really thinks Holy Word is a big-time college; you really believe in Brother Earl's teachings or your parents do; or you can't get into any other college anywhere—that's the group that includes most of the Beats."

"Yeah, so?"

"Well, so nothing. Except the Beats pretty well understand what Brother Earl's counseling sessions are about. They tell me Brother Earl doesn't start usually until late September. So the fact that he wants to see you in the first week of the semester, well you know, there may be something to your being Brother Earl's type."

"I think I'm going to throw up."

"Very funny."

"Chicken salad," Jim said, and he dashed to the men's room.

When Jim returned to the table, Phil had been through the cafeteria line again. "I brought you a milk shake. I thought that might settle your stomach." Phil reached into his bookbag and extracted a jar of marmalade.

"Don't you just hate these little packages of jelly they always have at these cafeterias?" Phil pushed the little plastic tubs of jelly off his plate of hot biscuits. "Now the thing is, the Beats tell me that Brother Earl likes to do tricks in his office. He evidently gets some special charge out of that. But he will take you to the motel if you hold out."

"Hold out?"

"If you were a True Believer you could have a scruple about doing it on holy ground. Or if you were a Hick you could think it has to be dark and you have to have a real bed to do it. But I think you'd do better as a Beat, in which case you imply that you expect to be taken for dinner and drinks before you'll come across."

Yeah, Jim thought, *that's something you'd know about. Dinner, drinks, maybe a few years' free room and board in his townhouse. Play a man out, lead him along, spend his money. I'm sure you know all the techniques. But you should remember I don't know that stuff. I know nothing about being cheap.*

And that was true. Jim knew nothing about being cheap because Jim never had been cheap. Jim had always been free.

Jim looked carefully at the fire alarm box. He had no idea how he would signal Phil. And he had no idea how to string Brother Earl along. Turn Brother Earl down cold: Jim knew how to do that. He had done that to plenty of men, some of them even more repulsive than Brother Earl. Yield to Brother Earl immediately: Jim knew how to do that. But string a man along? Of course, that had been done to Jim quite a number of times. Jim just had to hope he had learned something from those experiences.

When Jim got to the guard booth in the center of the hall, he carefully double-checked to be sure he presented the guard with the Holy Word ID and not the Reservation membership card. The guard hardly glanced at the ID.

"I'll buzz the door when you get to it," the guard said. The guard indicated a staircase. At its top was a solid, dark wood door. Naturally there was no room number or title plate. Everyone would know it was Brother Earl's office.

Jim climbed the stairs. They were very steep. Brother Earl's visitors were supposed to arrive breathless and dizzy as well as awed. Jim reached for the crystal doorknob. The door buzzed.

Trying to look as if he were only closing the door carefully, Jim found to his relief that the door opened from the inside without the buzzer.

Jim had rather expected to find a secretary or a receptionist. But all there was, was a gurgling aquarium, leather-covered sofas, a little end table with a big brown glass ashtray and an assortment of Brother Earl's tracts carefully fanned out, a small door that opened to what was obviously a lavatory, and a bigger door ajar revealing Brother Earl. Brother Earl was sitting at his desk, bent over a large, obvious, white leather and gold-leaf-covered Bible.

As if he were startled by a sudden awareness of Jim's presence, Brother Earl looked up sharply. "Oh. Come in. Come in." As if he meant to conceal what he had been doing, Brother Earl closed the Bible and, while standing up and making a sweeping gesture of welcome, slid the Bible into the lap drawer of his desk and closed the drawer with his knee.

"Jim, isn't it." Brother Earl said. But it was not a question. Brother Earl took Jim's hand and shook it.

"Yes sir." Jim was a little surprised. He was not disgusted by the contact with Brother Earl's flesh. Brother Earl was white-haired and a little flabby. But evil slime did not drip off him. He had, in fact, a kind of animal vitality. Jim could not help but realize that in his various adventures he had sometimes done much worse than Brother Earl.

Of course, Jim thought. *The seven-hundred-foot lamb, the free-will offerings in exchange for the bits of prayer cloth, the blessing ointment, the Expect-a-Miracle oil from the Holy Land: Even the dumb rednecks don't buy that stuff for what it is, but on account of the charm of the salesman. If evil were ugly and repulsive it wouldn't be such big business.* Perhaps the strain of such profundity showed on Jim's face.

"Oh well, Jim. Please have a seat." Brother Earl indicated a peculiarly Western piece of furniture, a sofa of draping cowhide and simulated wagon wheels, tattooed with branding marks: Rocking R, Bar X, Lazy W, Star Cross, XIT, and Circle A. The coffee table seemed to be a piece of glass, balanced in some mysterious way on two half wagon wheels. The standing ashtray was of the same brown glass as the ashtray in the outer office, but it was perched on a branding iron as if the iron were burning into the bottom of the glass. The ashtray looked as if it had never been used. Jim stared at it a minute, trying to read the brand. Then he remembered that the iron would be a mirror image. *Bar BQ, of course!*

"Feel free to smoke if you like."

"Oh no. I was just admiring the ashtray."

Jim wanted to sit on the far end of the sofa, in the corner, but he thought it better to stay as near the door as possible. The cowhide cushions sighed under Jim's rump.

"If only I had more time," Brother Earl began. "I used to know all of the students here."

Know, Jim thought, *in the biblical sense.*

"But things have gotten out of hand." Brother Earl closed the door. Jim heard an extra click as the door closed. "I mean the college has grown beyond my expectations."

When Brother Earl stood away from the door, Jim glanced at it. Jim could not see a lock. There was an ornate glass knob. But no keyhole. No obvious button. Still, Jim was certain that the extra click had been some kind of lock. Perhaps like the buzz lock on the outer door, this one did not lock from the inside either. *Better not count on it.*

"Let's see here, Jim." Brother Earl opened a file folder that had been lying on his desk. "It says here that you are a graduate student. You did your undergraduate work at the University of Houston?"

"That's right." Agnes had thought it would be futile to try to conceal Jim's Texas origins. But evidently she thought mention of Hogg University would rouse Brother Earl's suspicions. Perhaps she knew too that Jim was completely familiar with the University of Houston campus.

"You were in classics at Houston. A good preparation for seminary. You can read the New Testament in the Greek?"

"Yes."

"Ah, perhaps you know an old friend of mine. Tony Hargrave? I think he's in classics at Houston."

Which way to go on this one? It could be a trap. Maybe there is no Hargrave. Maybe Brother Earl happens to know the name of the department chairman and his name happens to be Hargrave. Maybe Brother Earl really does know a Hargrave and really isn't sure that he is in classics. There could be lots of reasons I don't know Hargrave. But if I say I know him, first there could be no Hargrave and second, if there is a Hargrave, Brother Earl could ask me something about him I don't know.

"No. I don't think I know him. It's a very large school." *Which it is. No doubt even in a small department like classics there are people who graduate without ever knowing the leading scholars.* "Maybe I would recognize him if I saw him."

"Oh? Well perhaps he has retired. I last saw him twenty years ago when our crusade visited Houston. There are some charming buildings on that campus. I remember especially the student union building. I believe they called it the Cougar Den."

Let's see. Twenty years ago I would have been . . . well, very young, Jim thought. *But I know about the old Cougar Den. Of course Brother Earl would remember it. It was the principal point of procurement of college men. Or so I've been told. If that's what he means I better encourage him a little at this point.* "Oh yes. Everyone talks about the old Cougar Den. It must have been something. But they tore it down long before I started there. They have a new Cougar Den. But it doesn't have the same . . . atmosphere." *That ought to be plain enough.*

"What a shame."

"Everyone says it is a shame." *He's got the message. Now the dance begins.*

"I'm afraid you'll find our college very dull after you've been to a place like Houston." Brother Earl closed Jim's file.

"Oh, I'm not so sure. Human nature is much the same everywhere." Jim eyed the door again.

"Yes. And temptation can be found anywhere."

"That's true." Jim noticed that Brother Earl's window, which seemed so dark from the outside, appeared perfectly transparent from within.

"I know it's especially hard on young men. Cooped up in those little dormitory rooms. The lack of privacy. The many constant sources of titillation. The hours of inactivity in class or trying to concentrate in the library." Brother Earl removed his coat and hung it on the back of his chair. Yes, there was a little roll around his belly, but his chest was massive and his shoulders were by far wider than his waist.

"You're right. And sports and cold showers can only go so far." Jim leaned back in the sofa and spread his legs slightly. He began to think that he would not necessarily need too many zebra pills when the time came. A horrible thought occurred to Jim: *It might even be fun.*

"I know I'm right. Hardly a day passes that the environmental services staff doesn't turn up some kind of evidence. Liquor bottles, rock and roll records, condoms, even the vilest sorts of publications."

"Oh?" Jim inquired.

"Yes indeed. Let me show you. These things are so vile, little wonder even our own good Christian students are led into temptation." Brother Earl went to his filing cabinet.

And what if it turns out to be fun? If Phil can make his living servicing old Agnes, why shouldn't I have fun at this? I mean, it's just once. I could make those pictures sizzle. If I can get him to the motel.

Brother Earl handed Jim a folder. Jim flipped through it. *Now here's another problem.* The pictures in the folder were all torn-out pages and clippings from girlie magazines. Some of them were foldouts from the supposedly class magazines. Some of them were exceedingly vulgar black-and-white pages from pulp magazines. *Should I pretend to be turned on by this stuff?*

That Cougar Den talk should have told Brother Earl what I'm into. But maybe he prefers to think he is seducing

straight men. Phil says Brother Earl is bisexual. Go figure
what a pervert is going to like.

No, I can't get into this stuff and I don't know how to
pretend I'm into it. If Brother Earl wanted an innocent to
corrupt he should not have picked a graduate student from
Houston. Besides, if I know the score it should be easier to
bargain for the motel.

"Surely these things don't tempt very many," Jim said,
not feigning in the least his disinterest. "Bad as they may
be, these kinds of magazines—these are pictures from
magazines?—perhaps have a certain fascination for adolescents. But they are common enough in society. Surely a college man has become bored with them."

Brother Earl smiled. "I suppose that's true enough in
Houston. But our environmental services people find a lot
of these. Our young men, often, aren't exposed to this sort
of thing until they get away to college."

"Oh, that explains it."

Brother Earl went to the filing cabinet again. "We find
much worse, too. And frankly, I don't know how our
young men get ahold of material such as this. It's not the
type of thing you find in convenience stores." Brother Earl
took the girlie file from Jim and handed him another folder.

Jim opened the folder. The first picture was a black-and-
white page torn from a magazine. It showed a young man in
a crew cut, bound and gagged and hung upside down. Tit
clamps, too. The second item was a brochure for an all-male
video titled *Engorged*. Judging from the color stills, it was
aptly named. Jim could not have feigned disinterest if he
wanted to, which he did not, as it certainly seemed he was
about to come to an understanding with Brother Earl. The
next things in the folder were black-and-white glossies
from an old-time studio. The subjects were Athletic Guild

types: young men in posing straps. Then there were a couple of foldouts of video stars in color. Jim recognized some of them.

Then there was a picture of Jim himself. Jim was startled. But he just stuck a finger in the folder at that point and continued flipping through the pictures.

It was a four by five of me having sex with a man.

Jim did not think it was possible. *Well, I could have been drunk.* Jim was not really looking at the things in the folder anymore. He just continued to flip through them, hoping Brother Earl would not notice the finger stuck in the folder, marking the spot. Then there was another picture of Jim. This time it was clear who Jim was having sex with. *It's a picture of me having sex with a younger Brother Earl.*

Brother Earl had returned the girlie folder to the filing cabinet and now stepped closer again to Jim and the sofa.

Jim stuck a second finger in the folder and flipped on to the next item. "I see what you mean," Jim said, trying not to gasp. "This is much stronger stuff."

It can't be me. I've never been drunk enough to go to bed with Brother Earl without knowing it. And when Brother Earl looked like that I must have been a child, if I had even been born.

Jim flipped through a couple more items in the folder. Brother Earl seemed to be standing right over Jim. Then, there it was again. A picture of Jim very explicitly engaged with a younger Brother Earl. *No. It's not me. The guy has a tattoo. I've never had a tattoo.*

Jim thought he could feel Brother Earl's breath on his neck. Jim flipped to the next picture, which was a relatively innocuous MonoGym ad. *Wait a minute. I know that tattoo.* Then there was another shot of the young Brother Earl and the tattooed man.

Good grief, Jim thought, *it's Daddy!*

186

FOURTEEN

T HE old gardener seemed to wilt in the afternoon sun as he hoed and raked in Trinity Garden. The sun beat down on him. He became more and more stooped under his wide-brimmed straw hat and he spent more and more time leaning on his rake or his hoe, whichever instrument he was wielding at the time.

Phil paced back and forth along the arc of Trinity Mall that was nearest the spoke of sidewalk that led to the ad building and the door beneath Brother Earl's window. After the swirl and bustle of the change of classes subsided, Phil became uncomfortably conspicuous. He glanced up at

Brother Earl's window as often as he dared, although it was obviously impossible to see into Brother Earl's office.

Jim's interview with Brother Earl seemed to be taking forever.

Jim flipped to the next item in the folder. Brother Earl sat next to Jim on the sofa.

"Yes," Brother Earl said, "this is stronger stuff. And you can see how someone might be aroused by it. I have to admit, I can see the attraction someone might find for some of the models."

Oh, oh, Jim thought, *Brother Earl's about to make his move. No wonder, either. I'm sweating and breathing hard. But Brother Earl doesn't know the real reason. Time to put on the brakes and make a play for the motel.* "Then I'll admit, too, in a more comfortable setting I probably would find some of this stuff irresistible."

"This is one of the most secure places on campus," Brother Earl said in an entirely new tone of voice, a tone of voice more suited to expressions like "C'mon," "Please," "Nobody can see us here," and "No one will know. I'll be very gentle."

"I'm sure. But I wouldn't feel right about it. Not here." *No point in talking in code any longer.*

"Another time we could go somewhere. But right now, nothing complicated or messy. C'mon. Please."

Now he's not Brother Earl anymore. He's just any other man. But how to get him to the motel?

"But it would be so much nicer. You know, somewhere with a shower and a real bed. I just don't feel right about it here." But the fact was, Brother Earl's voice, Brother Earl's excitement, and the very hot pictures in the folder were beginning to produce an obvious physical effect on Jim, one Brother Earl surely had noticed.

The photos. Wait a minute! Those must be the photos!

188

There's no need to get Brother Earl to the motel. I only need to get the photos out of here. What a vain old queen Brother Earl is! He got the photos. But he couldn't bear to destroy them—photos of him and Daddy. I've only got to get out of here with the photos.

"C'mon." Brother Earl was tugging at the crotch of his trousers in the manner of a little boy who cannot find the restroom. "C'mon, Jim. We can plan to go out another time. I can see you're as hot as I am. Nobody will know."

Got to count on the door being locked. What was it Thomas said? When Agnes has got the photos she can call the shots. "Well, maybe."

"C'mon, Jim. It will be all right."

"Do you mind—I mean, would you be offended if I looked at the pictures? I mean, it's so difficult for me to concentrate here."

"I don't mind at all. That's why I brought them out. In fact I'd like it if you would." Brother Earl reached for his own belt buckle.

"No!" Jim shouted. "I mean, please slow down a minute. Wait for me to pick out my favorite pictures. You're getting ahead of me. Just give me a moment and I'll help you with that."

"Oh yeah, yeah. Please hurry."

Jim shuffled through the folder, bringing the four four-by-five pictures he had seen together. Fortunately Brother Earl was not paying much attention to the folder but had begun licking Jim's right biceps and was nudging Jim's short sleeve up with his nose, evidently laying the groundwork for an assault on Jim's armpit.

"Oh yeah, Earl, that's great," Jim whispered, not entirely insincerely since Jim had always gotten more out of his armpits than most people do. "Yeah, Earl, now please stand up and let me take off your pants."

Earl stood. Jim loosened Earl's silver buckle but did not entirely remove it. He unzipped and unhooked Earl's trousers. Tenderly Jim lowered Brother Earl's trousers and boxer shorts until the belt was even with Brother Earl's knees. Earl seemed as transported as when he went into a healing frenzy.

Then Jim jerked the belt tight, fastening it in its tightest slot, hobbling Earl's knees.

"Wha—" Earl hollered.

But Jim had grabbed the branding iron ashtray and the four-by-five photographs.

The old gardener had seemed to be dozing, propped against his rake, but he appeared to jump a foot when the smoky glass exploded out of the chancellor's window and the brown-glass and wrought-iron missile plummeted to the spoke of sidewalk beneath the window. As Jim shoved the photographs out the window—the photographs proved impossible to throw—Phil saw that they were photographs. If they were photographs following the shards of Brother Earl's window and the ashtray, then they must be *the* photographs, however they had come to be in Brother Earl's office and however Jim had obtained them. Phil dropped his bookbag and ran toward the ad building. Then he remembered he had some of Agnes's mailers in his bag and ran back for one of them.

Nothing at all seemed to happen for a long time as the photographs took a bit of breeze, sailed and fluttered, swooped and swelled, dived and rose, touched the grass by the spoke of sidewalk and tumbled until they were caught, each at a different spot, along a low-lying hedge. At just that instant the ad building began to throb with alarm horns and flashing lights.

Phil reached the first photograph, picked it up, and

looked at it. Evidently satisfied, he blew at the end of the mailer to open it and carefully slid the photograph inside. Phil got to the second photograph. Jim was pulled away from the window and into the darkness of Brother Earl's office. Phil secured the third photograph and the fourth. Then the door beneath Brother Earl's window popped open. The two uniformed men were only twenty feet from Phil.

Phil ran. Phil ran toward the hub of Trinity Mall. The uniformed men ran after him. When he reached Trinity Mall, Phil ran across the freshly raked dirt of Trinity Garden. The officers seemed to be gaining on Phil as they approached Trinity Mall. But the old gardener appeared to be dazed by the excitement and stumbled into the officers' path. One of the officers slammed into the old gardener, and in the tangle the other officer tripped over the rake. The officers scrambled to their feet and were after Phil again.

The old gardener helped himself up with the rake handle, shook his head under the wide-brimmed straw hat, and wearily began to rake over the fresh footprints in Trinity Garden.

"You son of a bitch. You're working for Agnes, aren't you?"

Jim shrugged. He was handcuffed to one of the wagon-wheel arms of the sofa and his mouth was covered over with adhesive tape.

Brother Earl flipped through the file folder one more time. "Aha. You missed one of them." He held up a four-by-five photograph that had been near the back of the file. "No matter. The damage is done."

Good, Jim thought, *it did work. And he admits it.*

"You know, if you were twenty years older, you could be Thomas. I don't know why I didn't see the resemblance." Brother Earl looked at Jim and back at the remaining photograph three or four times.

Thomas. Then it was Daddy in the pictures. No wonder.

But of course Jim did wonder. He wondered if Agnes had not known. *Of course she knew. That's why it had to be me, not Thomas the houseboy who is pretty much my same type.* He wondered about all of Agnes's houseboys being named Thomas. He wondered about his father and Brother Earl. It was a tantalizing sensation, this wondering. It was not like being completely in the dark, when it is pointless to ask questions, when he did not know enough to know what to ask.

"Yes. You're the spitting image of Thomas. And I wasn't so bad then myself." Brother Earl sighed and put the photo back in the folder, put the folder back in the filing cabinet, and pushed the lock button. "Old Agnes. She must be pushing sixty now. Or past it. If she'd only been content to stay in her place. You know she's wrong. She could have had all her fun on the sly. If only she wouldn't rock the boat. She's wrong. You can't flout society's standards. Whatever you think, whatever the theories, society will never, never permit men to be lovers. All you can do is rock the boat. You make people suspicious. You make people aware. You make it dangerous for everyone else.

"Yeah. You hate me. I didn't invent society. I didn't invent Western legal tradition. But I'm a practical man. Get yourself a good position. Have your fun on the sly. It's the only way. If you don't tell, most of them won't even know it exists. Some of the others will wink at it or look the other way. Society will tolerate some fooling around. Society won't tolerate a slap in the face. Go on and hate me now. You'll learn sooner or later."

* * *

The old gardener had just about raked the last of the footprints smooth when they came back. The two officers maneuvered Phil by his shoulders. Phil's hands were cuffed behind his back. Phil bucked and twisted, but the officers held him firmly and pressed him ahead. They pressed him across Trinity Garden, leaving more footprints in the raked soil. And behind them came another young man, a young man who seemed very pleased with himself.

They all four walked across Trinity Garden, leaving fresh footprints, walked up the spoke of sidewalk, and entered the ad building through the door beneath Brother Earl's window.

The old gardener removed his canvas work gloves and fished in his pocket for a red bandanna. He removed his straw hat and wiped his brow. He replaced the hat and the bandanna, leaned wearily on the handle of the rake, and clicked the handle of the rake with his two-inch nails.

FIFTEEN

THOUGH Brother Earl's trousers were still unzipped, Security Officer Matthews could not think of how to say so under the circumstances. He nudged Security Officer Andrews.

"Did you forget something when you left the men's room?" Andrews ventured. "Sir?"

Brother Earl looked abstractly at Andrews. Andrews lowered his gaze slowly to Brother Earl's crotch.

"Oh." Brother Earl zipped his fly with a single quick motion. "I must have forgotten it when I went to the men's room." Brother Earl returned to the other side of his desk while Matthews cuffed Phil to Jim's free wrist. When Matthews looked away, Jim resumed his surreptitious struggle to loosen the arm of the sofa to which his other wrist was cuffed.

"The student who assisted us in apprehending him is waiting outside," Matthews said.

"Yes? A student? Good." Brother Earl put on his coat. "I want them both strip searched. Give me an accounting of everything they have on their persons. Make it a very thorough search. Do I make myself clear?"

"Yes sir."

Brother Earl opened the door and stepped into the waiting room. Donald was staring into the aquarium, watching the bottom of a big black snail slide over the glass.

Donald looked up and, recognizing Brother Earl, stood.

"No, no. Please remain seated. The officers tell me you assisted them in apprehending the thief."

"Thief? I should have known. What did he steal?"

"Some important documents belonging to the university."

"Oh. Well, I'm really the one who caught him. He was hard to hold until they got there. They aren't very fast."

"I see. Of course that is how it would be. You can't expect these grown men to keep pace with a strong young athlete like yourself. I didn't get your name."

"It's Donald. Donald Wilton."

"Donald. You are a student at Holy Word?"

"Oh yes. I'm a sophomore in sociology."

"Yes? Well I'm sorry I haven't had a chance to meet you before. I've always tried to have a talk with each of the students here. But the undergraduate colleges have grown so. I don't always get the opportunity. I hope you will be able to come to see me in the next few weeks."

Donald thought his radar must be malfunctioning. *Surely*

there wasn't an edge on the invitation. Not Brother Earl. Then maybe the stories about his interviews are true. I'd thought that was something we had made up. Wasn't it? The radar insisted: *OLD GOAT**OLD GOAT* "Yes. I'm sure I would like to do that. Sometime." *"Sometime, like "never," if you read me like I think I read you.*

"Well, Donald, be that as it may, it is very important that we recover the documents, including some photographs, that the thief took from my office. Did you see the boy do anything with any photographs?"

"No. He had something in his hand. An envelope. A brown envelope, about yea by yea." Donald demonstrated the dimensions with his thumbs and forefingers.

"Good. What happened to the envelope?"

"I don't know. He had it when I first saw him. Then he turned the corner at the student union. When I caught up, it was gone. He was just standing there like he had forgotten anyone was after him."

Brother Earl's eyes narrowed with suspicion. "How was it, Donald, that you happened to join the pursuit?"

"I saw the cops—I mean, the officers—chasing him and shouting. I didn't know he had stolen anything. I figured he must be up to no good. I think we should all try to assist the police if we can."

"Of course, of course. Now tell me where the thief was, exactly, when you finally caught up to him."

"You know where the bike racks are, by the door to the cafeteria? He was standing right there by the—That's it! That must be it!"

"It must be what?"

"He was standing right by the mailbox. He was just standing there. He stopped to drop the envelope in the mailbox. That's my guess."

"Sounds like a very good guess to me. Thank you, Donald. You've done a great service to the college. I hope we can find some way to show proper appreciation." Brother Earl patted Donald's thigh.

Donald was surer of his radar. The hand had landed a little too high on his thigh and had stayed there a little too long. "Uh, if that's all for now, I've got a class."

"Of course you do. Donald Wilson, right?"

"Wilton, sir, Wilton."

"Thank you, Donald. You may go."

Brother Earl did not move. Donald had to squeeze sideways against the wall to avoid brushing against Brother Earl.

When Brother Earl entered his office again, Phil and Jim were standing in their underwear, their shirts draped on the links of the cuffs between them.

"Here is the list, sir." Matthews handed a legal pad to Brother Earl. Brother Earl glanced at the pad and tossed it facedown on his desk. "What time is the mail picked up at that box by the student union?" he asked.

"You won't get away with it, you closet case . . . you hypocrite . . . you—"

"Gag him too."

Matthews held his hand over Phil's mouth while Andrews peeled a strip of adhesive tape from the roll that had been found in a first aid box when it proved necessary to gag Jim.

"The mail pickup?" Brother Earl asked again when Phil's mouth was taped as securely as Jim's.

Matthews shrugged. Andrews said, "I'm not sure."

"Well, get over there and find out. And stop the pickup."

"Stop the pickup?"

"Stop the pickup."

Andrews began slowly, "I'm not sure we have the authority."

"You have my authority. We must regain those vital documents. Yes, both of you go. Do whatever you have to. I'll take the responsibility. No, secure that one's other hand first."

The officers struggled for several minutes to thread one of the pairs of handcuffs through the arm of the sofa and force Phil's free hand into the wristlet. When they were done, Phil and Jim were cuffed back-to-back and stooped over the end of the sofa. Brother Earl stood at his window until he saw the officers leave the building by the door below and head for the student union. Then he bent behind the desk and opened a bottom drawer.

"First some establishing shots," Brother Earl said. He lifted the viewfinder to his right eye. The flashbulb twinkled at the boys in their underwear and the camera spit out a square of glossy paper. Brother Earl shifted his position to get a full-frontal shot of Phil. The flashbulb twinkled again. "Some establishing shots, and then we'll see how your equipment compares."

Phil discovered that if he let his right arm go slack, Jim could swing at Brother Earl with the arms that were not fixed to the sofa. That and Phil's legs kept Brother Earl at bay until the phone rang.

"Reverend Richards speaking. . . . Uh-huh. And what time was it you apprehended the suspect? I didn't make a note of it. . . . Then it's probably been picked up? . . . I see. . . . No, you all stay put for another half an hour to be sure the driver isn't just late. You know the mail service. . . . Don't worry about them. No sense in wasting more of the university's time. My private agency will carry the ball from here. . . . Yes, in fact, there's no point in writing the details in your shift report. Just note that you did an errand for me. . . . Good. Good-bye."

Brother Earl flipped through his Rolodex. "Agnes hasn't

got me yet. And you boys are my insurance." He dialed a number.

"Let me speak to Pete. . . . Reverend Richards. . . . Reverend Richards, you know, Brother Earl. . . . Pete, this is Earl. . . . Yes, I'll be there tomorrow night. . . . I expect so. Look, Pete, I've called about a matter of grave importance to the Knights. The afternoon mail from the campus mailboxes, has it arrived there yet? . . . Okay, lookit, it's got to be gone through piece by piece. There are some documents of the most damaging sort concerning the Knights. . . . Yeah, I know. But you know Titus would give us a warrant if I asked him. There just isn't time. . . . Find the documents and we'll paper it over afterwards. Offer a reward. Say it's national security. In a way it is. . . . Well, it's a brown envelope, about—"

Brother Earl squeezed the telephone receiver between his shoulder and jaw and held out his thumbs and forefingers in imitation of Donald's gesture.

"About five and a half by eight. . . . Odd-sized. More than likely it's addressed to Austin or somewhere else in Texas, but I can't be sure about that. Get anything and everything in an odd-sized brown envelope, and this is important: Don't open the envelope yourself. . . . No, it's not a matter of not trusting you. We have to—have to have our lab go over it to be sure someone else didn't open it before you got it. . . . There's a lot riding on this, Pete. Give me a call at the studio or at home as soon as you get ahold of it. I'll send one of our guys that you know to pick it up. . . . Yeah, I'll see you tomorrow night and do whatever we have to do to cover your ass. Now get going."

Brother Earl hung up the phone and picked up the instant camera, but his wristwatch began to play "Rock of Ages" in electronic tones.

"Later than I thought," he said to himself, and to the

boys he said, "I'll make one more call to put you two on ice. You're in luck. You're going to be the special guests of honor at the Klavern."

Jim had found no give in the arm of the sofa.

The engineer flicked his mike switch and turned up the pot beneath it. "This is the Holy Word of God Radio Network." He punched the theme cartridge and brought up the organ music until the VU needle hovered in the red area. After three phrases of pipe blasts, he lowered the level a bit and leaned toward his mike.

"Christian brothers and sisters throughout the Americas, this is your Holy Word of God Broadcast Cathedral!" Three more phrases of the unrecognizable hymn gave the engineer time to cue up the cough track.

"Now on this day which God has made, your pastor, the world-renowned Brother Earl, will speak to you from the beautiful campus of Holy Word of God University and Technical Institute in Osage, Oklahoma. Now, brothers and sisters, Brother Earl!" The timing was right and the last of the taped organ chords dissolved.

The engineer twisted up the pot of the cough track. After four coughs mixed with sounds of hymnals closing and papers shuffling, the engineer pistol-cocked his finger and shot Brother Earl's cue.

"Brothers and sisters in Christ, my text for today is from the Book of the Preacher: 'Cast your bread upon the waters and after many days, you will find it.' Yes, cast your bread upon the waters. . . ."

Rosey Sutton was nearly certain. He was nearly certain he had found the envelope. He had felt its odd shape when he reached into the bag to grab the next handful. He pulled his hand out of the bag. He saw that the odd-shaped envelope was brown. He dropped the rest of the envelopes back into the bag. The brown envelope was addressed to Austin.

Rosey was about to holler, already spending the reward money in his head, when he noticed the name on the envelope. He thought there was something special about the name. He had seen the name somewhere before, if only he could remember where. *No need to hurry,* he thought. *As long as I've got it, can't no one else find it. That reward will still be there. It might even go up.*

He picked up a stack of mail and put it on top of the envelope. His hand was big enough to conceal the bottom envelope, although it stuck out of the stack. He continued to make the motions of searching. As the brown envelope came to the top of his stack, he looked at the name again and shuffled the envelope to the bottom of the stack. He looked around carefully. No one had noticed.

Finally he was pretty sure he remembered. He unbuttoned a middle button of his shirt. When he bent over the bags again, he slipped the brown envelope into his shirt. When he stood again, he rebuttoned the shirt. Sure enough, for all the starch in the shirt, the envelope did not show.

Empty-handed, he walked past Peter Bullock and the coffee machine and went into the men's washroom. After he had thrown the bolt on the door, he took his wallet from his hip pocket. He turned through the pictures until he saw his father's face smiling at him through the frosty plastic. Gently he pulled the folded, crumbling, tattered white paper from behind his father's picture.

Some of the stains on the old certificate, he imagined, were his father's tears of joy. He remembered the old white-haired man sitting in his sickbed, so weakened, so frail, clasping the white paper to his bosom, weeping, and

201

gasping out the verses of one of the old, old songs, lining them out and then singing them again as he had for so many years in front of the congregation.

No one knew how the old man had known that the sunny Port Gibson morning was the morning of the day. They did not get the newspaper, and Mama had not told him. But he knew. They found him sitting on the edge of the bed, trying to catch his breath, the trousers of his brown, best suit half on his shrunken legs. He was fumbling painfully with his maroon tie. Mama tried to put him back to bed, but he would have none of it.

Mama sent the boys out of the room and closed the door. Behind the door, the old man raised his voice to her as loud as he was able until he started coughing. The boys could not make out the muffled words. Mama had a tear on her cheek when she came out of the room. She said: "Rosey, son, get on your Sunday best. Raymond too."

Rosey protested: "Oh no, Mama. It could kill him."

"You heard me. I been his wife these forty years and I know his mind. It'll kill him for sure if he don't."

Raymond and Rosey put on their Sunday suits. When they were dressed, they found the old man in the rocker in the parlor. Except for a few fair Sundays when Cousin Jay had come for them in his pickup, the old man had not been out in the sunlight for three years. The boys each took an arm and carried their father out of the house.

They carried him down the gravel path to the highway, up the hill, past the private white boys' academy, and down the hill toward town. In town the highway was called Church Street. They carried him past the bombed-out synagogue, past the Presbyterian church with its golden finger for a spire, past the other churches where the old chains still decorated the colored balconies, and down to Main Street. The truth was, the jeers and taunts from the passing cars scared Rosey, but he did not want Raymond to see that.

They carried their father to the square. In front of the Confederate monument, a great big young man sat in a folding chair behind a flimsy card table. The armed federal marshal stood by. Father would be carried no more.

One agonized step after another, pausing to lean on his cane, Father approached the little card table, the papers on it flapping in the breeze. A sister from the church saw the old man coming. She shooed the young folks out of line. Step by step, the old man came closer to the young man whose flesh hung over the seat of the folding chair. In the square, all of them but one watched the old man's painful progress. Some prayed that he would make it and some doubted. But the marshal's eyes darted from window to window and bush to bush.

The levee was not so far away. The levee was not as much as a mile away where the NIO had found the body of the last man, the Jewish college boy, who had come to sit in a folding chair behind a card table.

The fat man shuffled his papers. When the old man reached the table at last, the young fat man spoke to him. The bright fat man adjusted a piece of carbon paper in his book. He turned the book around, handed a pen to the old man, and pointed to the line.

The old man signed.

The man in the folding chair signed too, creased the paper in the book, and tore out a leaf. He handed the white slip to Father. Father tried to thank him. Then the man stood, the tallest, fattest, brightest man that Rosey had ever seen. He shook Father's hand. "Congratulations, sir," the young man had said. "Praise the Lord," said the sister, "Author of Liberty."

Yes. Rosey had been right. There in the lower right corner of the paper, below his father's shaky signature, was the name, writ bold in purpling ballpoint ink: "Angus McKinney, Special Federal Deputy Voter Registrar for Mississippi, June 19, 1965."

Rosey opened his shirt and removed the envelope. The address was "Angus McKinney, 124 8th Street, Austin TX 78701."

Rosey knew he would never know the truth of it. He knew he did not know anymore what national security might be. He knew he could use the hundred dollars. But he knew what he was going to do.

He slipped the envelope into his shirt again and left the washroom. The next time he moved a bag to the pile of those searched twice, he slipped the envelope from his shirt and thrust the envelope deep into the bag.

The producer jabbed the engineer. The engineer opened his eyes. Without looking at the clock, he could tell from Brother Earl's tone that the sermon was winding down. The engineer shoved the free-will offering promo into the cartridge player.

"... And after many days, you will find it again. This is your pastor, Earl Richards, blessing you for your prayers and for your free-will love offerings. Join us again next time for your Holy Word of God Broadcast Cathedral. Your announcer will tell you how to address your offerings. Now, good evening to all of you from Osage, Oklahoma." Brother Earl drew his finger across his throat. The engineer twisted the pot down and cut off Brother Earl's mike.

Rosey was quiet all through dinner. Afterward he sat on the porch in the old rocker for a long time. Ginny wondered why he kept opening his wallet and unfolding some piece of paper.

PART THREE

SIXTEEN

ONE day at the Reservation is much like another. Eight patrons, four night workers and four career alcoholics, compose the board of directors, so called, and each of them has a customary place. The interruptions are routine: the same coffee-breakers dashing whither and whence, every day at the same times; the same long-lunchers taking their particular cocktails; and the beertruck drivers making their rounds and considering themselves, rightly by Osage standards, especially cosmopolitan for daring to perch on gay bar stools to accept complimentary cans of the merchandise.

All day, every day, the Reservation is dim. Strong light is unkind to the old, red, flocked wallpaper; the old mahogany-veneer bar; the old, black, vinyl-covered bar stools; and the faded, gold, padded carpet.

Osage is a small, dull town in so many ways. Osage ever knew but one gay bar: the Reservation. The untraveled suppose that all gay bars are like the Reservation.

But the Reservation was designed to be one of a kind of bar, the kind of bar called elegant in cities where bars are numerous enough to fall into types: disco, country, leather, glitter, crossover, waterfront, hustle, quiet, show, video, drag, and elegant. The Reservation had been modeled on an elegant bar in Cleveland. The elegance is that of the culture. Not a simple elegance, not a quiescent elegance, but an elegance of velvet this and plush that, of scarlet and gold, and of antiqued mirrors. It is an elegance gaudy only in decor, not in decorum. In Cleveland in an elegant bar, neither drag nor shorts nor muscle shirts nor yelling "Mary!" across the bar is allowed. But such things are common in the Reservation because in Osage the Reservation is not the elegant bar. It is the only bar.

At night the red digits of the clock glow so that each customer can absorb his dose and fall in love before closing time. In the morning the clock is extinguished. Days, if any of the regulars had some special desire to mark the passing of the hours, he might observe the comings and goings which are as reliable a standard as any of the eight expensive watches—three Rolex, five reputed Cartiers—that the board of directors wear.

The occupation of the board—their mission, their vocation, their calling, if you please—is the training of new bartenders. It is a Sisyphean task.

Days, the Reservation is constantly supplied with new bartenders. This one is called Patrick.

Patrick stands nearly six and a half feet tall. He is slim but sinewy and tanned. His hair is golden blond, but his mustache verges on red. His upper chest, as it shows from his half-unbuttoned cotton Hawaiian-print shirt, is bony and hairless, and the cheeks of his ass pursed low in the thighs of his ill-fitting jeans.

No one knows why morning bartenders never stay long at the Reservation. True enough, the wages are miserly, the management surly, the customers exasperating and ugly, and the tips paltry. But the Reservation is air-conditioned, the labor is not backbreaking, even a congenital fairy can consider himself butch in the context of the clientele, and nothing is said if there is still a whisper of mascara about the eyes at opening time. It is not as if the morning help were apt to be lured away by offers of a better, more lucrative shift at another bar. In Osage there is none other.

Mysterious, really, that the morning bartenders never stay. Not only do they not stay, but also they evaporate completely.

Perhaps the morning bartender has been seen around before. Perhaps not. One morning he is installed: shorn and pressed, on his best behavior, eager to learn everyone's name and drink.

A week later, he shows a wrinkle here or there and a few hairs out of place, and he has learned it all. All of it. Everyone's name. And drink. And peccadillo. Especially the peccadilloes. He has the look of college students who have remained undergraduates too long. A morning bartender is soon jaded.

One morning he is late. Then he misses a day and makes excuses. He is late three days running and makes no excuses. Then—the remarkable thing for a small, dull town like Osage—he is never seen again.

No one ever sees him again.

Didn't he have a roommate? Didn't someone or other have his phone number? Wasn't someone sent to pick up his final paycheck?

No one has any information. Travelers never encounter him in the big cities, where any smart boy would go. His likeness never appears in the magazines, slick or pulp, or in the pornographic videos or eight-millimeter films. Vanished.

Whom the gods would obliterate from life's book, they first send to tend bar at the Reservation in the morning.

This one's name was Patrick and it was his third day. He was not yet familiar with the routine, nor yet convinced of its unrelenting inevitability. So he did not know to be astonished that Willard entered the bar when it was only half-past noon.

Ellenor had been amusing herself by ordering cocktails with cryptic names, concocted of liqueurs in esoteric combinations. She thinks this is good for a few laughs when a morning bartender is still fresh. The Good-and-Plenty was Ellenor's subject. A Good-and-Plenty by Ellenor's lights is a shot of anisette covered, not exactly layered, with a shot of Kahlua and finished with a splash of soda. It is served with four cocktail straws. Properly, the Good-and-Plenty is sucked up from the bottom all at once. Hence the name.

The two that Ellenor had bought for Patrick had been good. And more than plenty. After sucking up four herself, Ellenor began to feel them. She thought of changing the lesson to cream drinks for a while. But what little cream there was had taken on an unfortunate aroma. The moment before Willard walked in, Ellenor found herself at something of a loss.

Everyone was at something of a loss to see Willard enter and take his stool so much in advance of his usual hour. Everyone but Patrick, and Patrick was put on notice by the sudden flatfooted silence in the bar.

Ellenor recovered herself quickly and, with the smug self-assurance of a queen in a club that takes her checks, rapped on the bar with the earpiece of her spectacles. Patrick attended at once. Ellenor ordered a pair of Orange Blossoms, one to be delivered to Willard who certainly would not join Ellenor since she was sitting three stools away from the place known as Willard's corner.

Naturally, Patrick had to ask what an Orange Blossom was. Ellenor gave him the recipe of an Orange Blossom as it is made at the Reservation—a gin screwdriver with a dash of Triple Sec—knowing it was pointless to tell him that a proper Orange Blossom contains a half-teaspoon of powdered sugar and is served in a glass frosted with powdered sugar and garnished with a translucent slice of orange.

The Reservation did not have the powdered sugar. It was futile to raise the issue with the bartender or with the management, known to friend and foe alike as Her Nibs, because Her Nibs had never grasped the fundamental law of the bar business, which is that your dozen or so regulars will make or break your bar.

They pay the rent. They pay the light bill. They leave the tips the help can count on. While it is pleasant to have the pretty boys throwing around daddy's money, they and their lucre are as ethereal and fleeting as their youthful looks and summer tans. The substance of the bar business is your regulars.

That fact of life may occur to Her Nibs in the event the Reservation ever has any competition. In that case the Reservation will have powdered sugar or the Reservation will revert to the seedy warehouse whence it sprang.

A garnish, of course, was out of the question.

Such Orange Blossoms as Ellenor described were a snap for Patrick in spite of the Good-and-Plenties. He lifted a Bevnap from the spiraled stack and with a flourish presented one of the cocktails to Willard. Willard handed him a folded sheet of paper and nodded in Ellenor's direction.

Patrick took the paper to Ellenor, extracted the price of two Orange Blossoms—which he figured to be two juice highballs, never mind the Triple Sec—from the array of currency under Ellenor's handbag, and returned to stand across the bar from Willard to await the verdict on the Orange Blossom.

The paper was of the cheapest photocopier quality and mustard yellow. Ellenor noted the feel of the paper's surface, like that of Ping-Pong balls; put on her spectacles, letting them settle far down her nose; and unfolded the paper. It was a leaflet.

It was a Ku Klux Klan leaflet.

Ellenor was unsurprised. While much about Willard is enigmatic and impenetrable, Ellenor had been around long enough to know a precious little, and among the things she knew was that Willard was employed, which itself was more than most people were certain of. Moreover, she knew he worked as an estimator for a quick-print shop, though as appropriate for a price-competitive business they had given him a somewhat loftier-sounding title.

She was not surprised that Willard would have a sample of the leaflet, nor in the acrid savor of the political climate was she surprised by the leaflet itself.

The leaflet was similar to any number of Klan leaflets that had shown up of late. There was the illustration of the normal—that is, white heterosexual—family: husband, wife, son, daughter, and babe in arms of indeterminate sex. Across the page was a misty blot containing a number of unattractive men, some of them drooling. No question that these were the perverts. Between, in the middle of the page, was the robed Knight, mounted and evidently calling his unseen legions to battle against the leering mob. All very *Birth of a Nation.*

Beneath this was a great block of tiny gray type.

Ellenor had first found such a leaflet in the seat of a public conveyance. She had been so infused with the spirit of know-your-enemy that she had not waited to locate her spectacles in her handbag: "All the Italian men carry exactly this type of bag. Very practical," she always said. But squinting at the tiny type as the bus rocked and started and stopped and swayed and stank had given her a bad case of motion sickness.

Or some other ill humor: It was a fulsome little tract.

In the manner of tracts, it said the same thing over and over in sentences and paragraphs built upon the same formulas, varied only by the choices of pejoratives. Most of the epithets were entirely familiar and transparent. "Sodomites," "effeminates," and "queers" Ellenor understood very well. Some of the words were quaint or bizarre: "nances," sometimes rendered "nancys," "gay blades," even "sissies." The gist of it was that the Klan did not much care for homosexual people, which Ellenor already knew.

Yet some parts of it Ellenor could not understand at all. Some recurrent phrases seemed to have special meaning not evident from their denotations. Other phrases were unexplained. Such as the claim that male homosexuals had some particular desire that women, even against their will, be forced to have abortions.

Ellenor wondered about the logic to that. She read the part that suggested that male homosexuals wanted to rape white women.

Ellenor thought probably this was merely a rhetorical error occasioned by the refitting of homophobic terms in the boilerplate of an old-fashioned racial slur. But maybe not. Perhaps initiates were privy to an explanation.

It was, after all, a tract. No doubt it was fraught with meaning for those who already believed every word of it. But queers raping women? Wouldn't that perplex even those inclined with sympathy to the Klan's view? Ellenor saw that such leaflets could not inform her of anything useful concerning the enemy.

But the leaflet that Willard had brought to the Reservation had a peculiar headline, even for a Klan leaflet.

"Confront the Homosexuals!" it said.

And it said the date—today, Ellenor noted—and the starting time for a Klan rally on Caney rise, to follow a covered-dish supper.

"Confront." That was the word that bothered Ellenor.

Surely it is impossible to confront people in their absence. If one is to confront homosexuals, one must have homosexuals to confront. And what homosexual, except for the closet cases under the sheets, would dare to venture onto Caney rise in the midst of a Klan rally after dark?

It might be a figurative "confront." After all, when leftist tracts had said "Confront the Warmakers!" hadn't that really meant sit in the hot sun all day, smoke dope, and listen to folksingers? Even a figurative "confront" was not good. The Klan and Brother Earl were on the move, supposing, as Ellenor did not, that Brother Earl and the Klan were not one and the same thing. "Confront." She did not like the sound of it.

Ellenor raised an eyebrow and looked up at Willard. Willard looked pleasant and abstracted, as he always looked. Willard dredged the cocktail straw through his Orange Blossom, though not in fact vigorously enough to mix the melting ice with the orange juice and liquor. He took the straw out of the glass, tapped a drop back into the cocktail, considered the straw for a moment, and laid it across the ashtray.

Immediately Patrick whisked the ashtray away and replaced it with another, although except for the straw Willard's ashtray had been perfectly clean because Willard does not smoke and no one else presumes to use Willard's ashtray. Only Willard uses it, and he uses it to receive his cocktail straws. Without it, Willard would not know what to do with his cocktail straws any more than blue-haired ladies seated in the nonsmoking section of a restaurant know what to do with their used tea bags.

Willard nodded at Patrick, who was still waiting to see if the Orange Blossom was correct. Then slowly, Willard turned toward Ellenor, took a sip of his cocktail, smiled as he does when he cannot avoid making a remark, and said: "No. I don't know what it means. But it was a rush job to change the headline."

That, clearly, was all Willard intended to say.

Ellenor sighed at the mystery and ordered Girl Scout Cookies around the bar, except for Willard, who would never drink such a thing. Of course, Patrick did not know how to make them. Ellenor remembered that the cream had turned and changed the order to Tootsie Rolls, which she patiently explained.

Willard bought his own Orange Blossom for his second round and, when he was done with it, departed.

At three Patrick went off duty and Charlie with the big pecs put a newly counted cash drawer into the register. At four-thirty Willard returned unremarkably. At ten of five the after-workers began to drift in after work and Ellenor excused herself to walk two blocks to the new plaza, a many-fountained thing that Osage had installed in hopes of rejuvenating the decaying part of downtown. Rather off the beaten path, they had also installed a little hut with public restrooms.

By six Ellenor had returned to the Reservation, where the after-work crowd was becoming rowdy. It seemed dreary enough to Ellenor, who soon found herself explaining the business about the toga party and that Edwina was coming as a woman who was coming as Nero who was coming in drag. It hardly made any sense to begin with and Ellenor suspected she was not conveying the senselessness of it, but after all, toga parties are tired and Edwina's plans were the only aspect of it that might be portrayed as a novelty. Little that it was.

"No, no, no," Ellenor corrected the inquirer, "Edwina isn't coming as Nero. The woman Edwina thinks she is will—"

"Told you I'd get them." Donald intruded. Ellenor had not noticed his arrival.

"Get who?" Ellenor asked in spite of herself.

"That imperial pageboy or whatever you call him and that little blond hussy."

Ellenor did not remember immediately, so she cut Donald off. Donald had not proved to be as amusing as some had thought he might, and Ellenor had considered striking him from her list.

"Now. Starting from the beginning, Edwina is coming as a woman, but that woman is doing Nero in drag. Get it?"

"Yes. I suppose I see." The questioner realized that he had not really been all that interested in the first place. The essential thing was that a role at the toga party had been found for Edwina. The questioner looked up as if he had just seen someone he had been waiting for, bowed slightly to Ellenor, who nodded, and took his leave.

Ellenor resettled herself on her bar stool and took a moment to rearrange her spectacles, paper money, handbag, and cocktail before she consented to turn her attention to Donald.

"You remember the tall, black-haired one," Donald began again. "It turned out he was staying in my dorm but he didn't remember me. You said he was an imperial tribune before that blond witch waltzed in here and stole him from under my . . ."

Yes. Ellenor remembered. Ellenor remembers important things. So she listened and nodded and murmered "Yes, go on" in the pauses.

Something about the law of large numbers and monkeys composing Shakespeare occurred to Ellenor. It occurred to her because for one time in her life she knew, as if she had shaken a jigsaw puzzle in its box and poured it out in perfect order, a complete picture.

Ellenor was vain about knowing things. Very vain. So vain that when she did not know a thing, she made it up. And since she was an old, rich, powerful queen, whatever she made up soon became fact.

If she wished to know that a boy was a closet case, word got out that she knew it. Hairdressers told matrons that it was sterling truth, and matrons told daughters not to waste their time. Chicken hawks flocked to the boy with every enticement they could invent. Girls had nothing to do with him and men importuned him at every turn. Soon enough, it was true.

If Ellenor said someone were leaving town, he might as well start packing.

Ellenor was vain, but she was not stupid. Once in a while she caught herself recognizing one of her own prophecies on its way to self-fulfillment. Then, vain as she was, she had to ask herself whether she knew what she knew or not. But this time, as she listened to Donald's story, she knew what she knew and she knew that she knew.

When Donald finished, Ellenor remained quiet in a reverie of self-satisfaction.

"Well?" said Donald.

Ellenor rubbed the bridge of her nose, tapped her spectacles on the bar, and put the spectacles on. She ordered another drink and swiveled in her bar stool to regard Donald full face.

"Well?" Donald said again, this time a little nervously.

"Well, I see, dear. Let me just review this tale of yours to be certain I have grasped the salient points.

"First . . ." Ellenor paused to down the whole of the fresh cocktail and nod at the bartender while she still had his attention.

"First, an imperial tribune was lodged in your dormitory at that homophobic institution which you attend because you cannot get admitted to any other college anywhere. The tribune is obviously on a secret mission because he confided in none of the local community leaders such as myself.

"Second, he is now unaccountably missing and the indications are that he was not expecting to leave—because his effects remained undisturbed in the dormitory overnight and then, so you say, with a great to-do his belongings were seized by Earl's rent-a-pigs this morning, leaving no trace that such a person ever existed. Have I got it so far?"

"Really, Ellenor—"

"Third, Earl is fomenting the most vicious anti-queer campaign that anyone can remember, even in this very backward little town in this troglodytic state.

"Fourth, yesterday you observed the tribune's companion being pursued by Earl's rent-a-pigs and with your

218

matchless athletic ability and thick skull you delivered up one of our own people into the hands of the enemy."

"Ellenor!"

"Fifth, nowhere in this little escapade, which is supposed to have involved a theft, is there any evidence of the legitimate authorities having been consulted. Sixth"—Ellenor took the mustard-yellow paper from her handbag—"here is a leaflet for you to peruse at your leisure. And seventh, you and I very soon are going to have a very very serious grave talk, at which time you will probably come to curse your mother's womb that it brought you to such a day."

"No! You don't understand."

"For once I do understand. Finally I understand one thing completely and absolutely."

"Ellenor—"

"Good-bye, Donald. And when I say good-bye, Donny, you understand, I say good-bye not only as Ellenor, but I speak for the entirety of the A list."

"You're wrong, Ellenor."

"Yes. I have been wrong, much as it pains me to admit it. In the past I have sometimes been wrong. But not this time. Now, Donald, it is good-bye."

Donald made a scene. He denounced Ellenor. He renounced the A list. It was all very unseemly, even as Reservation scenes go. Sympathetic eyes assessed Ellenor, who remained above it all. They half pitied Donald, poor deluded thing who only made it worse by prostrating himself before the throne of fate.

Then he was gone.

Ellenor removed her spectacles and ordered quarters. Peculiar, since Ellenor did not play pinball and always brought her own imported oval cigarettes. Peculiar, since drink prices were round dollars and Ellenor always tipped in folding money.

While Charlie stacked quarters on the bar in front of El-lenor, she searched through her handbag until she found her address book. There was a way, her long-distance company had written in a brochure, to punch up code numbers and charge a call from any pay phone. Ellenor wished she had paid attention, but she had not. She was an old-fashioned girl who still called a refrigerator an "icebox" and referred to coins as "silver." Naturally she made a show of not counting the quarters Charlie had stacked up and of leaving her folding money and her handbag unattended at the bar.

In the alcove, by the door where Jerry still presented himself as doorkeeper and flexed his arms, Ellenor read the instructions on the phone three times to be sure she understood. She dialed the number of Agnes's red line and put quarters in the phone.

"Hello," the young voice said. If you had the red-line number you did not need someone to say "Agnes's residence."

"Hello. I need to speak to Her Imperial Majesty."

"I'm sorry, Madam is not available at this time."

"But this is a matter of the utmost urgency. How can I get in touch with Agnes?"

"I'm sorry, I cannot say."

"Will she be home soon?"

"I am unable to provide you with that information."

"Is she in Austin? I'm calling from Osage City."

There was a telling pause. "I am sorry. I cannot say where Madam is at the moment. Can I take a message?"

"Never mind. I think I know all I need to know."

"May I say who called?"

"If I'm right or if I'm wrong, it won't make any difference by the time she gets back."

"I am sorry that I could not be more helpful."

"I'm sure you are." Ellenor hung up the phone. She read the instructions again. She stopped to ask herself if she could be wrong. She found a Houston number in her book. No, she was right and she knew it. She dialed the Houston number and dropped her quarters into the phone.

"Magdalena's Slagheap Bar. It's your nickel."

"May I speak to Chief?"

"May you speak to what chief?"

"May I speak to THE Chief, sir?"

"That's better. Hold the horn."

Ellenor could hear the phone being clunked down on the bar, and over the phone she listened to groans and the whack, whack, whack of leather and flesh until the Chief picked up the receiver.

SEVENTEEN

O H no, mister. Here, have some more. It will just go to waste otherwise." Ann McCain found another breast within the mound of fried chicken parts. She grasped it with her tongs and laid it on the pile of chicken on the man's cardboard plate. "Lord knows," she said, pushing her rhinestone-spangled trifocals back on the bridge of her nose, "there's a world of plenty."

In the clearing on Caney rise was a world of plenty.

Plenty of brisket and ribs, deep-fried crusty chicken and catfish, barbecued turkey, stuffed eggs, potato salad, corn on the cob, cornbread, biscuits, plain white bread and buns, hot dogs, apple pies, cherry pies, chili beans, meat chili, baked beans, three-bean salad, green beans with bacon drippings, Spam and onion pie, rhubarb cobbler, fried eggplant, hush puppies, cole slaw, two-gallon jars of iced tea, two-gallon jars of Kool-Aid, canned beer on ice, new Coke, old Coke, diet Coke, Dr Pepper, cucumber pickles, cauliflower pickles, cherry peppers, ripe olives, corn relish, radish roses, hot candied yams with big melted marshmallows, fudge cake, fudges with nuts and fudges without, bags of greasy potato chips, baked potatoes, mashed potatoes, sweet potato pie, french fries, bowls of onion dip, egg pie with bacon and cheese, melted Velveeta dips and sauces in long steamy pans, sausages in molasses, creamed peas, creamed corn, creamed chicken, chicken pie, tuna casseroles, chicken casseroles, chipped beef casseroles, casseroles without names and casseroles manqué, home-canned fruit, ready-bought fruit salad with added sliced bananas and tiny pastel marshmallows—a world of plenty.

Ann McCain turned her attention to the next man in line. Though the sun was setting, the man sweated in his white rayon robe, its blue-lined hood wet and drooped over his back, altogether appearing as the photographic negative of an academic ceremony at a black college.

"Oh, it's Petie Bullock," Ann exclaimed, "as I live and breathe! Why I haven't seen you in a month of Sundays. Are you still with the post office?"

Bullock nodded, but Ann's mouth had sprinted past.

"And Janie was asking me only last week, or maybe it was before that, what I heard of the Bullock boy. You know, we just can't think of you as all grown up—But here, please have some more of my chicken. Made it myself from Grandma Cantrell's recipe—No, take some more, please.

Don't hurt my feelings. I just don't know what I will do with it all if folks don't eat some more of it. Lookie, here's a nice thigh."

The Ford was a venerable pickup, '49 or thereabouts and in mint condition. It was in mint condition, but no better. The black paint looked black and shiny, but it was not the hand-rubbed black of classics restored to better than they had ever been. If Truman were still president, one would guess to look at the pickup that it had just been driven from a big-city showroom out through the dusty Oklahoma by-ways that run direct to the compass points and meet at crisp right angles, out to where some farmboy GI's dream had reclaimed his father's birthright from the dustbowl, out to where a man is hard pressed if forced to choose from among his wife, his best dog, his pickup, or his good right arm, out to where "banker" and "bastard" are synonyms.

But Harry's gone.

To those who looked at the pickup and thought, it seemed extremely odd. Where could that truck have been to save it from the single certainty in all the mystery of time passing? The battery was new enough, and the spark plugs and the blackwall tires. But as to the truck itself, everything was as it was when the UN took Pyongyang.

Trailing a cloud of dust, the pickup came. The pickup came on toward the radio antenna.

The radio antenna grew out of the ass of a plain white Dodge Dart, which was parked in the rocking shadow of a pump bob, where grass grew along the fencerow. The pickup slowed as it approached the base of the antenna. The white-hooded figure in the pickup strained in the late sun-light to make out the silhouette of a cowboy who was rest-ing his rump against the Dodge, a shotgun crossed over his arm. The pickup stopped and honked. The man stood up.

Utterly gracelessly, the huge robed and hooded figure dismounted from the Ford's cab. The cowboy had been studying the pickup's license tag.

"Jesus, you're a big un," said the cowboy.

"Yep. They grow them big in Texas."

"I don't recognize your truck."

"I'm from Texas."

"Them is out-of-state plates."

"Yep, I just drove up from Texas."

"You aren't from around here."

"No. I'm from Texas."

"You're a long way from Texas."

"I know. I just drove all the way."

"Them is Texas plates."

"Yep, that's where I drove from."

"Sos you just drove up from Texas."

"Shore did."

"I see." Still cradling the shotgun in one hand, the cowboy drew a Bull Durham pouch from the rear pocket of his jeans. "Well, what you doin here?"

"I drove up for the big event."

"What big event?"

"The Klan rally."

"What Klan rally?"

"The Ku Klux Klan rally. The one tonight on Caney rise. You know, confront the homosexuals."

"So why are you wearing that white robe and white hood?"

"Because I'm going to the Klan rally, the one on Caney rise tonight. I drove all the way from Texas to go to the rally on Caney rise."

"Now, now. There's no need to raise your voice with me. I have to ask you these questions because it's my job. You see, we're having a Klan rally tonight on Caney rise.

225

That's just up the road a piece. And I have to stay here and make sure no busybody outsiders are sticking their noses where it don't belong."

"Oh, well, I didn't mean to get short with you. I think I understand now."

"What's that? What do you understand?"

"That there's going to be a Klan rally tonight."

"Who told you that?"

"You just told me that. But I told you first. I told you that's why I drove up here all the dadblamed way from Texas and that's howcome I'm wearing this dogblasted white robe and white hood."

"Are all you Texans so short-tempered?"

"Sorry. Runs in the family."

"Then you did know about the Klan rally before I told you."

"Yes. I did."

"Well, if you knowed about it then I guess it's all right."

"Good."

"Not so fast. What's that on your robe?"

"Just some stitchin."

"Well I can see that. But what kind of critter is that?"

"That's a chimera."

"A chimera?"

"It's mythical."

"Mythical? Well I'm not so sure."

"You know, like grand dragons, imperial wizards, like that. Well, I'm the White Knight of the Green Chimera."

"What's that mean?"

"Entertainment committee."

"Oh." The cowboy licked the cigarette paper and rolled the cigarette closed with his free hand. "Got any whores?"

"No, I don't got any whores. Does it look like I got any whores?"

226

"Now, now. I asked you not to raise your voice with me."

"I'm very sorry."

"That's better. Now, you say you're on the entertainment committee."

"That's right."

"So where are the whores?"

"I didn't bring no whores."

"Why not?"

"Because you can't bring whores from Texas to Oklahoma. It's a violation of the Mann Act."

"The what?"

"The Mann Act."

"Don't seem very manly to me."

"Maybe not. But it's a federal statute. Now, you don't want the NIO down on us, do you?"

"Course not."

"Well, that's why I didn't bring any whores."

"We got perfectly good whores in Oklahoma."

"I'm sure you do."

"State's full of whores."

"If you say so."

"Well?"

"Well what?"

"Sos howcome you not to bring any Oklahoma whores? Ain't they good enough for you? Or is that a violation of the Woman Act or something?"

"I didn't bring any Oklahoma whores because I don't know any Oklahoma whores. I just drove in from Texas this afternoon for the Klan rally."

"I see." The cowboy lit his cigarette and began slowly to walk around the truck. When he reached the tailgate, he turned sharply to face it and to stare at the bed of the pickup, which contained a fading drab tarp, held down with limestone rocks, and evidently something under the tarp. "There's something under the tarp."

"Yes. Yes there is."

"Well, what is under the tarp?"

"See for yourself."

The cowboy extended the muzzle end of the shotgun and snagged up a flap of the tarp to reveal a bit of brown cardboard. "Cardboard boxes. You got cardboard boxes under the tarp?"

"I do."

"I see." The cowboy flicked his cigarette away. "There's something in them boxes, ain't there?"

"Yep. You're right."

"What's in them boxes?"

"See for yourself."

"Then you won't mind if I take a look?"

"No. Go right on ahead."

The cowboy raised the shotgun quickly and the tarp flicked back on itself, revealing the sides of three boxes, each imprinted with the dark figure of a chained, naked supplicant and the bloodred legend "Middle Passage Bourbon."

"It says it's bourbon," the cowboy said.

"Yep."

"You got bourbon whiskey in them boxes?"

"Yep. Twenty cases."

"Well then, what exactly are you doing out here in the middle of nowhere with twenty cases of bourbon?"

"Taking it to the Klan rally."

"What for?"

"To drink."

"Now, now. Wait a minute. You can't tell me that you're gonna drink twenty cases of bourbon at the Klan rally."

"Not by myself. Not all of it. I told you, I'm on the entertainment committee."

"So?"

"So the bourbon is for entertainment."

"Oh. But you didn't bring any whores?"

"No. I'm sorry. I didn't."

"Seems like a waste to me. All that whiskey and no whores."

"Can't be helped."

"Maybe not."

"Well, go ahead and take a bottle for yourself."

"Aw, I couldn't. Could I? I mean it wouldn't be right."

"Of course it would. It's for the membership."

"That's what I mean."

"Well, you're a member."

"How did you know that?"

"Well if you're not, what are you doing out here with a shotgun and a radio asking me all these questions?"

"Well it just so happens that I am a member. So there."

"In that case, get yourself a bottle of whiskey."

"All right then. Don't mind if I do." The cowboy pushed one of the boxes to the side of the pickup, walked around to the side, tore open the box, and took a bottle from its cardboard pigeonhole. "But you know, I still have to ask you about your gloves."

"Take another bottle, if you like. There's a world of plenty."

"Your gloves. Most men in these parts don't wear white gloves like that."

"Oh, the gloves! Are you sure you don't want another bottle? There was an accident at the plant."

"So what about the gloves."

"Nitric-acid burns. I have nitric-acid burns on my hands."

"So?"

"My hands hurt. And they look like hell."

"Like what?"

"Like, you know, like see those nicotine stains on your fingers."

"Where?"

"Right there on your trigger finger."

"Oh yeah. What about em?"

"The burns look like that except all over and splotchy. Besides, they smell like shit when I take off the gloves."

"Did you get workman's comp?"

"No, course not. You apply for workman's comp and they fire you and put you on this list sos no one else will ever hire you."

"Oh yeah. I heard of that. That don't seem right. That's not fair. That's like discrimination."

"Isn't it just."

"What?"

"Yep. It's just like discrimination."

"You sure you won't miss a second bottle?"

"Well, I don't know. How many more checkpoints?"

"How many what?"

"How many more guys with guns between here and Caney rise?"

"Don't worry none about them. I'll radio you clear through."

"Well then, help yourself."

"Do what?"

"Take as much liquor as you want."

"Is three too many?"

"No. Three would be just fine."

"No whores comin down the road then?"

"Not that I know of. Sorry."

"Well that rally lasts almost till dawn."

"I know."

"And I'll be out here with this liquor all by myself."

"That's a shame."

"I mean, you don't happen to have any real good magazines? Some you'd be willing to trade me? I've got some, but I'm tired of them. I mean, you being on the entertainment committee. Or maybe a deck of them playing cards, like I saw once in Dallas."

"Sorry. But I do have a fresh tube of K-Y."

"Qué-why?"

"It's in the cab. I'll toss it down. You'll figure out what to do with it. Just use your imagination."

"My what?"

"Oh, never mind."

"And so Janie said to me, 'It's been awhile since Kate passed away.' And you know, Petie, our hearts went out to you, but Janie is right. It has been quite some time. And you know, I recall you used to be sweet on Janie's Sarah and Sarah's had her troubles too—cruel wicked tongues being what they are, I'm sure you have heard—but we've all got a past and thank goodness it's behind us. So you know Janie was thinking that you might like to come over for a home-cooked meal sometime with her and Sarah and Sarah's boys. You know the boys go to bed early and Janie's a heavy sleeper herself. You know Sarah really has been losing a lot of weight lately, and Sarah really isn't looking for another husband, but she does like to dance, you know what I mean. And you know grown-up adults have got to be adaptable to situations. I'm sure you know that no one would speak an ill word if—Oh my, listen to me go on. I'm just holding up this line. Janie's number is in the book.

Sarah is staying with her. Have another piece of chicken. Lord knows, there's a world of plenty."

The children were getting cranky with hunger. The tiny ones, some in tiny white robes, some in coveralls, looked for their mommies among the aproned women in the serving line, dashed from table to table, and chased each other squealing and mewling through the line of men.

The older children gathered at the start of the line. The bolder of them, when there seemed to be an opening, grabbed cardboard plates from the stack and stood at the end of the line. "Stop that!" said a blue-haired woman, as if correcting a naughty puppy. "You know better than that. Wait until the men are served."

"Paul!" A man at the end of the line called into the clump of adolescents.

The clump parted and yielded Paul, a strawberry-blond boy of fifteen, bare-chested and sunburned.

"Come on, Paul, and get in line. You did a man's work today."

Paul hung his head and blushed through the sunburn. Behind him, his best friend shoved him forward. Paul stumbled.

"Paul, did you hear me, son? Come on and get in line."

Paul came to join the line, moving slowly, pulling his T-shirt on and leaving the boys behind.

EIGHTEEN

A T last, in the clearing on Caney rise called the parade
ground, no one could be found to absorb another
morsel from the bowls, platters, and pans on the
shaky card tables. Men and boys hugged their bellies,
belched in concert, and said, "Well, cousin, I believe I've
hurt myself this time for sure." The women returned to
the serving line with an undertaker's frame of mind: to put
the best appearance on the remains.

On excuses, which Ann McCain saw through clearly
without sparkledy glasses, the wives contrived to humiliate
her by sending her home with stacks of sliced roast beef and

ham. She had noticed that some of the women who had piled their plates with pie and potatoes had avoided her chicken on the plea of watching their diets.

Ann was bitter about her poverty. She was bitter that they knew. She was bitter that a simple, honest life had reduced her to being the object of charity.

She objected. "You know I live alone. I don't know what I will do with all of this." But she did not object too strongly. She did know what she would do with all the leftovers. She would live on them for the rest of the month.

She wrapped the offerings and her chicken in once-used foil and stacked the glistering argentine bundles on her pan. She carried the pan to her old Chevy in the parking lot. She laid the pan on the frayed, tobacco-smelling upholstery of the backseat of her late husband's last car.

He had wanted to buy one more car, one more car he could really take care of once the kids were grown and gone. He had never quite managed it, though he fancied himself a horse trader and spent many of his last Saturdays at the car lots. Ann, while she wished he had gotten his wish, felt at ease with the old boy-worn Chevy, which was free of modern conveniences she thought she might not understand.

As she locked the Chevy again and rechecked the doors, Ann noticed men in white robes unloading boxes from an old-fashioned pickup. Her eyes were not so bad as she sometimes made out. It was whiskey.

Ann did not approve. Ann did not much approve of the men's drinking beer with supper. If their wives said nothing, it was not Ann's place to object. But drink was only part of what Ann did not approve of. There was a time—and this Ann would say whenever she gained a sympathetic ear—there was a time when the Klavern was for all the family. First there was the picnic, then the speakers, and then the one big ceremony, only one cross illumination. In those days, full of the inspiration of the fiery cross, everyone went home, husbands with their wives, fathers with their children.

Ann did not like the new way of doing things.

The Klavern was running late. The children's cross was supposed to have been illuminated at sundown. It was fully dark before the last of the dishes and the food was removed and the cars packed with the folding tables, blankets, lawn chairs, balls and bats, and empty ice chests. Then it took nearly an hour to robe the teenagers and those of the little bitties who had not been playing in their robes, to assemble everyone, to fire the generator, and to adjust the public-address system. By the time all was in place for the children's ceremony, it was after ten o'clock.

The four-eyed ingenue who had won the essay contest declared that she could not read by flashlight. And she had not quite committed the essay to memory. She insisted she could not recite under the present conditions.

"Do you want to be grounded for the rest of your natural life?" Her mother attempted to reason with her.

"No, Mother. Please. I can't," Melissa Marie Bissonet whined. Melissa Marie thought that if she could not read her essay, perhaps Poor Ginger Taylor, the runnerup, would be called upon.

"You are doing this on purpose, aren't you? You wait until we are here, with all of my friends watching. Then you pull this damned-fool stunt."

"I'm not doing it on purpose. I can't. I can't stand up there with a flashlight. I can't read it."

"And these men. Do you realize that your father does business with these men? What do think this will do to his business. Do you think money grows on trees?"

"Please. I can't. I just can't."

"I can read it perfectly well. I don't see why you can't. Don't you remember it at all?"

"Some."

"I begged you to memorize it, didn't I?"

"I tried. I tried and tried. I just get some of it mixed up."

"What if I prompt you?"

"What's that?"

"I'll read along since I can see it perfectly well with the flashlight. If you get stuck I'll whisper the next couple of words."

"Oh no. People will see. People will hear. I'd be embarrassed."

"You'd be embarrassed! You'd be embarrassed!" Mrs. John A. Bissonet cradled her face in her hands and shuddered.

"Oh God, Mother. Don't start crying. I'll do anything, anything. I just can't read it."

Mrs. John A. Bissonet sighed deeply and looked up. "Well, how about if I get behind your robe on my hands and knees? On my hands and knees with my arthritis, where none of your trashy friends can see me, sos you won't be embarrassed. Then do you think maybe, just maybe, you could manage to give one piddling little speech in order to save our standing in this community and your father's business, which he has slaved over all these years to build up so that you can have nice clothes and a decent car to drive and prospects of marrying a man besides that human garbage you insist on going out with?"

Melissa Marie appeared to be giving it serious consideration.

So it was that while Brother Earl made his introductory remarks, Melissa Marie stood directly behind him. When he moved aside, Melissa Marie stepped forward, her mother scurrying cockroach-style under the cover of Melissa Marie's white robe. Melissa Marie smiled graciously at Brother Earl as he twisted the microphone stand one way and then the other so that the microphone was level with her chin.

" 'Our White Heritage,' by Melissa Marie Bissonet," the girl began. "What our white heritage means to me is an America strong and free. . . ."

That was all Melissa Marie could recall. She was mortified. Worse, she knew why she was mortified. God was punishing her for letting her mother help write the essay. Melissa Marie knew that Poor Ginger Taylor should have won.

"A family America . . ." her mother hissed.

"What our white heritage means to me is an America strong and free. A family America . . ."

"Based on God's plan . . ."

"What our white heritage means to me is an America strong and free. A family America, based on God's plan of one woman and one man united in sacred matrimony. . . ." Melissa Marie began to sob audibly.

"You little ninny! I'm going to slap you silly the minute we get home," Melissa Marie's robe snarled. "A family America, bulwark against . . ."

Of course Poor Ginger Taylor should have won. She should have won because she wrote her own essay. She should have won because she had to wear funny clothes that people were not supposed to laugh at because she was always called Poor Ginger Taylor because her father had never seen her and was an MIA and probably dead but you were not supposed to say that and because her mother was too palsied to sew properly.

"What our white heritage means to me is an America strong and free. A family America, based on God's plan of one woman and one man united in sacred matrimony. A family America, bulwark against the chaos of heathen perversion and red communism—"

Melissa Marie threw up on the microphone.

It was a world of plenty she brought up. Plenty to soak the bunting. Plenty to pool up on the rostrum. Plenty to wash ominously toward the edge of the platform so that the first row of listeners backed away a bit and then backed away quite a bit more. Plenty to drench Melissa Marie's robe so that her mother stood up suddenly. Plenty of vomit to slick the rostrum over so there was no footing and Melissa Marie and her mother slipped and, clawing at each other, went down in the ocean of it.

Naturally, Rufus Thoraksen took it personally.

Clearly, the condition of the microphone and the rostrum made it impractical for Rufus to be introduced to the rally. They all knew him anyway. But since he would not be introduced, they would not learn the reason that Rufus had been afforded the singular honor of illuminating the children's cross. They would not get to hear his modest, laconic remarks on the occasion, denying that he had done anything special, displaying heroic embarrassment at being singled out.

It was like something Melissa Marie would do on purpose, except that she would never do anything so embarrassing to herself.

In any event, the hours he spent practicing to cast his voice into its lowest register, the paring of his remarks, and the rehearsing at the mirror of the bashful shake of his head with the little, almost imperceptible chivalrous bow—all of it wasted.

If that was wasted, then wasted too was the denouncement of the pervert boy Robin and the nasty auto-da-fé at juvenile court. All wasted and washed away by Melissa Marie's dinner.

"Git it lit, or Ah'll do it mahself," Peter Bullock ordered.

So Rufus reluctantly fired the children's cross without his introduction, without the proper ceremony, and without the proper reverent attitude.

The little cross burned for a long time—long enough to remove the visible remains of Melissa Marie Bissonet's award-winning essay. But the soprano declared the smell too overpowering, and she declined to approach the microphone to lead the singing of "Our White Knights of Christian Virtue." No volunteer could be found to attempt the melody a cappella.

No one then was sure when the ceremony of the children's cross was over. The little ones hardly had to be encouraged to be properly impressed as they gazed open-mouthed at the fiery symbol. But a few of the older boys cast covetous eyes at the huge, unlit cross, the one being saved for the real ceremony, the men's ceremony. The lesson seemed quite clear: In cross burning, as in all things, the men keep the good stuff to themselves.

As the last flame on the little cross flickered out, some of the women began to move about with flashlights. Others, waiting for the anthem, stood quietly, trying to maintain the proper reverence among their children and the children nearby. At last a hooded man fumbled in the darkness with the microphone switch and announced much more loudly than he had intended because the amplifier was still set for Melissa Marie's demure voice, "Go. The ceremony is over."

"Go. The ceremony is over," echoed from the low places around Caney rise.

The small groups began to sort themselves out around

the flashlights. Most groups were of two women and their respective children, doubled up for the ride home in order to leave half the vehicles for the men. The littlest children were overly tired and cranky. The older ones were overly excited and boisterous. The cars were cramped and the pairs of women in the front seats sat silently, watching for cars they were supposed to follow or the ones supposed to follow them. Not a few of the women, already weary, with a night ahead of unloading the car, trying to get the children into bed, doing the dishes, and then waiting, waiting perhaps until dawn—not a few wondered if Ann McCain were not right: The old way of doing things had been better.

Near to midnight the last of the taillights of the manless caravan left the crushed-shell parking lot and shrank far down the curveless blacktop.

For a moment there was silence.

The sliding bay door of the panel truck shrieked. Phil awoke with a start from the dream his mind had started when the voice boomed "Go. The ceremony is over." Two white, cone-shaped creatures stood at the bay door.

"On your feet," one of them commanded in a muffled voice.

Though there was only the moonlight, the glowing embers of the children's cross, and the flicker of the kerosene lanterns hung from widely spaced branches around the parade grounds, Phil blinked in the camera darkness of the van and nudged Jim. "Wake up. Wherever it is, I think we are here."

"Come on. We haven't got all night," said one of the Klansmen, perhaps the one who had spoken before. He grasped the chain that connected Jim's leg irons to Phil's and hauled Jim and Phil to the bay door.

Jim stumbled as the Klansman tried to stand him up, not

so much on account of the leg irons as because his foot was asleep. The Klansman leaned Jim against the van, and after some debate among the hooded men a ring of keys was produced. One after another of the keys was tried until at last the leg irons were removed. Then the Klansman stood Jim up.

Jim and Phil, still doubly handcuffed together, were led crabwise a few feet to a nine-foot, creosoted stake, and after much jingling and fumbling and dropping of the keyring one of the handcuffs was opened for a moment and then relocked. There they were, Phil and Jim, the homosexuals to be confronted, back to back against the stake and much too near, Jim thought, to the huge cross, padded with burlap and smelling distinctly of petroleum.

But just then no one was confronting the homosexuals on the parade ground on Caney rise. The two Klansmen closed the bay door of the panel van and drove away. Jim and Phil were left to wonder and to listen to the shouts and laughter as the Klan confronted, at initiation campfires in little clearings around the parade ground, twenty cases nearly of Middle Passage Bourbon.

A long time passed, or so it seemed.

"So this is a Klavern," Jim said. "I thought somehow that it would be very different."

"Obviously this is much before curtain time," Phil answered.

"What do you think they are doing?"

"Getting stoked up, it sounds like to me."

A breeze was coming from the rostrum. Jim sniffed. "Smells like some of them have been overstoked already."

Phil turned his head as far as he was able and inhaled. "Oh, ick. Smells like . . ."

"Exactly." Jim had been looking at the towering cross. "They are going to burn us, aren't they?"

"I don't think so."

"Then you think they'll let us go?"

"Of course not. They'll kill us later."

"Oh wonderful."

"We would have been all right if only Earl hadn't had a connection in the post office." Phil sighed. "I thought when I got the photographs in the mailbox that we were home free."

"But now we're dead meat."

"Sure looks that way. But this will really get Agnes pissed when she finds out about it. I'm sure she'll find a way to get Earl. She's got to. That's the important thing."

"The important thing is that we will be dead."

"Oh Jim, don't you see? We're just two little people in a world gone mad. We don't really matter. What counts is that sooner or later people will see the real nature of people like Brother Earl and everything he represents. And when they do they'll get together and wash away all the bigotry and corruption and hatred. One day the little gay children will frolic on the playgrounds of the world with the little straight children, and they will never know that once they were supposed to hate each other. One day people will be judged not by the gender of their bedmates but by the content of their character, and a 'faggot' will once again be just a stick of wood."

"Oh Phil, you're such a dreamer."

"Yes. I have a dream."

"If only we had met in a different time and place. If only I had met you before . . . you know, before you met Agnes, before you started working for her or whatever you call it, before—"

"Oh Jim, I think you still have the wrong idea about Agnes and me."

"No. Don't explain. I know about these things. And

most of all, it really doesn't matter anymore."

"It does matter—"

Phil was interrupted by a loud bass voice from a distance.

> *O there will never be a faggot KKK!*
> *There will never be a faggot KKK!*
> *Floral designs they may toss,*
> *But they won't light the fiery cross!*
> *'Cause there'll never be a faggot KKK!*

Other voices, rather haphazardly, joined the bass as the chorus was repeated twice more. Evidently no one could remember the verse, or the verse had not been composed yet. The choruses were separated by strings of dum-de-dums. No doubt that the voices were coming nearer.

"Brace yourself," Jim whispered, "here they come."

Four of them stumbled out of the bushes behind the great burlap-wrapped cross. One was very tall and heavy-set. One was extremely short. The other two were average sized, so far as Jim could tell for the white robes ballooning in the breeze. Each of the men brandished at least one open bottle of Middle Passage Bourbon.

"Hot damn! There they are." One of the men pointed at Jim.

"Well I'll be!" exclaimed the big one.

"Yup, queer as they come, I hear."

The men came closer.

"Wow! You know, I seen em on TV from San Francisco, but I never thought I'd get to see one up close."

"Which one is the man?"

"How the hell am I supposed to know? Aw hell, ain't either of them men. They're both faggots."

"I mean which of them plays the man?"

"That's it. How the hell do any of em ever figure it out?"

The short Klansman had walked around to Phil's side of the stake. "This one's bound to be the girl."

"Oh?" said the big one. "How can you tell?"

"See? He's real narrow at the waist. And about hairless. But mostly, look at those hands. See the fingers? Whatya-callit, artistic hands."

The big one stepped closer to Phil and lifted Phil's hand as far as it would go in the handcuffs. "Yep, now I see what you mean."

"O gawd, don't touch em." The little Klansman turned his head away in disgust.

"Yeah. Oh well, no harm done. I'm wearing gloves."

"I'd burn em if I was you."

The parade ground was beginning to fill again as clumps of white-robed men came from the surrounding bushes. Most of the men had bottles.

"Then this one must be the one that's supposed to be the boy," one of the averaged-sized Klansmen said from Jim's side of the pole.

"Yeah," said another, "and that bothers me. Do you think we could tell if we didn't know?"

"Sure we could. I guess. If we saw him walk."

"Yeah."

A sharp bang drew the Klansmen's attention. Someone was trying to start the generator again. The generator rumbled and stopped. "Son of a bitch!"

In a moment, with a whirr and a sputter, the generator turned over again, backfired, rolled over a few times slowly as if it would die again, but it did not. The hum of the amplifier rose again and the feedback whine pierced the darkness.

"Hey, we better get around there. Looks like it's time," the big Klansman said.

The four exchanged swigs of bourbon from each other's

bottles and stumbled around the rostrum, leaving Jim and Phil alone.

"All right everybody, let's assemble on the parade grounds and get this thing going." It was Brother Earl's voice and the click of the microphone being turned off.

"Jim," Phil whispered.

"What?"

"I've got the keys."

"Why didn't you say so before?"

"I didn't have them before. One of them passed them to me just now."

"Then let's get out of here."

"It's the whole ring. It will take a while to find the right one."

"It's a little short, simple one."

"I know. There's four or five like that. But first . . ."

"First what?" Jim asked aloud.

"Sh! First, we've got not to run off the second we are loose."

"What do you mean? That's the idea, isn't it?"

"Yes. But we are surrounded and we don't know which way to run. We don't even know where we are."

"Then when do we get out of here?"

"I don't know. Give me some slack on your left side. No, I mean your right side." Phil got one of the keys into the keyhole of the handcuffs. The key would not turn. "I think we will know when the time is right."

"How?"

"I don't know. We'll know at the time."

The microphone clicked on. "Can't you guys do better than that? Come on, straighten up those rows. . . ." It was a block of wobbly ranks and staggered files that Brother Earl surveyed on the parade grounds of Caney rise. "I'm not going to give my address until there is better order. You!

You stand that man up or get him off the parade grounds."
Brother Earl shook his head. *Modern times,* he thought. *I bet they didn't put up with shit like this at Nuremberg.*

At last Brother Earl saw that the Klavern was in as good an order as it was going to be in. Indeed, it was in danger of degenerating. He chose to overlook the occasional upturned bottle stuck in the mouthhole of a white hood.

"Brethren . . ." Brother Earl began.

"I've got it," Phil whispered to Jim. "Now remember, don't break loose until the right time. I'll hold the cuffs together so it looks like we are still caught."

"Fellow White Knights of the Fiery Cross, honored guests from the Knights of the White Camelia, tonight I speak to you of the danger which is as great as any we have faced in our role as the protectors of the white race.

"You know that tonight we are called to confront the homosexuals. You know that homosexuality is an abomination in the eyes of God. You abhor homosexuals as I do and the damage to our social fabric they do by their very existence."

A little orange light flickered behind Brother Earl.

"But you may wonder, why now? What is the pressing need to concentrate our moral vigor to eradicate homosexuals and homosexuality from our society at just this time?

"Shouldn't we first do something about the way the colored races continue to pervert the natural order, setting up niggers in positions of authority over white men? Shouldn't we deal with first things first?

"Yes. Of course we should. But I tell you, homosexuality is the most dangerous tactic now being used by the colored races in their campaign to rule the world. What is homosexuality but race suicide? I ask you."

The orange light behind Brother Earl grew brighter.

"That is why niggers and the niggers' agents have infil-

246

trated our public college campuses to draw our young people in, to trap students in a foreign way of life, to spread the disease of faggotry—"

A flare of orange light stopped Brother Earl. He turned around. The great cross was alight. Flames raced up the gasoline-soaked rags to the top of the thirty-foot pole and spread out on the arms of the cross.

"What the hell? Not yet. Not yet!" Brother Earl's voice bellowed through the amplifier, roared out of the speakers and echoed from the low places. Just as the flames billowed in full flower, the flaming symbol rocked with a groan, righted itself for a long moment, and slowly, slowly began to arc down toward Brother Earl and the assembled Klan. "Jesus Fucking Christ!"

White robes scrambled out of the way of the flaming fiery whomp. Flames hopped and splattered over the parade grounds.

"Wow!" said Jim.

"This must be it!" Phil yelled. He opened his fists so that the handcuffs dropped to the ground. He turned to shake the awestruck Jim back to his senses, but Phil found his nose buried in the white rayon robe of an enormous hooded person.

"You okay, hon?" the huge figure asked. "Then follow us. The carriage awaits."

"What?" asked Jim.

"It's Agnes," Phil answered.

"Yes," Agnes said. "Jim, you drive." Agnes pressed the Ford's keys into Jim's palm until by reflex he closed his fingers around them.

"Good. Come on now." Agnes pulled the boys into the shadows of the trees and shrubs.

Agnes seemed to glide through the thicket, pausing only to wait when Jim got caught in one of the creepers or stumbled over a root. "Hurry. Watch your footing," she urged. "It won't be long until they figure out what has happened."

Several minutes later Agnes stepped out of a bush and onto the crushed shell of the parking lot. "Goodness, where did we park now?"

"No, not again, Agnes," Phil whined.

"Don't say it that way. We will only get more rattled."

"What is it?" Jim asked.

"Agnes has forgotten where she parked. It always happens."

"We know it was around here someplace. It's a pickup."

Jim looked around the parking lot. "Agnes, they are all pickups!"

"No. Only most of them. It's a black '49 Ford."

"Then that must be it." Jim pointed.

"Why yes, child!" Agnes squinted in the direction Jim indicated. "We believe you are right."

Jim ran ahead. Phil had only to walk briskly to keep up with Agnes. By the time they'd reached the venerable Ford, Jim was seated in the cab. "Well, start it!" said Agnes as she scurried around the hood to the passenger door. Phil got in first to pull Agnes in. Agnes carefully scooped up her robe so that it would not get caught and slammed the door.

The three of them sat in the cab.

"Why don't you start it?" Agnes asked.

Jim twisted the key to show her. "It's dead."

"Dead! Why that can't be."

"But it is," Jim said. "Dead as a doornail. It won't even turn over."

"The starter," Phil said, "you know you have to use the starter."

"Starter?"

"It's a button. See there?"

248

Jim pushed the button. The engine of the venerable pickup turned over and started.

Jim had seen the lights for a long time, just little specks, far behind the venerable Ford. He looked at his watch. He did not know when first light was on an Oklahoma September morning, but he thought it could not be long. Jim pressed his foot against the accelerator until he was certain he had gotten all out of the pickup that it could give.

Still the lights behind got bigger and brighter.

"I think they are following us," Jim said.

"Huh?" said Phil, who had been mesmerized by the miles and miles of direct blacktop highway and deep gray, featureless countryside.

"He said, they are following us," Agnes said. "We've been watching in this mirror and we think so too."

"It could be someone else," Phil said in a manner full of hope.

"It could be someone else, but we don't think so. We take it, Jim, that you are getting everything out of this old thing that you can?"

"Of course. How long until dawn?"

"Until sunrise we don't know, but the east has been getting lighter for at least twenty minutes."

"Are you sure?"

"Of course we're sure. You just keep your eyes on the road."

The lights grew larger and brighter.

"Agnes, look in your mirror," Jim said. "Aren't those cab lights?"

"You're right. It's another pickup. One with all the trimmings."

"Whose would it be?"

"In Oklahoma it could be anyone's. But yes, Earl has one with running lights. They are catching up."

In Agnes's mirror, a snake-tongue of flame forked out of the cluster of pursuing lights. "Duck!" Agnes shrieked.

The first ping came from the roof of the venerable Ford's cab. The little pops came from behind. Jim slid down in the driver's place as far as he could.

"Phil! Under the seat. Hand us the plastic box."

Wedged between Agnes and Jim, Phil had to burrow to get a hand under the seat. "I don't find it."

"More over to the driver's side. Hand it to us."

"Ouch!"

"Did they hit you?" Agnes asked.

"No. Something under the seat bit my hand."

"Nonsense. The box has only come open. They've got sharp points. There are about a dozen of them. Carefully get me a handful."

"What?" asked Phil. "What are these?"

"They are jacks. Except they have very sharp points."

More pops came from behind them. The Ford pinged from tailgate to cab.

"Jacks?"

"Yes, jacks. You know, onesies, twosies, threesies."

"Oh. *Jacks.* Here. Hold out your hand. Here are four of them."

"Yes. Good. Look for the rest." Agnes sat up suddenly, thrust her arm out the window, and threw the jacks as nearly as she could directly up.

More pings from the tailgate.

Agnes ducked again.

"I've found five more."

"Good. We're not sure if the jacks failed to clear our truck or whether they are shooting lower."

"Going for our tires?" Phil asked, gingerly dropping the jacks in Agnes's open palm.

The old pickup boomed and screeched. Jim knew what it was; he felt the explosion of the tire through the steering wheel. He braced himself and struggled with the wheel. The venerable Ford stayed on the road.

"They've got us now," Phil said. He turned to peek out the rear window of the cab. The headlights seemed to gain speed as they drew nearer and nearer. "This is it."

Suddenly the headlights veered sharply to the right. In a moment came the thudding shockwave. The road behind the Ford was empty.

"What was that?" Jim shouted.

"Jacks," Agnes said demurely.

NINETEEN

BLACK rubber fell in the wake of the imperial pickup and lay on the Oklahoma highway like a flattened, vaguely reptilian creature. The ka-thudding of the right rear tire gave way to a rusty rasp.

"Agnes, this won't do at all." Jim's death grip on the steering wheel carried the violent vibrations up his arms and into his chest.

"How much farther can we go?" Agnes asked.

"A few miles, maybe. But the farther we go, the less likely we'll be able to fit the spare. It will bend the rim or something. I guess. Hell, I don't know."

"Then as long as we are beating a walking pace, let's put as much distance between us and that rifle as we can." Agnes watched the wreck behind them in her side mirror. Smoke rose from the ditch. She could not tell whether anyone got out.

Agnes twisted in her seat and squeezed her head and shoulders through the window. Treading on a bag of egg salad sandwiches next to Phil on the seat, she achieved a perch in the window of the pickup. From this vantage Agnes thought she saw a bit of orange flame on the pursuer's truck before it disappeared below the horizon. Then a horrible thought occurred to her.

"Phil, hand us up our bumbershoot," she shouted. In a while Phil found the umbrella and placed it in Agnes's free hand. With some difficulty, she extracted it from the cab. Leaning further back than she thought elegant or safe, Agnes probed the spare tire with the tip of the umbrella.

Agnes squirmed back into her seat in the cab. She bucked back to adjust the drape of the white robe, lowered the visor to use the mirror, and repaired her coiffure. "Gentlemen, we have some unfortunate news."

"Agnes." Jim's voice quavered as the shaking of the steering column vibrated his body. "What at this point qualifies as unfortunate news?"

"Gentlemen, it is our sad duty to inform you that our spare tire has joined its ancestors."

Phil laid his forehead against Jim's shaking shoulder. Without thinking, Jim turned from the road for a moment and kissed a silky curl.

"You mean they shot it out too?" Jim asked.

"That, or it was flat to begin with. In any event, there is no pump."

"I see." Jim scanned the flat, direct, southbound road ahead. "How far are we from a town or a crossroads or anything?"

"We really could not say. Provincial geography is not our strong suit."

"Damn it, Agnes. I don't suppose you have such a thing as a map?"

Agnes gasped. She had seldom heard that tone from a man and not at all for many years. She opened the glove box and began shuffling through it, giving a flustered account of her findings: "Let's see . . . tissues . . . San Antonio-Austin map . . . Twits . . . Eastern United States . . . I'm getting warmer. . . . Yes, here we are. Oklahoma-Texas."

A jolt bumped Agnes's head against the roof of the cab. A fin of sparks arced from the tail of the pickup. Jim turned off the ignition. They sat quietly and still in the Oklahoma morning.

"What is it?" Agnes asked.

"Mechanics is not *my* long suit," Jim mocked, "but I'd say it was the axle or something equally irreparable." Jim jumped from the cab and began kicking the pickup in every vulnerable-looking spot.

"Jim!" Phil yelled. Agnes touched Phil's arm and shook her head. Phil supposed for once that Agnes was right. They sat in the cab. As time passed, Jim found fewer and fewer vulnerable spots. Finally he sat down on the running board and panted for breath.

Agnes and Phil got out and spread the map against the hood. The southern breeze pinned the map and carried a deep, distant droning rumble.

Seeing that Jim was exhausted, Agnes ventured: "That's the trouble with maps. They are really quite useless unless you know where you are to begin with."

"Let's see that." Jim got up.

Agnes stood aside.

"Any idea at all?" Jim asked.

A curved nail traced an inch-long path on the map. "We are probably somewhere on this long, bleak stretch. But whether we are closer to one end or the other, who knows?"

Agnes stepped back from the map and peeled off her Klan robe. "White is simply not our color," she mumbled to herself and tossed the robe into the cab. Then, unconsciously absorbing a sound like distant thunder, she picked up the umbrella. She arranged the bow of her iridescent green polyester blouse.

"Anybody remember seeing a distance marker?" Jim looked hopefully at Phil. Phil shook his head. "That's about the old ballgame, isn't it? He's got the pictures. It's only a matter of time until they catch up with us. The highway patrol is as likely to be in Brother Earl's pocket as not. Right?"

"We are afraid so," Agnes admitted. "But there is something . . ."

"Yes, go on."

"He could be after us out of spite. He's not known for being especially magnanimous in victory. But what if . . . what if he doesn't have the photos? If he thinks we've got them, that is almost as good as our having them. Better, in a way. Because if he only thinks we have them, and we don't, then he can't find them even if he gets us."

"That's right," said Phil, "if I followed it all."

Jim thought for a moment. "He's not playing like he has all the cards, is he? Even in Oklahoma, shooting us on the highway would be taking a big chance if he had already won. Okay, let's not let on that we don't have the pictures. It may buy us time once they catch up with us. I don't see what good it will do in the long run, but it can't hurt." Jim looked up. "What is that noise, anyway?"

The background drone had become a roar. Somewhere,

from the south, something was coming. Far down the road, above the vanishing point, rose a pillar of dust and smoke, pink on the left in the rising sun.

"A cyclone!" Phil shouted.

"Nonsense, child, the sky is blue." Then Agnes noticed that she was still carrying the umbrella in her hand. She cast it away. She strained at the southern horizon. "Get up on the truck, Phil. Our eyes aren't what they used to be—and never were."

Phil boosted himself onto the hood of the truck and, using Jim's head as a stepping-stone, arrived on the crest of the cab. "Well?" Agnes inquired, even before Phil had found his footing.

"I can't make out anything, but it's sure getting louder."

Agnes rummaged under the seat in the cab. "Here, here is a dime-store glass. See if it helps." Agnes handed the toy to Phil.

Phil held the PeeWee Pirate glass to his eye. "Yes, there's something, but I can't make it out. Everything's shaking."

"Well, check the rear first," Agnes directed. "Let's not forget what we're about."

Phil surveyed the north. "Can't be sure. Looks like two of them are walking this way."

"Shall we make a run for it?" Jim asked.

"They are still real far away and not moving fast," Phil reported.

"Try the south again," Agnes urged.

Phil turned to the south again and lay on the roof of the cab, propping the glass with both hands. "Two flags."

"Flags?" Jim asked.

"That's what it looks like. One's green. No . . . yes . . . Dad, it's the Jade Ensign!"

"Dad?" asked Jim.

"The Jade Ensign!" shouted Agnes. "Quick! What's the other?"

"I don't know it. A kind of purple triangle."

"Dad?" Jim asked.

"Of course! Not purple—lavender. A lavender triangle. Child, it's the Hell's Fairies! We're saved! We're saved!"

"Dad, break off the aerial and give me your bow."

Agnes tied the end of her green bow to the whip of the aerial and handed it to Phil. Phil stood on the roof of the cab and waved the aerial in a great figure eight.

At the head of the double column of bikes, Chief stood over the saddle of Mama Hog. He thought he'd caught a glimmer of jade far ahead in the early sunlight. He shook his head and stood for a moment more to relieve the soreness of a night in the saddle. Maybe Ellenor was being hysterical. Probably nothing was wrong at all. Yet the urgent despair of Ellenor's call had convinced him to come. At least he could calm her down a bit.

As he was about to lower himself back onto the engine of Mama Hog, the glimmer was there again. He goosed his throttle, and Mama Hog pulled ahead of the deafening thunder of the forty other bikes. Soon he picked out the shape of Agnes's old pickup, a ribbon of green waving above it.

Chief looked over his right shoulder at the lavender flag that flew from the eight-foot sissy bar of Beast's bike. He knew the jade banner was beside it on Mad Dog's bike. He raised his left hand and let it fall. Throttles spun in the column behind him. Mama Hog and her forty sisters flew up the highway toward the imperial person.

Phil saw Chief's hand signal. "They've seen us!" Phil handed Agnes the aerial. Agnes rescued her bow and began trying to restore it to her outfit. Phil slid off the roof of the cab and onto Jim's shoulders. While Jim stared dumbly to the south, Phil climbed down his body.

"Phil, help us with the bow. It won't lay right." Agnes snagged a nail on a loose thread. "Damn. Where is that hairbrush? Phil, are you listening to us?" Agnes looked up. "Oh. We see. Never mind."

Jim cradled the snow-blond head in his hands. Phil looked up at him.

"You called Agnes 'Dad.' "

Roses shone in Phil's cheeks. His pink lips barely parted. The Athenean eyes grew deep. "Yes, that's right."

"You are Agnes's son?"

The smiling muscle at the left corner of Phil's mouth twitched. "Yes. I think you've got it."

"But I thought . . . you're not . . ."

"You thought I was Agnes's little sexpot."

"No . . . well, yes, something like that."

"Nonsense. I'm not even her type."

"But you're blond."

"Mother was a blonde. And you can see that Agnes is real light. Bright. High yellow. Café au lait. However you say it."

"You call her 'her' so easily."

"Agnes stayed pretty much in the background—I mean, I knew who he was and all. But Agnes didn't want, you know, to influence me unduly. They had some funny ideas back then. But once it was clear I was going to turn out all right, she started letting me hang around court."

"Still, didn't you think you were sort of obliged to follow a destiny?"

"Jim, did you *look* at the photographs?"

"Yes."

"They were lovers."

"My father and Brother Earl?"

258

"No, silly. Your father and Agnes. That's how Agnes got around the South: They pretended she was your father's driver."

"Oh."

"Now, what about destiny?"

Jim looked south, down the highway at Mama Hog rushing toward them. He could see the grin on Chief's face, the double column advancing, and the red morning sun on the jade banner. Jim's hand rested on Phil's loin. He looked back into the gray eyes. He thought that Ganymede in his flower was not so sweet.

"I guess," Jim said, "I don't need to know anything more about destiny."

Mama Hog threw herself into a skidding stop in front of Agnes, kicking up a shower of loose gravel. A pebble bounced and rolled up to the toe of Agnes's red, snakeskin boot. Agnes's regal bearing was unperturbed.

"Agnes, gal," Chief grinned broadly, "what kind of trouble are you into now?"

"There seem to be a couple of men back yonder." Agnes nodded to the north. "They had at least one rifle. Oh, and there may be a few of our little jacks in the road."

Chief hauled Mama Hog onto her stand. "Okay. I'll get Rabbit and Jake to look into that." Chief pulled off his right glove and held three fingers in the air. The third rank of the double column peeled out and headed for Mama Hog.

"Watch this column turn, Agnes. They've been working on it." Chief waved his arm in a circle over his head.

The column slowed as the bikes approached the pickup. Mad Dog dipped the jade standard as he came abreast of Agnes. The turn was a model of precision, except for Beast's laying his bike down and skidding into the ditch. Chief paused in instructing Rabbit and Jake. He winced.

"The poor thing," Agnes said. "Aren't you going to help him?"

"Beast is all right." Chief turned back to Rabbit. "Watch out for Agnes's little tank traps. Got it?" Rabbit nodded. "Okay, boys, go get em."

Rabbit and Jake hopped on their bikes and headed north, around the waiting column.

"Now what, Agnes?"

"We haven't accomplished our mission. But we best put Oklahoma behind us for now."

"What do you want to do with the truck?"

Agnes looked at the truck and shook her head. "It's a shame. A classic, you know. But right now it's expendable. We had better ditch it."

"Beast! Front and center!" Chief hollered. "Beast is going to love this."

"After what the poor man's been through? Really, you ought to be more sensitive to the condition of your troops."

"Agnes, I said that Beast is all right."

Beast presented himself. He was almost as tall as Agnes. The matted mass of his black hair joined the matted mass of his black beard in a great fuzzy ball.

"Poor thing. Did you hurt yourself?" Agnes asked.

"Gee, heh-heh, I guess I did some." Beast held up his left forearm, which appeared to be spread with raspberry jam. "Haw, pretty good, huh, Chief?" Beast giggled.

"I told you so," Chief said to Agnes.

"Sorry. We should know better than to tell you your business." Agnes reached for the pearls at her throat and realized she was not wearing any.

Chief nodded. "Beast, put the truck in the ditch."

"Put the truck in the ditch, Chief?"

"You heard me. Put. The truck. In the ditch."

"Gee! Wow! Heavy duty! Outtasight!"

"Beast was overly impressed by the sixties," Chief explained. "Better get them out of the way." Chief pointed to the lovers. "What's with them, anyway? They've been like that since I got here."

Agnes clasped her hands in front of her chest. "Our latest experiment in matchmaking. What do you think?"

"Very nice. Which one of them is the fem?"

"Even they don't know for sure. Times are changing, Chief. You need to try to dispose of that old-fashioned stereotypical thinking. It's politically incorrect."

"Can't help it. I'm no chicken, you know."

Agnes looked closely at Chief. He had a few more lines around the eyes. No question that he was graying at the temples. But his short frame was as tight as ever. Agnes sighed. "It's been a long time, Chief."

"Yeah. Okay, I admit I miss the old days. I liked being a perverted rebel a whole hell of a lot more than being an alternative lifestyle." He winked at Agnes. "Hey! You two! Break it up. Beast is about to do something cataclysmic to the truck."

Jim looked up vaguely.

"Agnes, the dark-haired one is the spitting image of your Tom."

"He ought to be. A chip off the old block."

"Really?" Chief almost asked what had become of Tom but thought better of it. "Okay, Beast, have at it."

"He's not going to do it by himself?"

"No, he only wishes he could."

Beast walked up to the driver's side of the cab and gave the truck a good pop. The truck rocked on its springs. "This'll be a piece of cake. Come on, guys. On three."

Beast and five other Fairies began rocking the truck. On the ninth oscillation it tipped and rolled onto its side. Beast stood back and scratched his head.

"This is rich, Agnes. Beast hasn't thought this far."

Beast shoved a tire. The truck did not even vibrate.

"Piece of cake, Beast?"

"Gee, Chief. You going to say something nasty to me again, ain't you? Go ahead. Say, Beast, you could fuck up a wet dream. Say, Beast, you ain't got the brains that God gave a screwdriver. Go on. Like water off a duck's ass. I'm used to it."

"Well, Beast, you did about top yourself this time. But I guess it's partly my fault. I saw what you were going to do and didn't stop you. Reckon the forty of us can deal with this?"

"Guess so, Chief."

"Then no harm done."

"Gee, Chief, I hate it worse when you are nice to me."

"I know."

In the business district, the Austin mail begins to move early. Gene yawned and stretched and looked for his coffee cup. Someone had thrown it away. The pot was empty. Might as well get going, anyway.

Gene decided to kill a few more minutes by rechecking the sorting of the bundles. Seventh Street seemed to be in order. He looked at Eighth Street. It was okay, except the regular bundle was broken by an odd-sized brown envelope. *Damn,* he thought, *sooner or later everyone will have to use standard envelopes, and standard envelopes only.*

He looked at the envelope. *Aha, for Agnes. Good.* He would have an excuse to ring the bell. He could say the envelope would not fit the box.

Maybe the Japanese one would come to the door again. That would be nice. *A cup of coffee. Maybe even an amaretto. Better yet, amaretto and coffee in the hot tub again.*

This route is not so bad. No dogs. And Agnes's place at the halfway mark.

At last the truck lay in the ditch. Rabbit and Jake came down the road. Chief looked around.

"Well, Agnes, can you think of any reason to delay our getaway?"

"There are the transportation arrangements." Agnes nodded toward the lovers.

"Wouldn't do to split them up, huh?"

"We think it might be impossible."

"Okay. Bobby is still mellowed out from his birthday party. I think I can prevail upon him to give up his bike. Hey! You two! You got gills or what? Either of you know how to operate a bike?"

"I guess I can manage," Jim admitted.

"That's really confidence-inspiring. I want to hear 'Yes sir, Chief.' "

"Yes sir, Chief."

"That's more like it. Okay, Rabbit, what's the deal?"

"The lady was right. Two men and a rifle."

"Well?"

"They had an accident. And their boom-boom got broke. Nasty bikers runned it over."

"And over and over," Jake put in.

"Good."

"Chief?" Agnes had been examining the line of bikers. "Chief, excuse us for asking. But that one, that one near the end of the line: Have our eyes gone at last, or is it an RG?"

"A real girl? Yes, Agnes. Meg! Come over here." Chief kicked a pebble. "I guess things are changing with us too."

"What d'ya want, Chief?"

"I want you to meet somebody." Chief turned to Agnes.

"Agnes, this is Meg—except for Bobby, the newest Fairy."

"Pleased to meet you . . . uh, sir?" Agnes glanced sidelong at Chief. Chief nodded.

"Meg, this is Her Imperial Majesty Agnes, Empress of the Jade Chimera."

Agnes extended her hand. Meg kissed it. "Honored, ma'am."

"How did that come about?" Agnes asked when Meg had gone.

"Oh, she kept hanging around. After she whupped Beast we about had to let her in. Woman can do very impressive things with a length of drive chain. Okay! Everybody mount up! Bobby, you ride with Rabbit."

Chief straddled Mama Hog and kicked her up. "Come on, Agnes. Sit those tired old buns up here." Chief slapped the seat behind him.

"You say you are tired of them?"

"No, ma'am. But when we get back to Austin, we'll see if I can make them tired of me."

"Chief, that sounds to us like an indecent proposal."

"Ain't no kind of proposal. It's a fact. Laws of Chivalry, Article III, Section d: 'Rights of Knights Regarding Damsels Successfully Rescued.' Now get your big ass up here right now, gal. Wrap your arms around me and see if you can soothe the ache I get thinking about old times."

"Keep talking like that, honey." Agnes draped a thigh over Mama Hog's saddle. She put her arms around Chief's waist. "Damn, Chief, you weren't kidding. Will it keep until we get back to Austin?"

"It will if you don't move your hands too much."

"There's nothing quite so sweet as seeing old friends again, is there?" Agnes kicked the heels of her red snakeskin boots against Mama Hog's frame. "There's no place like home. There's no place like—"

The rest was drowned in the thunder of forty-one bikes rolling south.

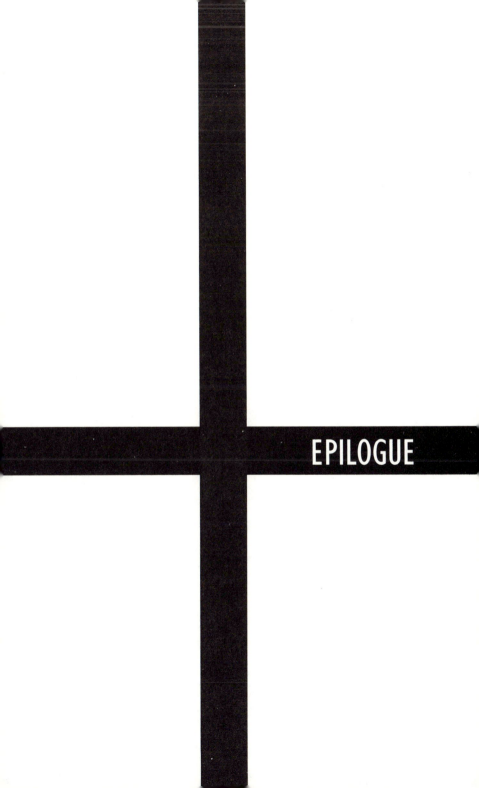

EPILOGUE

TWENTY

THE old beige Fairlane honked again. "Okay, keep your garter belt on, Myrna. I'm coming. I'm coming," yelled the Duchess of Waterloo. She knew she could not be heard. At the last moment, she remembered her handbag. But then her keys were missing. It turned out they were still in the door.

The Baroness DuBastrop continued to press the horn. No one paid much attention because the rising orange moon shone on the highest of all Austin holidays: All Hallows' Eve.

"All right, Mary. Enough is enough." Waterloo let herself into the car. Her red wig had fallen a little over one ear, her left cheek was angry with a leprous affection, her right with a complementary adjustment of rouge.

"Well we're late already," Bastrop said. "I certainly hope we will be late enough."

"An hour by the time we get there. But take it slow."

"Have you got our invitations? You know her house-boys are always so snotty."

"Right here in my handbag." Waterloo peeked to be certain.

"Well"—Bastrop took her eyes from the road for a moment—"what do you think?"

"Think? What is one to think? Installing a mere boy as heir to the Jade Throne, ending the queenly tradition, inviting all the riffraff bikers in the state to the Halloween cotillion. Think? I think she's finally flipped her very cheap and tacky wig."

"You have to give her credit, though. She shut up Brother Earl in a big way."

"If it had been me, and it certainly should have been, he never would have gotten out of control in the first place."

"No doubt."

Waterloo turned around suddenly in her seat. She turned back. "My dear, I could be mistaken. But I would swear there is a gorilla in an MG following us."

"Oh yes, you are quite correct. Strange, he's been following me for days. Well, not *that* strange. The MG has been following me. But this is the first time there's been a gorilla in it."

"Whatever do you suppose the reason is?" Waterloo opened her compact in order to study the situation better.

"Don't bother. This one will never live to be as old as he looks. Really, I can't imagine that he thinks he has a chance with me."

270

There is no accounting for taste, Waterloo thought.

Mae West and W. C. Fields waved from a passing car. His nose lit up red. Bastrop honked and waved back. Presently the Fairlane found the Seventh Street exit. The blue MG followed. Bastrop looked around at the stoplight by the police station.

"Where are we going to park the chariot?" Waterloo asked.

"I thought we would put it under the highway there. And then we can walk. These days we won't have any problems on the streets. Remember when come Halloween we would be the strangest thing you could see all night?"

Yes, dear, Waterloo thought, *and that's still what they say about you in the bars any night.*

The gorilla did not follow them into the parking lot under the highway but drove the MG around the block. Bastrop parked the Fairlane. They got out. As they approached Agnes's townhouse, they encountered the heavy cable of television trucks. Police were trying to form a line in front of Agnes's door.

"No," Bastrop said, "I think we better go to the VIP door off the alley. We have invitations, after all."

The gorilla was following them from a discreet distance.

"But what is all of that going on around Agnes's door?"

"I imagine it's the demonstration. The Caucus has been threatening for months. They even sent a silly pair of clones to ask me to denounce the cotillion. They know there's no love lost between me and Agnes. But denounce the cotillion? How naive of them!"

"A demonstration. How quaint. Takes me right back to my college days."

In college, wondered Bastrop, *what did you demonstrate against? The Kaiser?*

Something did not seem quite right to Waterloo as she

stood in the doorway, surveying the great hall. Cups and glasses were still neatly stacked on the bar. The decorations were still in place. Somehow there did not seem to be enough people in the great hall. Finally she caught the eye of a passing Thomas, the Japanese one.

"Hello, ladies," he said. "How exceptional that you should be so very punctual."

Waterloo could see. That was what was wrong. She was on time. She dug into her handbag for the invitations. She compared the invitations to her watch and looked puzzled. Since she was still blocking the VIP door, someone in the crowd shoved her from behind.

"Why don't you step in, honey, so the others can get by?" asked the Thomas.

"Because I am waiting to be announced."

"Come on in. Everybody knows who you are."

"I am waiting," sniffed Waterloo, "to be announced."

"Very well," said Thomas. He turned to the three dozen people in the great hall and raised his voice: "The Douche-ass of Waterloo and the Barren-ass DuBastrop!"

Waterloo snarled and proceeded to the bar. The dam burst. The crowd at the VIP door rushed into the hall, including, amid the taffeta and chiffon, a gorilla. Bastrop seized a seabreeze and wandered in the hall until she saw someone she thought she knew.

"Mary," Bastrop indicated the stage, "what are those?"

"Those are the entertainment, specifically selected by His Highness, the heir apparent."

The Retched Pukes hit The Chord all at once. Suddenly the great hall seemed much smaller. Then the Retched Pukes hit their Other Chord and strummed it a bit. Emetick removed the microphone from its stand. The Retched Pukes returned to The Chord. Emetick's lips curled toward the microphone.

272

Don't give-a me sex.
Give me a punch with your fist.
Cause I won't know you love-a me
Till you break-a my wrist.

Drunk Daddy love.
Drunk Daddy love.
No, I'll never get enough
Of that drunk Daddy love.

"Myrna, they look tubercular to me."

"Where have you been? Mars? It's all the mode."

"I mean, they don't look well enough to bury."

"That's it. These young people won't leave a burning building until they are made up to look positively cadaverous."

It's the only love I've known.
It's the only love I need.
So come on, drunk Daddy,
And make-a me bleed.

Drunk Daddy love.
Drunk Daddy love.

My god, thought the gorilla. *At last a clear statement of their torture methods.* The gorilla crowded its way closer to the stage in order to better receive the message that was so clearly intended for it.

I don't want your huggin.
I don't want your kiss.
I just want you to use me ...

"That bitch!" Waterloo shrieked in Bastrop's ear.

Bastrop turned to Waterloo. "Did you say something?"

"I said I found out how she did it," shouted Waterloo. "I saw someone else's invitation. She had ours printed separately. Ours were printed for an hour and a half early."

No, I'll never get enough
Of that drunk Daddy love!

Emetick flung the microphone over limply as the Other Chord wrung the ending out of the song. The lighting in the great hall began to shift in a quite amorphous way. The guests found their attention drawn to the parquet dais. Then the light drew itself into a tight focus. Agnes stood.

"Happy Halloween, ladies and gentlemen. Welcome to the forty-seventh annual Halloween cotillion of the Jade Court. The bars are open. There will be entertainment of a more traditional sort later, and of course we hope you will remain for the investiture. But first, affairs of state. We will now receive the delegation from Osage." Agnes gestured to the Japanese Thomas.

"Osage?" hissed Waterloo to Bastrop. "This is quite a coup if the old gal has pulled it off."

"Lady Ellenor of Osage and party," announced the Thomas at the door. The delegation of three approached the parquet dais. First was the presiding light of the Reservation, Ellenor. Her escort was a younger, darker man with braided hair. He led the third member of the party by the hand: Donald.

Ellenor curtsied before the throne. "Your Imperial Majesty," she began, "I have come to say that we are sorry. All of us now know that you always had our best interests at heart. Through great risk to your own imperial person, you saved us a great tribulation. I have come, then, to pay tribute and to renew the ancient bonds which placed Osage under your protection."

"I'll be damned. She did pull it off," Waterloo whispered.

"Very graciously put, Ellenor." Agnes fluttered her dragon fan.

"Yes, well," Ellenor went on, "and as a symbol of our renewed allegiance, we have brought this wicked child to serve at Court for a year, in hopes that you can teach it some manners."

Donald wrenched his hand free. "That's what you say, you old biddy."

Lady Ellenor glared at Donald. "Child, shall I repeat certain elements of our little heart-to-heart talk, right here in front of everybody? Don't think I won't."

Donald sneered.

Agnes snapped her fingers. The red-haired beachboy appeared at her side, wearing his formal black chamois. Agnes cleared her throat discreetly and spoke to Donald: "Look here, child, perhaps your reluctance to join us at Court stems from a misperception of conditions here. This is Tommy." Agnes used her fan to indicate the beachboy. "He will be in charge of your rehabilitation. For one year you will absolutely be under his direction and you must obey him day and night and do exactly what he says."

Donald's eyes grew big as he took in the broad, brown-flecked shoulders, the knotted nipples, the blue veins on the biceps, and most of all the black chamois bulge.

"You mean," Donald asked hopefully, "that I am a slave to his every whim? That I must yield immediately to his every desire? That I must do whatever he says, no matter how disgusting, degrading, or vile?"

"You got it, honey." Agnes winked. "Goodness, Ellenor, what a bright youngster. We are sure all of this will work out for the best. A sociology student we understand?"

"Yes, ma'am."

"Excellent. We have a little project in the local sociology department for which the child seems eminently suited. Tommy, why don't you take the child to the roof garden and try to reconcile it to its state of bondage."

"That's right," Donald said eagerly, "I am almost inconsolable."

Tommy offered his arm to Donald. Donald took hold of the arm with both hands. Tommy led their way through the crowd.

"Now Ellenor, we see perfectly well that you have got your act together in Osage. We have been living in the past. Tomás, bring us the instrument of independence."

"Independence!" Waterloo gasped. "Mercy, Myrna, can she do that to us?"

"We heard that." Agnes regarded Waterloo with disdain. "Yes, we can do it. *L'état c'est moi!*"

Bastrop whispered to Waterloo: "It's all the French she knows except *oui.*"

Agnes picked up the quill from the silver tray and fixed the pince-nez on her nose. "Let's see here," she mumbled as she studied the parchment page. She dipped the quill and found the spot at the bottom of the text where she signed: "*Agnes Regina.*" Tomás blotted the signature. The Swedish Thomas dripped wax and nodded to Agnes. She pressed the chimera ring into the blob of wax.

"You, Ellenor, are created regent until your group has a chance to act upon this new state of affairs. We expect you will be queen."

"That is not for me to say."

"You are much too modest, Ellenor. Be sure to join us on the dais for the festivities after the investiture."

Tom had rolled the parchment and handed it to Agnes. "Your Imperial Majesty." Ellenor curtsied again to receive the document.

"Ladies and gentlemen." Agnes looked up. "Liquidating the empire is thirsty business. Now that these proceedings are closed, let us give our attention to the entertainment and liquor for a while. We are very fortunate to have tonight the very great blues artist Mr. Crumbelly Croissant."

The lighting of the great hall again lost its focus and wandered about until all at once it drew together on a washtub upturned on stage. As if dozing, Crumbelly sat on the washtub with his ukulele. Suddenly Crumbelly looked up. He raised his lavender-colored glasses and looked at the crowd in the great hall. His eyes sparkled mischievously.

"Everybody say: Mary, Mary," he shouted at the crowd. The hall responded: "Mary, Mary!"

> *Everybody say: Mary, Mary.*
> *Come into this ole meat rack bar,*
> *Everybody say: Mary.*
> *Same old gals, think they be a star.*

> *Everybody say: Mary, Mary!*
> *Everybody say: Mary, Mary!*

The gorilla shouldered its way through the mass of flesh in the temporary plywood corridor behind the stage. The third door it forced open revealed Emetick in front of a mirror, removing makeup from his tit with cold cream. The gorilla pressed through the door into the small dressing room and removed its head.

"Hey, uh . . . cat," McThacry said.

"You got a problem, fuckhead?" Emetick grabbed another wad of tissues from the box.

"I heard your song and I got your message."

"You got my message? Look, it's Halloween and I already have a date."

"No, I mean that Daddy song. I want to help you. I really want to help you."

"Okay. But it will cost you. And make it fast." Emetick stood and faced McThacry.

"You don't understand. I'm not one of them."

"Then forget it, bubba. I only roll over for love."

"I want to help you get away from them. They're doing bad, terrible things to you."

"Yeah, I know. But they're the only band I've got. I'm thinking of going back to country and western anyway."

"Which one organizes it?"

"What?"

"Who is behind it all? The beatings. The song. What do they do to you?"

"Geek, what are you on? I'd like to get about half as much of it as you've had." Emetick leaned over to wipe more makeup from around his eyes.

"You know, breaking your wrist. Making you bleed. Like you told me in the song. The message of the song. You meant it for me, right?"

"Ka-duh! Space city." Emetick sighed and looked up from the mirror. "Look, I don't usually explain my material. But it's like a protest song. About child abuse. Get it?"

"Yes. Yes, I do get it. I know. I know." McThacry tried to project a look of deep, vigorous, manly concern.

"Okay. Okay. It's Halloween. You must need it bad. If I give you what you want, you'll go away quietly?"

"Sure. Don't worry. They'll never find out."

Emetick pulled the two-inch brass ring on his zipper. The straining flesh behind the zipper popped out. "There it is. All you want."

"What? Cattle prods? Electrodes? Scars?" McThacry knelt to better examine Emetick's evidence.

"Emmy, Agnes would like you to . . ." Black-haired, blue-eyed Thomas stood for a moment in the door. "Oops! Oh, pardon me!" Thomas turned away quickly and had half shut the door. Something about the muddy-colored crew cut on the gorilla kneeling in front of Emetick. "McThacry? It is McThacry!"

McThacry twisted around, still holding Emetick's privates in his hands.

"McThacry, what are you . . . No, never mind, it's perfectly obvious what you are doing here."

McThacry looked slowly from Thomas back to Emetick's organ. He had not found any scars yet. He looked again at Thomas. Then he realized. This situation could be misinterpreted.

Thomas smirked. "Oh well, after all, it is Halloween. Enjoy it, hon." Thomas stepped back through the door and closed it. It was a great temptation, but Thomas turned his back to the door and slid down the corridor between the bodies of the members of the third band.

Everybody say: Mary, Mary.
Been comin in this bar since I was trade.
Everybody say: Mary.
Now I buys the drinks if I wants to get laid.

The investiture went well enough, except that Waterloo developed a coughing fit, which was cured when Chief trod on her toes. The final duties of office discharged for the evening, Agnes could join the celebration of the holiday under a lesser title. The last band had completed its set when Agnes stood at the doorway en masque. When the black-haired, blue-eyed Thomas came near she grabbed his arm.

"You're fired," she whispered. "You may ask us to dance."

"May I have the honor of this dance, ma'am?" Thomas beamed. "Jim told you, didn't he?"

"It wouldn't do for him to keep a secret like that from his mother-in-law."

"No, I guess not."

"Did we ever remark how much you resemble Jim?"

"And Jim's father?"

"Well, yes."

"Lucky for me."

The antique, bubble-light jukebox clicked and hummed. A girlish voice began a song about a place where bluebirds fly. The mirrored ball began to spin.

This is ridiculous, Thomas thought. *Who can look the least bit butch while dancing with a six-foot-seven queen?* Thomas sighed, laid his head on Agnes's chest, and closed his eyes.

Long after the bands have packed and gone, after the lovers have fought and made up, once the singles have found their tricks or lost them or done them already, when the balloons have fallen and been burst, many hours into All Saints' Day, the brave remaining souls who can still stand gather around the parquet dais.

A cappella, as they always have in the drag courts of the nation, they sing together their time-honored, if politically incorrect, song of pride and defiance:

God Save the Nelly Queen!